MIAMI NIGHT NURSE

LESLIE JANE LINDER

Copyright Notice

The Miami Night Nurse Copyright © 2025 by Leslie J. Linder. All rights reserved under International and Pan-American Copyright Conventions

This book is a work of fiction. Any references to real people, events, establishments, organizations, or locales are intended only to provide a sense of authenticity and are used fictionally. All characters, and all incidents and dialogue, are drawn from the author's imagination and are not to be construed as real.

To the extent that cover images depict a person or persons, such person or persons are merely models and are not intended to portray any character in the book.

By payment of the required fees, you have been granted the nonexclusive, non-transferable right to access and read the text of the e-book on screen or as printed in the paperback edition. No part of this text may be reproduced, transmitted, downloaded, decompiled, reverse-engineered, or stored in or introduced into any information storage and retrieval system, in any form or by any means, whether electronic or mechanical, now known or hereafter invented, without the express written permission of the author.

Book Cover Design and Interior Formatting by 100Covers.

EPIGRAPH

...I have never been caught. I have rarely been sorry. I am friendly. I am responsible. I am invisible. I blend right in...
— Patric Gagne

CHAPTER 1

Happy hour, or what they ended up putting in its place at the bars up in Boston instead of an actual discounted drinking period, was over for the evening.

A few decades ago, on this very same street, on another damp autumn night, a young woman was accidentally run over and killed by her drunk-driving friend. Their whole group had been over-served during a rowdy after-work drinking game. The ensuing public outcry at the woman's death prompted state legislators to take a closer look at how alcohol consumption was being promoted in drinking establishments across the state. New laws were put in place to regulate drink pricing during these early evening cocktail hours.

On this particularly dismal, rainy Friday night, long after that mostly forgotten 1983 fatality, groups of people were beginning to spill out on to the dark, wet November streets. Some of the young women wobbled a little on their red-soled high-heeled shoes and reached out to take someone's arm. The clusters of financial district workers sheltered for a few moments under the awnings and the dripping pots of ferns hanging near the doorways of the bars and restaurants while they shook open their umbrellas. Some waved down taxis, preparing to head out to get something more to eat; others thought they would maybe just go home to Brookline or Arlington. It had been a long, stressful work week at the banks and the brokerage houses.

The guys were loud and a little loose after a couple of hours of drinking and arguing with their coworkers from accounting and IT about how the Patriots' draft picks were working out and where interest rates were going to go next. Their hopeful but increasingly sloppy flirtations with the female servers and with the women in their groups had played themselves out. The clouds of breath they exhaled into the cold air smelled of martinis and IPAs and seasoned wings and sliders. They left behind plates spilling over with oyster shells and piles of wet, crumpled paper napkins on the wooden high-top bar tables.

A cool blonde dressed in a short, clingy black dress was still sitting near the back of one of the fern-y, dimly lit joints. It was one of those places that seemed to attract mostly finance guys. He noticed she was making no move to leave. The group she had been with, or maybe she had just been sitting near them so he had assumed she was one of their party, had moved on several minutes before, carelessly dropping keys and change from their pockets. Another guy in a dark suit was eyeing her too, poised on his stool like he was thinking about going over to try his rizz on her.

Sean Mallory decided right then that he'd better make his move before any of the other guys who were sitting alone at the bar got up the nerve to give her their line of bull. What was the absolute worst that could happen? He would just go straight home to his wife if things didn't go his way. Not much at stake here, not really.

He leaned across the damp bar and motioned for the bartender. The bartender cocked his head and listened for a moment. Then he backed away and shrugged.

"Never saw her before."

"What's she drinking?"

"Nothing that I know of. Water."

"She's gorgeous. You don't see that silvery blond hair every day. I wonder if she's Swedish, or something. Maybe a tourist here to walk the Liberty Trail?"

The bartender shrugged again. "Take your shot."

"You think so?"

The bartender nodded. "What do you have to lose?"

Possibly my marriage, Sean thought, slipping off his wedding ring.

The bartender caught his move and smiled. He worked his way down to the other end of the long bar, wiping the smooth, shiny top as he went, picking up the stray empties that the tech crowd had left in wet clusters as they'd headed out the door.

Sean strolled over to the blonde and stood uncertainly next to her table. She kept scrolling on her phone and didn't seem to be picking up on his presence.

"May I join you for a drink?" he asked quietly.

"I don't think so," she said, quickly looking around the bar and then standing. She picked up her purse and slipped the strap over the left shoulder of her bright red coat.

"Too bad," he said. "I sure would enjoy spending some quality time with someone as pretty as you."

"Hmm," she said, smiling faintly as she headed toward the front door.

He watched through the street-side window as she waved down a cab at the curb, and then, after short second of hesitation, he hurried out to the sidewalk.

He fumbled with his umbrella, trying to avoid the puddles on the wet concrete, and motioned for one of the white taxi cabs cruising down the street. He stepped from the curbside directly into the back seat to avoid soaking his Christian Louboutin's in the small river of gutter-rain. He snapped instructions to the driver to follow the cab that had just turned left at the light. The cabbie arched his head back to check the traffic and then pulled an illegal U-turn on the black, rain-slick pavement.

This one was driving unusually slow for a Boston cabbie. Sean inhaled impatiently and asked the guy to please try to move it along. Fortunately, after a couple of miles, Sean spied the blonde's cab pulling over in front of another bar. This joint was located in a pretty ritzy neighborhood of high- and medium-end brick condominium apartments. His cabbie made a skidding stop maybe fifty feet from where the blonde's driver had let her out, splashing rainwater over the curb.

"Watch it, ya fuckin' douche," shouted some kid in a Red Sox cap and jacket.

The blonde turned her head to look and saw Sean struggling get out of the cab without soaking his expensive shoes. She smiled, maybe at him he thought, and then put up a small umbrella and began strolling casually down one of the brick side-streets. He followed her. The street led into a dark, tree-canopied residential enclave dimly lit with faux gas lanterns set on posts. She stopped walking after maybe seventy-five yards and stood near the doorway of one of the ridiculously expensive rowhouses. She watched his tentative approach.

He felt anxious as her eyes settled on him, and more than that, foolish and doubtful. What could he say that wouldn't make him sound like a stalker, maybe a dangerous bad guy? He felt a twinge of shame at the realization that what he was doing might be frightening her. Still, he'd come this far. What was the worst that could happen? He'd been told 'no' before. Not a big deal.

"Hi, there," Sean said, as he caught up with her. He stepped a little to the left into a circle of yellowish light cast by one of the streetlamps so she could get a good look at him. "Don't be afraid. I saw you in the bar. I really wanted to talk with you back there, but you left before I could get up enough nerve to think of something to say that wouldn't make me sound like a jerk."

"You said something. You asked me if I wanted a drink, and I said no. Then you followed me here."

Did her voice sound cold? His smile shivered and left his face. I should just go home and forget the whole thing, he thought. But maybe she was smiling a little as she'd said it, just a flicker around the edge of her lips?

"Do you live here?" he asked.

She shook her head. "No."

He waited, but she didn't elaborate. "I'm sorry for intruding on your privacy. Now I feel stupid for even being here."

She looked up and down the street and then asked, "Did you want to come inside for a drink? Get out of the weather?"

He nodded quickly. "If you think it would be okay…"

She shrugged. "Why wouldn't it be?"

He took a deep breath. The whole scene felt unreal, this beautiful woman, a total stranger, standing outside with him on a quiet, historic Boston street on a slightly spooky autumn evening. A light rain was still coming down. Wispy halos of mist hung around the streetlamps. Puddles on the brick pavers beneath the lamp poles reflected the lamps' dirty-yellow light.

He just didn't do things like this, the impulsive pursuit of a beautiful woman. What had gotten in to him? Susan was at home waiting for him. How was he going to explain things to her if it got very late?

He followed the woman in the red coat up the short front walk. The pavers were laid out in the same slightly uneven pattern as the damp, red bricks on the street.

He stood behind her at the doorway, admiring the curve of her legs in her very short skirt. He put out his hand, palm facing up, as if to cup her bottom. But he didn't actually touch her as she leaned over just a little and pushed her hips back. She put the key in the lock and undid the dead bolt. He tilted his head a little and thought he maybe caught a glimpse of her panties beneath the hem of her skirt.

What would happen if he did just slide his hand up there, right now, under that short little skirt? Did she want him to? Is that why she was bending like that with her butt pushed out? Would her panties already feel wet to his fingers?

What was he even doing here? This wasn't like him at all. Susan would be sitting in their living room in Arlington with the lights dimmed, smoking and drinking bourbon on the rocks. Or maybe pacing. Maybe she would have already angrily thrown out the ruined dinner if she had cooked something for them. Or maybe she had her sister over, or possibly a friend, possibly that woman Carol who was married to one of the State Street managers, and they'd been talking and snacking on cheese and fruit and drinking lots of cold white wine and hadn't even thought about him or about dinner at all.

The door to the condo opened and he followed the blonde in the slick red raincoat into a small, high-ceilinged living room.

"So…" he said, with what he hoped was a seductive smile. He was feeling even more doubtful and on edge now that he was in her private space, because she just seemed so…cold. She wasn't acting drunk or sexy or flirtatious. She was just being matter of fact. Maybe she did this all the time. Maybe she was a pro. He didn't have much cash on him. Venmo?

He thought back to the bar. She hadn't offered him any encouragement at the happy hour. How had he even gotten the idea that he should follow her? This honestly wasn't like him. But here he was, a little uncomfortable but a lot aroused by her ice-cold beauty. Women like her could be like tigers in bed, he'd heard.

"May I take your raincoat?" he asked, as if he were the host or somebody just trying to get a little bit more in control of the situation.

She looked up at him from beneath her lashes with what seemed like a condescending smile. "No, thanks," she said dryly, removing her red coat and hanging it on a brass hook by the door.

Her jersey dress clung deliciously to her curves. Her body looked trim and tight. He stepped up close behind her and immediately slid his hands up the sides of her ribs and took hold of both her breasts and squeezed them, pressing his hips against her buttocks.

She sighed and leaned back against him. Her weight pressing on him caused him to shift back on his heels; he moved to steady himself.

This was really going to happen. He felt himself stiffen some more, if that were even possible. Women these days had so much fakery: nails, lashes, tits. Sometimes, even their asses. This one felt like she was all real.

"Would you like to sit and talk for a while?" he asked, gesturing a little uncertainly down at the white leather couch. "Do you have anything to drink here?"

"No," she said. "Let's go to the bedroom."

She turned away and started pulling her knit dress over her head as she walked down the short hall leading to a darkened room. He followed her, stepping tentatively now. Was any of this even real? A gorgeous woman in a bar. He stalks her home. She invites him into her bedroom right away. It was like the set-up for the thin, cheesy plot of a porno video. He was the horny dude in the scene dying to take those bare tits in his hands. In his mouth. He was feeling like he might explode in his pants before he even got a chance to take it out and shove it in her.

She turned around to face him, watching his reaction as she unhooked her lace demi-bra and stepped out of her silky black panties. She kicked her underwear to a corner of the room. He'd first caught a glimpse of those panties back at the bar when she'd crossed and uncrossed her legs. Probably so had most of the other guys in the place. But he was the fortunate bastard who was here with her now. She was standing naked in front of him in just those sexy, red-soled high heels.

"How did I get to be the lucky guy tonight? Why'd you pick me, Baby?" he asked, looking into her guileless, clear blue eyes. She was like a lovely, slightly remote angel who had floated down from heaven.

"There's something about you that reminds me of someone I used to know."

"Who's that?" he asked. "Your boyfriend from high school? Maybe some rock star?" he joked.

He gasped as she pushed him down on to the bed and climbed on top of him, still wearing those shoes.

"No," she said. "Someone I didn't really like."

He grabbed for her tits again, but she swatted his hands away. She leaned forward, her weight on her hands and knees, and stretched out over his face, her bare nipples inches from his mouth. He snagged one of them with his lips and started sucking on it.

He felt like he was for sure going to come before he even got it in her. He grabbed her buttocks to try to position her right over his stiff cock. She pulled away just a little bit and her nipple slipped out of his mouth. Then she leaned down to the left, unzipped her purse that was on the floor near the bed, and took something out. She let him take her nipple in his lips again. He sucked on it desperately while he cupped her buttocks and slipped two fingers inside her. She was so wet already.

He kept trying to position her hips so his cock would slide right in, but she kept moving away just a little, adjusting herself, just teasing him, he thought, arousing him even more.

He was about to flip her off and enter her forcefully from behind, enough of her prick teasing games, his balls were about to burst, but then she abruptly pushed his face away from her tits and sat up tall on his thighs. She raised both her arms high over her head, hands together, and he fixed his gaze on her full, perfect breasts. Had he ever seen a more lovely pair?

He turned his face to look at their reflection in the dresser mirror. He could see himself stretched out on the bed with her sitting astride his thighs. He squeezed her buttocks with his hands, trying again to position her directly over his stiff cock.

It was then that he caught the bit of reflected light flash in her hand. He had time for one quick gasp as he realized what she was holding. Then she fiercely thrust her hands downward. The knife plunged into his neck, and he felt the hard, gleaming blade slice into his throat.

She inhaled and slit open his windpipe, giving the knife a hard tug as the blade got caught up on some gristle.

His body had gone rigid. He wasn't able to fight her off or even move in his state of shock. She was still mounted on top of him, looking down at his face with a curious expression. What was happening here? This couldn't be real. Incongruously, he thought of Susan waiting at home all by herself in the dark. Then, the woman astride him pushed a thick pillow down hard over his face and kept herself seated firmly on his hips as he bucked and struggled.

When he stopped moving, she removed the pillow and checked to make sure he was dead. His eyes were open and the look frozen on his face was one of stark surprise. She climbed off him, kicked away her shoes, and stepped in to the shower to wash away the blood splattered on her chest and arms and belly. As she dressed, her eyes scanned the bedroom and living room for anything she might have brought in with her. She wiped down the doorknobs and any other surfaces she could have touched. She leaned over his body, being careful not to get any more of his blood on her clothing, and cleaned the knife handle protruding from his neck with a bit of soap on a washcloth. She left the blade stuck at an angle in his throat.

Then she walked out the front entryway, leaving the apartment door unlocked and ajar. She was wearing his khaki raincoat with the collar turned up over her own red coat. She carried his black umbrella open and slightly tipped forward to shield her face. She walked over to the Park Street Station, her heels clicking rhythmically on the wet pavement.

The rain had settled into a light but steady drizzle. She hesitated in front of a trash receptacle and looked around. Then, she took hold of a thick section of her short, silvery platinum hair at the forehead and pulled. When the wig came off, she pushed it in past the trashcan's flap and shook out her own reddish-blond hair.

She walked down the steps to the platform by the tracks, the tapping of her heels echoing against the tiled walls, to wait for the Red Line train. As it pulled up, she tossed the man's raincoat she was wearing and the umbrella she'd taken from the apartment to a homeless guy sitting against the wall.

Two days later, the story was all over the papers and the television news programs. The tabloids screamed, *Jamaica Plain husband and father murdered in Beacon Hill condo!* News anchors soberly described the gruesome details as well as the victim's biography: *After a twenty-year career at State Street, he leaves a grieving wife and a daughter who attends Boston University.*

"You know what's so peculiar about this?" asked the elderly medical examiner who had been called to the scene.

"What?" asked one of the cops who had secured the murder room. Someone, a woman apparently, had called in the address from a payphone near one of the T stations.

"He still has an erection."

"No shit," said the cop, looking down at the body. "How is that even possible?"

The medical examiner shrugged. "It happens occasionally, but it's uncommon in circumstances like this. You might hear about it sometimes in cases of execution by hanging, or especially during choking kinds of kinky sex-play when it goes bad. Or with rope suicides. They used to call the medical phenomenon 'angel lust' back in the Middle Ages…I guess the idea being that the deceased guy's spirit was aroused, even though he was dead."

The cop shrugged. "Yeah, well, apparently it was the angel of death who came down to visit this dude. Hope she at least made it good for him while he was getting his rocks off."

"I don't think he actually made it that far," said the medical examiner, looking down at the body. "And we don't necessarily know at this point, not until we get the labs back, if it was a 'she' who did this."

"Any thoughts about a motive, then?" The cop gestured at the dead man with a flick of his head.

The medical examiner shrugged. "Not really. If it was someone he knew, then revenge, I'd assume, a crime of passion. If they were strangers or recent acquaintances, then who really knows?"

The cop nodded. "In probably half of these cases, there's going to be no way to identify the perpetrator from just the evidence at the scene."

The medical examiner looked up from the corpse at the cop. "So, I guess we'll never know?"

The cop shrugged. "We'll have to see. Sometimes this type of perpetrator can't stop at just one."

CHAPTER 2

I'm always on time for work, and I'm usually a little bit early. I never call in sick for frivolous reasons, only if I think I might be contagious. I'm thought of as a very reliable employee.

My normal shift these days is from 11pm to 9 am, three nights a week. I get paid for forty hours, even though my actual time on site only adds up to thirty. I get almost a month of paid vacation, plus various holidays, which I either take off or get paid double-time if I work.

The substance abuse treatment center where I'm employed as a registered nurse is located near the Atlantic Ocean, on the South Shore, a number of miles from Boston. There are some residential enclaves in the area, but we're mostly all by ourselves, set on a few acres of land with large expanses of cranberry bogs stretching for miles on three sides. On many nights, the mist has begun swirling in from the ocean as soon as the day started cooling off in the late afternoon, so by the time I arrive at work, the whole area might be pretty fogged in.

The cranberry bogs, if you don't know what those are, are basically marshy, somewhat groomed fields of low-growing cranberry bushes, acres and acres of them. No one really spends much time out there in the bogs, except in Spring for replanting and during the Fall harvest season. Sometimes the bogs get sanded in the winter, if they are sufficiently iced over. The farmers will normally come out and do periodic inspections of the crop, but that and everything else related to cranberries is always done during the daytime.

At night, wispy curls of ground fog rise from the wet bogs. On cool, still nights, a layer of ground fog tends to just hang there a few feet over the fields, shrouding the earth in a blanket of unsettled, lightly shifting clouds. If someone were standing out near the bogs at night, the mist might cover them from their knees down to their feet. I would imagine on nights like that, someone could come crawling along the sides of the bogs under the cover of the ground fog and get pretty close to the back of the treatment center before anyone would even see them.

Cranberry Pointe is what they call the place where I work. Please let go of any stereotypes you might have about drug and alcohol treatment centers. This place looks like a mid-priced, one-story motel with a lot of big glass windows. All the rooms, meaning the patient rooms, the meeting rooms, counselors' offices, the dining area, all of that, are laid out in a rectangular pattern around an open center courtyard. Out in that yard, patients can smoke and socialize when they aren't supposed to be somewhere else, all under the usually watchful eyes of the staff.

It's actually a pretty easy place to work the night shift. The patients are normally first admitted for a medical detox, and nowadays that usually means for either heroin or alcohol. Sometimes maybe for benzos, a prolonged detox experience that I really wouldn't wish on anyone who I didn't already hate. Occasionally it's just cocaine, or something else. The patients are all medicated to make sure they have a safe, medically appropriate detox, and then their dosages are gradually lowered on a specific schedule to wean them off whatever it is they came in on.

Some of them, particularly the opioid addicts, try to lie about how much they were taking on the street. When they do that, it isn't necessarily because they are trying to scam us into giving them enough medication to get high. Usually if they lie, it's just because they are afraid of not getting enough medication from us to completely cover their symptoms while they are going through withdrawal. Oh, sure, some of them still do want to get high and are plainly ambivalent about getting clean. Which isn't unusual. Not that many addicts or alcoholics get clean and stay clean from just their first detox. It's a tough disease. It usually takes more than one try for sobriety to stick.

My job as the night nurse normally isn't too strenuous. By the time I get to work, all the patients have been to the seven pm Twelve Step meeting and have had their evening medications. Most of them are in their rooms, in bed. The only ones I need to take special care of are the recently admitted patients who may be having a difficult time, medically, getting through their detox. If so, I'll need to check their vital signs more frequently and maybe call out to get a doctor's order for more of some medication.

We almost never get admissions at night, because all patient insurance must be pre-approved by the financial office, and our insurance clerks only work until seven pm. The only times that someone gets admitted as late as my shift is if their transportation to the facility was delayed for some reason, and in any case, Admissions would have had to have pre-approved them before we would let them inside. This is not an emergency facility, although on rare occasions we do get people transported here after they have been medically stabilized at one of the area hospital emergency rooms.

In other words, I normally work a quiet shift, and I prefer it that way. Doug, one of orderlies who moonlights here some nights from his day job as an emergency medical technician, is occasionally scheduled to work a shift when I am here. If it is one of those hoped-for quiet nights, we might go into the linen closet, which is really just a small room that stores piles of towels and thin sheets. It is conveniently situated just across the hall from my medication desk. We get half-undressed, and fuck. He is a tall, good-looking blond guy, and he's very good for a quickie. I don't know anything else about him.

The day shift nurses, usually two, are supposed to arrive before seven in the morning. I give them report and count the meds with the day-shift medication nurse and we sign off on the med sheets. Then, they both go in to morning meeting with the counselors and social workers while I finish my notes and grab a quick breakfast in the cafeteria. Usually, I'll chat about recovery stuff with some of the patients while I'm waiting for the day shift meeting to be over. Then, I get into my car and go home to sleep.

A lot of the patient histories at any rehab will tend to have a common flow: I was raised in a nice family/horrible family. I started getting high with my friends/older siblings when I was young. Things started to go downhill, but I kept right on using alcohol/heroin/cocaine. Then things got really bad, and I quit a few times, but I would always get lonely/quit going to AA meetings/start hanging around with my old friends who were still using. Then I relapsed and things got really, really bad. So here I am. I want to get clean, but I don't know why I keep going back out.

I guess one of my most memorable patients at Cranberry Pointe was Danny. That's his real first name, but whenever I talk about him, I always leave out his last name, both for professional confidentiality reasons and because I wouldn't want someone like him to be mad at me.

Danny just couldn't stay sober, as he told me one night when he couldn't sleep. He was coming off both heroin and benzos, so he was having a really rough detox. He wanted to quit using, but every time he did quit, the bad feelings would come bubbling back up, feelings that he just couldn't tolerate, along with terrible, vivid memories. And dreams about the devil, he said, nightmares that he woke from screaming and flailing.

During the last of his string of admissions, after I had thoroughly re-explained to him the strict confidentiality regulations that detox and rehab facilities are subject to, I was able to coax Danny into telling me a little bit more about what was bothering him so much that he couldn't sleep and he couldn't stay sober.

It turned out that Danny was (or is?) a hit man for what some people refer to up in South Boston as the Irish Mob.

"I don't feel anything, absolutely nothing, when I shove a gun in someone's face and pop him, not if I'm high. But whenever I'm not all fucked up on something, I start thinking about going to hell for all the things I've done. I can't tell you any of the specifics, because then I might need to pop you, too, but the guilt I carry for my sins is so bad that the only thing that ever helps me is the heroin or the booze. But I'll take whatever I can get my hands on. I need lots of it, some nights. Probably one time, I'll just end up OD'd if I don't figure out how to stay clean. Maybe that wouldn't be so bad. But it would just kill my old mother if I went out like that."

It was clear to me that Danny was feeling very hopeless about ever being able to achieve a lasting sobriety, and I could understand why. His long string of detoxes always ended up with him getting discharged from treatment and then him picking back up after a week or two. A vital cornerstone of the 12 Step recovery program is honesty, but Danny couldn't exactly be expected to sit in an AA meeting next to a suburban homemaker or a banker or a snitch out on bail and unburden himself about how bad he felt because of all the people he had killed for his living.

Since Danny was a true-blue Irish Catholic, I suggested that he should think about going to confession, maybe at a parish where he'd never been to Mass. He could tell the priest on duty everything he'd ever done, all his sins, without fear of going to jail or being targeted for being a rat by his fellow mob-members, right? Then, he could accept whatever penance the priest came up with in response to

Danny's confessions of murder and God knows what else. And receive absolution.

Danny's face brightened with an almost childlike smile. He loved the idea of cleansing his conscience of all his terrible secrets. He said he would gladly accept any penance the priest came up with, "honestly, whatever he says, anything," if it would help him live his life and hold on to his secrets without having to get wasted all the time. I could only imagine what some poor priest would feel like after hearing a detailed confession from a guy like Danny.

I'm sure that if I were a patient at a place like this one, I would want to hold on to some secrets of my own. You're supposed to learn how to get in touch with the feelings you've been medicating with mood-altering substances and become open and honest as part of the recovery process. If I were to get too open and honest with other people, I'd definitely wind up in jail. Which is part of the reason why I almost never drink or do drugs. Or stay in one place for too long.

Which is why I was moving down to Miami pretty soon.

About a year after our little talk, I got a note forwarded to me at my Miami job that Danny had written, addressed to me at Cranberry Pointe. It said he'd just received his one-year sobriety medallion at his home group up in South Boston. He thanked me effusively, included his private cell phone number, and said I could text him *if you ever need anything, really, anything at all*. He underlined the word *anything* twice. He also wrote that I sort of reminded him of his little sister, before she'd had three kids and gotten fat. And wound up in Oak Ridge Cemetery after she'd overdosed on quaaludes.

****

My own childhood was anything but great, but I'm not complaining, I'm just trying to be honest. I suppose *honest* might be too strong a word, but you can assume that anything I tell you is as true as it needs to be.

I was born into a reasonably normal family just outside of Boston. You hear about the Boston Irish all the time, as if every other person in Boston came directly from County Cork. In fact, Boston is less than one quarter Irish American. New York and Chicago have way more people of Irish background than Boston does. My Boston-area family was mainly of French and Scandinavian descent, and I had grandparents from Maine.

Or so they tell me. My parents both died when I was very young, so young that I'm not even sure if what I remember about them is based in reality or is just something I fabricated from the various stories I was told about them.

The first thing I heard when I asked about my family was that my father was a very damaged person with a tragic family history, and that my mother never would have died if she had only listened to my grandmother and not married him. Again, I don't know that for a fact; my maternal grandparents, who were quite old at the time they took me in, never wanted to give me very many specific details about what had taken place. I do know my parents both died on the same day, and that their death certificates said something about "death by misadventure."

For those of you who don't know, the implication of that phrase is that my parents took some kind of a risk that led to their deaths. So, the term suggests that it was way more than just an accident. That's all I knew at the time, and most of the people who might have been aware of more details, such as my mother's parents, are now dead and gone.

I stayed with my grandparents until just after I turned eight years old. Then, my grandmother got sick with breast cancer and died. So, I guess my grandfather, my mother's father, was actually the one who started the process that eventually resulted in me going to live at The Home. More about what led up to that later.

The Home is what all the orphans and stray kids called the place. So did some of the nuns. I don't know what its official name was.

It was a great big, old rambling place built probably a hundred years ago as a family farmhouse. It was constructed from local hardwoods and was still being heated by a huge coal-burning iron furnace located in the basement. The kids would whisper at night, "there goes Herman," when we would hear the maintenance man slowly scraping up shovelfuls of coal from the pile at the bottom of the coal shoot to toss into the furnace door. Sometimes in the mornings, Herman was still there, or back again, and we would hear him loading up the furnace for the day while we were eating our breakfasts.

By the time I moved into The Home with my sad little suitcase and a dirty white stuffed bunny that I was told my mother had given me when I was a baby, the big house had been painted a bright green. Certain shades of green are among my favorite colors now, but I've never liked the bright, grassy green that The Home was painted. It didn't fit in at all with anything else in the neighborhood, and we kids were ostracized enough in the community as it was.

I guess the moms and dads of the kids at the neighborhood school we attended thought we might have something their kids could catch. Like lice. Cooties. Maybe bad luck, or something even worse. Since we weren't well-liked by any of the kids with regular families, nor allowed to play with them, we used to try to gang up on them sometimes on the walk home from the elementary school. We'd regularly beat up any of those bratty little kids we could catch. I knew how to fight, but I hardly ever joined in, unless I was holding a grudge against one particular kid. Otherwise, I didn't see the point.

The nuns at The Home were definitely not mean. There was no corporal punishment, not even for really bad behavior. They were just "sad" for us, or "disappointed that Jesus has to look down and see us" when we did something wrong. All the little kids except for me would cry when they heard about Jesus being sad because of how bad we were being. I would fake my sniffles to fit in, but I understood from a very young age that I just didn't care a whole lot about what either Jesus or the nuns thought, at least not as much as most of the other the other kids seemed to. I might have still been numb from my parents dying. Or, it might have been something else.

Much later, right after Herman the coal man died, things changed for me. Basically, the grown-ups at The Home, and even some of the other kids, thought that I, who was only a twelve-year-old girl by that time, might have killed him. More on that later, assuming I remember to get back to the topic.

The best thing that ever happened to me at The Home was Jerry. He was another young kid whose mom had died. She had been killed in a car accident. So had everyone else in his family, all except for the drunk uncle who had driven their car into a bridge abutment under I-94 around seven pm at the tail-end of a normal Friday rush hour. Jerry was at a Little League practice when it happened or else he probably would have been in the car, too.

Jerry and I used to roam the acres of fields behind The Home almost every day after school. I was slightly obsessed with horses back then, so I would pretend I was riding a white Arabian stallion, or sometimes a coal-black quarter horse, while we were outside. I would run like I was trotting or cantering and had these little things that I would do with my legs to change to my gaits. Jerry kind of ignored it when I did my horse thing. He might have been embarrassed by my silliness.

Jerry was the only true friend I had back then. Or, maybe, ever. I could talk to him about anything. He told me all about his plans to move to Miami and become a cop and live in a house on the beach, just like in the *Miami Vice* re-runs we would watch on the big TV screen in the day room. He would be like Crockett, cool and well-dressed, he said, and he would catch all the bad people who had ever done anything to hurt me. He didn't really know much about my life, I didn't think, but maybe he'd figured out some things on his own.

I pretty much decided right then to move down to Miami, too, when I grew up. I probably got that idea because things became so much better for me after Jerry and I started our friendship. He was smart and quiet, and I felt safe with him.

I think I loved him all the way back then, in a way. He was the first boy I ever kissed willingly. He didn't chase me or tease me or make fun of me. Of course, for a long time, he would never show that he liked me in a special way in front of the other kids, which was fine with me, but I do think everyone knew.

Just after the Christmas when we were in seventh grade, Jerry flew back from a visit with some relatives he had down in Florida. He said his dreams were really coming true. He was going to be moving to Miami pretty soon and would be living in a house near the old Hialeah racetrack.

I was stunned. My best friend in the world was going away. I remember throwing punches at Jerry after he told me he was leaving. I was just so angry, and I was really trying to hurt him. He grabbed my wrists as I swung at him and then he told me that he would always love me, no matter what. He gave me a piece of paper, part of an envelope, that had his uncle's name and address and telephone number printed on a little return address sticker.

"He's a retired cop, and he said he would help me become a cop, too, if I still want to be one when I get out of high school. I want to go undercover, just like Crockett and Tubbs."

"That's not for six more years," I said, almost crying. "Why do you have to go to Miami *now*? I want you to stay here with me."

Jerry's aunt and uncle came up to take him away on the Thursday before the New Year. There was already snow on the ground, and the bitter wind sweeping down from Canada cut through my thin denim jacket as I watched them drive off. I raised my hand to wave goodbye to Jerry. I couldn't see well enough through the thin layer of snowflakes that had started to settle on the rear window of their car to know if Jerry ever turned around to look at me while I stood watching him start to fade away.

I believed at the time that I would be sad forever, but as it turned out, after a few days of missing him, I barely gave Jerry another thought for almost twenty years.

As soon as I turned thirteen, which was not too long after Jerry's aunt and uncle came to take him away to Florida, Herman started bothering me for real. If I were outside after school, he would usually come out of the cellar or from wherever he had been lurking. He'd look around. Then, if no one else was nearby, he would make a little *hiss-hiss* sound and motion for me to come over.

The first couple of times, I was curious to find out what he wanted. He was dark-haired and not very tall, and he had thick legs and arms. His hands and his hairy forearms and his face just about always had smudges of coal dust, and his work clothes were usually filthy. He would change into some cleaner clothes whenever he went off the grounds on an errand for The Home, but I think he must have lived in the coal cellar. He was almost always around. Sometimes on cold nights I would wake up hearing banging sounds coming up through the pipes, and the slow, harsh scraping of the iron shovel on the cement of the basement floor. I guess he was scooping more coal into the furnace door.

I wasn't really afraid of Herman, but some of the other kids were. I had no reason to complain about him for a long time, so I didn't. But I heard that whenever the other kids did say something, the Sisters would explain that Herman was one of God's special people, and we were supposed to make allowances for God's will. As far as I was concerned, he was a retard who had better keep away from me or he would be sorry. I told him so the same week that Jerry went away to Florida with his aunt and uncle.

What happened was that Herman came up to me while I was walking around outside by myself. I was supposed to be sitting inside doing homework along with the other kids, but I didn't feel like being made to sit on a hard chair in the dining room after being forced to sit in school all day. Plus, I was still sad about Jerry. So, I told the nuns I'd done all my homework at school and that I didn't have any left to do…but that the gym teacher wanted me to practice dribbling and shooting baskets, so I needed to go outside to the court.

I took a basketball out with me and listlessly ran some patterns on the cold asphalt and tossed the ball at the basket from a few different angles. I kept missing most of my shots, but I wasn't really trying, and I didn't care.

After a while, I noticed that Herman was watching me from behind some overgrown rhododendron bushes while I ran around on the basketball court. I ignored him for a while, because I wasn't particularly afraid of him. When he started making little whistles and perverted sounds, I threw the basketball hard in his direction and went back inside.

I told Sister Margaret that Herman was bothering me and that I thought he was trying to look at my underwear. Although, to be honest, I didn't know if he actually was or not. I just wanted to get him in trouble. That day, I was still wearing the little skirt I had worn to school. Sister Margaret looked down at my bare legs. She was troubled, I could see. Then, I started to cry, to ice the cake.

Sister Margaret patted my shoulder and said something like, "There, there, Cassandra, don't cry." She said that she would definitely talk to Herman again and remind him to stay away from the girls. I hadn't realized that he bothered any of the other girls besides me. No one had ever said anything to suggest that he had, and for some reason it had never occurred to me until right then that I might not be the only girl he annoyed.

The next day, Herman looked away when I saw him and he didn't say anything, but what I really wanted was to not have him lurking around The Home any more at all. So, I followed him to the outside basement door where I knew he had disappeared, and said, not too loudly, that if he ever did anything to annoy me ever again, I would set the coal room on fire while he was asleep down there. I told a couple of the other kids, Denise and Sharon, what I had said, because I wanted them to know that Herman wasn't going to keep getting away with bothering us.

A few weeks later, there really was a fire in the coal room. I told everyone that I truly didn't know how it had started. After the ambulance had left with its siren-noise trailing behind it in the cold night, the Sisters sat me down and asked me what I knew about the fire. I figured Denise or maybe that Sharon, she was kind of a snitch, must have said something.

Sister Anne was very angry. "The whole house could have burned down," she said. "That poor man."

I nodded, but I didn't say anything. I wasn't sure yet exactly what she wanted to hear.

"Are you even sad about what happened to Herman?" she asked.

"He shouldn't have been sleeping in there," I replied calmly. "Then he wouldn't have been hurt. Besides, no matter what, he should have made sure that the furnace door was closed properly. We could have *all* been burned up."

Sister Anne looked at me like she wanted to say something more. I waited. Finally, she said, "Go back to your room. Say your prayers. Ask the Lord to cast the demons from you."

I was a little surprised that Sister Anne thought I was the one infested with demons, so I said, "Maybe Herman was a demon. Maybe God was punishing him."

A week later, Sister Anne told me that I would be moving out of The Home and would be attending a boarding school up near the New Hampshire border "on scholarship, thanks to a generous donor." Later, I found out that the word "school" was a euphemism. It was going to be more like being in a private juvie than being in a school.

On the bright side, that place was really where I started to think hard about my future. I didn't want to keep getting kicked from one detention to another and I for sure did not want to end up being trafficked on the street, having to give blow jobs to whomever some skeezy pimp said. I hadn't ever really thought about things like that before, about pimps and stuff, or even known about them, but some of the older girls in the boarding school/juvie would talk about it sometimes.

Turns out, the New Hampshire place really wasn't that bad, once I established my cred with the other kids and embellished my backstory a little bit so that some of the meaner bitches would just leave me alone.

I managed to convince the counselors and social workers that I had "potential," and they helped me plan a route out for myself. I worked hard at taking advanced placement classes while I was in there so I wouldn't have to spend too long getting my college degree once I turned 17 or 18 and aged out of the "boarding school". I would need a solid career after I was old enough to leave the state child welfare/incarceration system, because there would be no one else to take care of me except for me. I was aiming to work in a field that paid well, had jobs available anywhere I might want to go, and one where I didn't have to take too much crap just to get a paycheck.

I looked online at some nursing schools and read about the many options that a registered nurse has for making a living. They can work in hospitals, clinics, nursing homes, rehabs, be a traveling nurse, a private nurse, a home health care nurse, or even an Army nurse, and so much more. There's demand, so that equals job security, and you can work just about anywhere in the country once you pass the NCLEX. For a while, I was even thinking about going to work in Hawaii. More on that, later.

So, that's what I did. I studied, and I planned, and I graduated just as I was aging out of the juvenile detention "school" with my high school diploma and a lot of college credits toward my BSN. I am probably that school's biggest success story. Maybe someday I'll go back there and volunteer to be a motivational speaker.

Once, while I was still living there, I was able to sneak a quick look at my records. The file said my diagnosis was Conduct Disorder. I don't think that was accurate. The description, when I looked it up online, said there must be "a persistent pattern" of antisocial behaviors, and gave a list of examples: theft, lying, harming animals or people, serious violations of rules, and so forth. Very little of it seemed to apply to me. I've never stolen a thing in my life, and nor would I ever hurt an animal, unless it was attacking me.

What *I* think it is, is that I just won't take a lot of crap from anyone. The only people I've ever tried to hurt in my entire life are people who give me a very good reason to. Well, sometimes people who have something about them that *reminds* me of the people who once gave me a good reason will also end up getting on my list. Or sometimes people who just have something that I want.

CHAPTER 3

Sgt. Jerald McIntosh, of the Hialeah, Florida PD, was cooling his heels in court waiting to testify in a series of DUI cases. The benches in the rooms were hard, and the air conditioning was always either too cold or on the fritz. Several of the glum-looking people sitting behind him had been arrested or ticketed by Jerry, all on the same Friday evening a few weeks before. When they'd noticed him walk in, every single one of them had slumped. Today, there would be no getting off or getting rescheduled because the arresting officer was a no-show.

People tended to pull out recklessly from the gravel parking lots behind the several bars located within a half-mile radius south of Miami Gardens Drive. They'd gun their vehicles up the street, squealing their tires, happy to be off work for the weekend, but now they were running too high a BAC to be legally driving. You'd think they would have heard that a cop was usually waiting somewhere nearby as part of a departmental effort to curb drunk driving within the city limits and they at least wouldn't be so flagrant about it.

The court cases were proceeding along today as they normally did. First offenders typically pled *no contest* or *guilty*. They were adjudicated, paid a fine, were assigned community service hours, had their license suspended, were required to attend DUI school, and, nowadays, had their vehicle impounded for a week or two at a significant expense.

Jerry sometimes felt sorry for the young, stupid kids and even for the older, seasoned drunks who were going to lose their license for a very long time, but he'd also been the first responding officer at collisions where babies and little kids had been crushed inside of vehicles. So, he didn't feel too sorry.

When Jerry had first moved down to South Florida as a boy fresh out of The Home, he had lived with his aunt and uncle for several years at their place near the old racetrack. After he got out of the army and became a cop, he bought a house of his own not too far away. He knew the neighborhood and many of the people who lived there, and he wanted to help his community become a safer place to raise a family.

The little house he owned had been burglarized twice before he replaced the rotting metal security bars on his windows with new ones that were up to code. He also installed a video security system. He was pretty sure he knew which kids had done it. That all stopped for good once he became a cop and was assigned a marked cruiser. He kept it parked out in front of his place when he had a need to take it home. The rash of burglaries pretty much ended, not just at his place, but also on most of the rest of the street.

The most common crimes on his beat were thefts of all kinds: motor vehicles, burglary, robbery, and their various statutory iterations. There were also assaults, rapes, and, occasionally, a murder. Drugs and alcohol were usually involved, but his work wasn't all that much like what was shown on *Miami Vice* unless they were busting a neighborhood drug dealer.

For a while, when he'd first joined the force, he had taken to dressing a little bit like Crockett when he went out socially…a pastel sport coat, some facial hair, his blond hair a little bit long for a cop…but he got so much shit from the guys at the station that he cut his hair short again and left the raw-silk jackets at home in the back of his closet.

On one hot, humid Friday, shortly before the court adjourned for lunch, Jerry's personal phone pinged. He didn't recognize the number, but a little while later, when he went outside to get something to eat, he listened to the message. It was from Cassie, a girl he hadn't spoken with in at least fifteen or twenty years. The voice message said that her name was "Cassandra, but you might remember me as Cassie," and that she was living in Miami now. She said she had looked him up online, had gotten this telephone number, and if he wanted to get in touch with her, he should call her. Her husky voice sounded only a little bit familiar, and he might have been imagining even that much.

After he thought about it for a while, though, Jerry recalled that he had given Cassie his aunt and uncle's contact information years before when he was packing up to leave The Home for good, so that must have been how she had gotten his cell phone number. His aunt was still alive and at that same number, although his uncle, his mother's brother, had passed away three years ago.

He wondered if Cassie needed something, and if that was why she had called, and how her life had been going. He was feeling cautious about just popping open some potential can of worms, but the more he thought about it, the more he felt that calling her back was the right thing to do. She might really need some help from him.

Or she might be doing just fine. That would be nice to hear. He was in pretty good shape now himself, after all, and they'd both kind of come from the same circumstances. Now he had a good job with a future and no current money problems. He owned a modest home in South Florida, and he was still only a little bit past thirty. Maybe Cassie was doing fine, too.

When he left the courthouse for lunch, he just sat outside in his car, remembering how Jerry-the-small-boy had told little Cassie that he would always, always, love her. The cop that Jerry had become was normally far more measured in his responses to things. He smiled, though, thinking about some of the talks they'd had as kids while they'd walk around out in the fields behind The Home. He wondered if The Home was even still standing. He bet it was. It had been a fine, solidly built old place. Even if the land around it was now being used for something else, maybe for a new subdivision, the big house should still be there. As his memories started coming in to focus, so did some of the intense feelings he'd had for Cassie as a boy.

He did want to talk to Cassie. He just didn't know yet if he actually wanted to see her. He'd also have to do some careful thinking about whether he should say anything to his girlfriend about Cassie. He sighed. Things had already begun to feel quite a bit more complicated than he liked.

Jerry had met his present girlfriend, Isabella, three years before, a few months after a girl he'd been living with for almost a year had told him that she wanted to be honest: she'd actually never finalized her divorce from her husband. And the dude had shown up here in town. And that she was moving back to Colorado with him in just a few more days. They were going to be growing high-octane weed out there as a joint business venture. She had laughed at her own pun like it was the cleverest thing in the world, had kissed Jerry on his cheek, and then she was gone.

Some of the guys in the precinct had grown tired of seeing Jerry moping around after the Colorado girl left town, so they had fixed him up with a cousin of one of the guys.

Isabella was smart and pretty. She worked hard at her day job in the county property appraiser's office, and she was taking night classes in Kendall at MDC. Having recently passed her state real estate license exam, her primary goal was to get into real estate sales full time as soon as she could. To that end, she often spent weekend afternoons and some evenings helping out at a broker friend's open houses in South Dade to gain sales experience.

All Jerry's friends liked her, and Isabella's family made him feel right at home. His conversational Spanish was actually very good by now, pretty much a job requirement for being effective as a cop in South Florida, and he enjoyed hanging out with Isabella's friends and family members.

The only thing he wasn't really crazy about was Isabella's jealousy. He'd grown up as a boy in The Home and then, later, as a young man in Hialeah, always having lots of platonic friendships with girls. He'd never thought anything of it, but Isabella didn't like him to have any close women friends. She thought that men should stick with men and women should stick with women as far as their friendships went, and she viewed other women, particularly younger, good-looking ones, as potential threats to her relationship with Jerry.

Jerry dodged her undeserved accusations and occasional jealous outbursts by just not talking about the women he interacted with at work. Also, he frequently changed the security code on his personal cell phone. He didn't feel like he was doing anything the least bit wrong, but he saw no reason to go around poking the beehive by giving Isabella any ammunition to feed her groundless doubts about his faithfulness. He'd never been with another woman once he and Isabella had gotten into the groove of a steady relationship.

After Cassie had gotten in touch with him, Jerry did some soul-searching about how to deal with Isabella's jealousy. He decided to just totally leave her out of the loop. He would arrange for any future contact with Cassie without telling his girlfriend anything about it. It wasn't until later that Jerry started to understand that many of the mistakes he'd made stretched back to that one little secret.

About a week after Cassie called him, the two of them arranged to meet out at the beach in a few more days for a quick lunch at a restaurant on the Intracoastal. Jerry had no idea what to expect, although Cassie had texted him a somewhat blurry photo of herself. She had said that she would also text him a description of what she was wearing on the day they were going to meet, to help him recognize her.

So, all he knew was that he was going to have lunch a woman he had last seen back when they were both about twelve years old. She'd said she would be wearing a black dress, probably, and that her hair was shorter and maybe redder than it had been when he'd last seen her long ago, waving goodbye to him as his aunt and uncle's car pulled away from The Home.

****

I'm not really sure what I was expecting when I went to meet Jerry. I saw a fit-looking blond guy wearing wraparound sunglasses sitting at a table under a blue and white striped umbrella out on the terrace of the restaurant. He was quite tan. He looked like he hit the gym pretty often. I was attracted to him right away, before I even realized that I was probably looking at my little friend Jerry from Massachusetts for the first time in maybe twenty years.

I wondered if he would recognize me. There were a few other women walking around, so it wasn't like I was the only possibility. I was wearing a black, sleeveless, form-fitting dress, but not slutty-black; elegant and expensive-looking black.

I've taken to ordering my clothing cheap, directly from China, so I have a lot of choices in my wardrobe. My current job as a nurse at a private Miami Beach rehab requires me to look like I'm the concierge at a very upscale hotel rather than merely a medication dispenser at a facility for rich junkies cooling their heels in detox. Yet, my outfits get messed up on the job pretty often: spills, stains, little rips, and so forth. Nurses have a lot of grunge work to do. Hence, all the clothes. I'm sorry if my clothes are made by underpaid wage-slaves in a factory that probably has exploitive and unhealthy working conditions, but I didn't create the troubling parts of the global economy any more than you did.

I could have just walked up to the guy sitting there who I thought might be Jerry and asked him straight up if it was him. For some reason, though, I wanted to see if he would recognize me. I don't know why it mattered. Anyway, I stood on the terrace of the restaurant, my hand on my hip, looking out at the ocean like a model on a photo shoot.

After a minute or less, some guy from the restaurant, the concierge, I guess, came over and asked if he could help me. He had that slightly lisp-y Cuban accent that I like. I looked over at Jerry and smiled. I still didn't think he knew it was me. Then I shook my head at the concierge, walked over to where Jerry was sitting, and said to him, "Hi, I'm Cassie."

I'll skip all the boring parts about our happy, chatty reunion. Suffice it to say that I felt my eyes were locked in to his for the entire time we sat there. Every time the server came over, it felt like a huge disruption of the charged atmosphere at our table. Jerry and I eventually stood up after a couple of drinks without even bothering to order food, went back to my new rental apartment situated just one block off Collins Avenue, and spent the rest of the afternoon in bed.

I didn't bring Jerry back to my place expecting anything amazing, but the sex completely blew me away. We just totally clicked in bed. His stamina and his intuitive responses to my little moans and gasps were perfect, just what I wanted and needed. I was so happy.

What I *did* expect, after, was for Jerry and me to start dating, just like a regular couple. He had been so warm and passionate that whole afternoon, but his eyes turned troubled when it was time for me to get ready to go to work. I had sort of a short swing shift scheduled, from six until midnight.

"I get off right at twelve, so if you want to stay here until I get back…" I said. That's when I noticed the look that was spreading across his face.

"Cassie," he said a few minutes later, after he got out of the shower. "I need to tell you something. Maybe I should have brought it up earlier. My girlfriend, Isabella, and I are pretty serious." He didn't exactly cast his gaze down at the floor, but he didn't meet my eyes.

I just stared at him.

He and this Isabella were so fucking serious that he had just spent the whole afternoon in bed with me doing things with my body that could have made us the stars of a long, lovely, sexy, romantic porn video. So *maybe* he should have said something earlier? And then, *then*, he'd gone into my bathroom and taken a very long, soapy shower to wash the smells of our sex and my perfume off his body? I held my temper, though, and gave him a little shrug with my left shoulder like I was cool with it and walked him to the door.

As soon as he was gone, I looked up this girlfriend online. She was, in fact, with a local real estate company, like he'd said earlier at lunch. I scanned the list of open houses that her broker was having on the coming weekend, and found one that an associate named Isabella was hosting in Country Walk.

I chose to hit that open house Sunday at what I guessed would be the most crowded time of day so that Miss Isabella wouldn't have too much time to focus on me individually. There were five cars parked in front of the house when I arrived. Perfect. The sellers must have priced it competitively.

I nonchalantly approached the front door, looking up at the gutters and eaves to see what kind of shape they were in, acting like how I assumed a normal house-hunter would.

Once inside, I signed the book with a fake name and my real cell phone number. Then, I went to look at the kitchen first thing, just like a typical woman looking at homes might do.

Isabella was short, trim, and was wearing very high heels and a gray tropical weight business suit. She had her long dark hair pulled back attractively. She was good-looking, but not in an out of the park home run kind of way. I felt a little better. After I checked out the bathrooms, Isabella approached me with a friendly smile.

"How do you like the place?" she asked.

"It's ok," I said. "I'm thinking more about a condo, maybe one near the beach. I don't have the time to keep up a yard."

"I have a couple of nice listings around Eighty-fifth and Collins," Isabella said. "Would you like for me to arrange a showing?"

I smiled. "Maybe. I'll let you know." I waved her business card, so she'd know I'd picked one up from the table.

Then, suddenly from out of nowhere, I got the feeling that I should probably just leave. Sometimes, I do get these feelings, and I've learned not to ignore them. My animal instincts, I call them. I snatched up another one of her business cards, nodded and pointed to my watch, and scooted out the front door.

I was barely in my car, just pulling away from the curb, when Jerry drove up. I'm sure he didn't see me. I just hoped he wouldn't study Isabella's sign-in list and recognize my real phone number that I'd written next to *Gina*, my fake name.

It wasn't that I was so embarrassed about stalking Jerry's girlfriend. It's not like he had the high moral ground at this point. I just didn't want to become a suspect later, if it ever came down to that.

I decided to wait in my car around the corner to see if Jerry would leave soon. If he did, then I might just go back inside the house and feign some more interest in shopping for a house or a condo. Maybe I could set up some private showings, or even just one, maybe at a different house or at a condo in a more isolated area, maybe on some dark, rainy evening when I'd be Isabella's only customer.

CHAPTER 4

"Hey, *mi vida!*" said Isabella. Jerry had strolled into the kitchen of the house she was showing, a warm smile on his face. "*Que bolá?*"

"Nothing too much. Just thought I'd stop by to see how you're doing."

"It's kind of slow. People are dropping by, but no real interest. There was a woman here a few minutes ago who seemed pretty interested. She said she's renting out at the beach for now; I guess she's new to the area."

"Do you want to go over to Paulo and Sara's after you close up?"

"Sure. Should I meet you there, or what?"

"I could wait with you here, and we could drive over together."

"I think I want to go home first and change. I'll see you over there."

A casually dressed young couple entered the home and stood uncertainly in the hallway.

"First time buyers, I bet," Isabella whispered to Jerry. "See you later."

Jerry gave her a quick kiss on the cheek and exited by the kitchen door.

After Jerry left, Isabella gave the couple a quick tour of the house and made sure they noticed how nice the fenced yard would look, even at night, with all the outdoor lighting the home sellers had installed. The smaller bedroom was staged as a baby's room. The wife looked pregnant, so Isabella made sure to highlight that space during the tour. The woman might have just been overweight, so Isabella didn't ask any intrusive questions, and the wife didn't volunteer anything.

As Isabella was getting ready to close up the home at the end of the open house period, the woman who'd stopped by earlier and said she was maybe more interested in a condominium apartment than a house, came back. She said she thought she did want to set up appointment to see a few of Isabella's recommended properties. They arranged to meet at a listing one of the other salespeople had out on the Intracoastal.

Gina was her name, the prospect said, Gina Petracelli. This Gina didn't look Italian at all, what with her greenish-blue eyes and reddish blond hair.

My ex-husband's name," said Gina, reading Isabella's expression.

"See you Thursday, Gina," Isabella said.

"I'll definitely call to let you know if anything comes up and I have to postpone, like if they call me in to work," Gina replied.

****

I actually was married once, but not to a guy with the last name of Petracelli. After I left foster care and The Home and juvie and all that behind me and had enrolled in a college up state to work on my nursing degree, I met a guy. He was in my Wednesday physiology lab, during my second year of course work. He was enrolled as a junior in pre-med, he said.

Jack Hartford was tall, dark-haired, and a total frat boy. He had gorgeous brown eyes. He told me he was from Marblehead and that he'd been a sailing fanatic ever since he was six years old. He also mentioned he had a pretty bad case of asthma and needed to always carry a prescription inhaler around with him. I told him that my family had died, but I didn't say anything about the Home, or about my stay in juvie. After we'd slept together a few times, he invited me out to meet his parents.

His father said that he thought I was hot, too hot for his son, and that maybe he was the one who should be dating me. He actually said that in front of both Jack and Jack's mother. Jack just rolled his eyes, and his mother took it in stride, so I assumed it wasn't the first time he'd ever both trashed his son and made a move on his son's date within fifteen minutes of meeting her.

His mom sat me down after dinner and brought out some old family photo albums. She showed me pictures of both sets of Jack's grandparents.

His great-grandfather, now deceased, had been a rabid antisemite and a racist, plus a good friend of the original Henry Ford. Jack had told me some of this family history before we'd even arranged to go out to see his parents, so that I wouldn't be shocked. I guess he knew from experience the directions the conversation with his parents would be likely to go. This same great-grandfather/buddy of Henry Ford had also been a member of the Ku Klux Klan, Jack had said, and I don't think he was kidding.

Jack's maternal grandparents were serious-eyed people who now lived out in the Berkshires during the summers and down in the Turks and Caicos during the winter. They'd rented Dick Clark's place down there in Chalk Sound one season right after America's Oldest Teenager had died, before they bought themselves a spacious condo on the same island, said Jack's mother.

"My whole family used to try to fly down during February school break," said Jack.

I took all this to mean that Jack's grandparents on his mother's side of the family tree were also loaded, but I didn't bite. I just acted cool about it, like I dated guys from rich families all the time, which wasn't true at all.

A few months later, after a lot of fun times together and a lot of hot sex, Jack and I surprised his family and a bunch of their Waspy friends by stopping in at one of his parents' regular Sunday pre-football game champagne brunches. We dropped the exciting news that we had flown out and gotten married in Las Vegas over the past weekend. The room went silent, and everyone's eyes shifted to look at my belly.

"I'm not pregnant," I said coolly.

Jack's father looked like arteries were going to start popping off all over his head.

"We'll see about that," he said, like he thought he had caught me in a trap and that an expanding belly would soon make my obvious lie public knowledge.

I insisted that I was definitely not pregnant and acted indignant and offended. My new young husband just stood there uncomfortably, shifting his weight from one foot to another. I certainly wasn't going to tell his parents that I'd been on birth control pills since my early teens, right after I'd left the Home for foster care.

A few months later, after it became evident that I was *not* pregnant, no one in Jack's family apologized to me. In fact, they started hinting that they'd like a grandchild and that we should hop to it.

The thing was though, I was finding that marriage, or at least this marriage, really didn't suit me. I had kind of assumed that marrying Jack meant that we would just move in together and continue to have a lot of sex. I would stay in school and keep working to finish up my nursing degree; he would do his premed course work and start applying to medical schools; we'd split the household chores. Then, at some vague point in the future, maybe after he became a doctor, we might move somewhere else, and have a kid, or something.

Turns out, though, that his parents had raised a pretty spoiled and not-all-that-motivated son, which I hadn't had much cause to notice prior to the marriage ceremony. So, after we came back from our Las Vegas wedding and honeymoon weekend and were living together in an apartment off campus, I ended up working a part time job, taking a full load of nursing classes which included long hours of practicums, and doing all the housework. Jack cut classes, and went out drinking with his friends at the campus hot spots almost every night while I was either at work or studying. He didn't graduate on time. Or even come close.

He would take a big huff off his asthma inhaler whenever I said that maybe he should party less and work more, and then made it seem like it was all my fault that he was getting so upset that he couldn't even breathe. I thought that the whole asthma drama was kind of over the top.

At what was supposed to be both our graduations, I was the only one standing there in a cap and gown, and Jack's father was pissed. Like it was my fault somehow that the boy *they* had raised continued to be in their pockets all the time and was wasting their tuition money by not studying.

So, I told Jack as soon as his parents had bugged off back to Marblehead, no doubt pouting all the way, that I was sorry, but I was done with both him and his family.

I flew out to Hawaii right after that conversation to take the national nursing exam. I had scheduled it all the way across the continent and the Pacific Ocean, because why not make it a fun experience? I felt I had earned a short vacation after all the years of work I'd put in, and I hadn't been taken on a proper honeymoon trip after we'd married. I guess my original plan had been for Jack to come along, too.

When I got back from Hawaii, Jack had filed for divorce. I assumed he'd made the move so that I wouldn't file first.

A while later, after I had begun working full time as a newly minted RN, I had imagined that I would just be able to put Jack and his very rude parents behind me. Turns out, though, that I was still pissed. Very pissed. And I stayed pissed off. I kept brooding about it. How was I even the bad guy in all this? I just couldn't let things stand the way we had left them.

So, one evening in October, after our divorce was final and the lawyers and the judge hadn't awarded me even one dime in the settlement because the marriage had been so short and we didn't really have any shared assets they said, I dropped over to Jack's place, unannounced, just to talk. And to clear the air, I said, although that was a private joke between me and myself.

Anyway, to make a long story short, Jack died of an asthma attack while I was there. I really, truly had had major doubts about the seriousness of his asthmatic condition. I had thought all along that he was mainly just being a drama queen about the whole thing, a big baby. My plan had been to simply go over to his place and test out my suspicions about that, nothing more.

Before I went to see him that evening, I had stopped by our local animal shelter. Dogs don't always like me. Cats do. I had spent the entire afternoon cuddling a whole bunch of affection-starved, unwashed cats and kittens against my sweater. Then, as soon as I showed up at Jack's place and he'd very reluctantly let me in, I sailed right by him, straight back to his bathroom.

"I have to pee," I'd said, and I grabbed up all of his rescue inhalers that I could find in there. When I came back out, he was already reacting to the cat allergens on my clothes, which, again, I admit did surprise me. I thought there was at best only about a 50/50 chance of my plan working. It was intended as more of an experiment, really.

Anyway, I snatched away the inhaler that Jack had pulled out from his shirt pocket before he even had time to take a single huff. He sank down on the couch with a look of shock. I yanked off my cat hair-infested sweater, tossed it over his face, and quickly pulled the sleeves tight and tied them around his neck. I stepped back a few feet so I could make a quick exit if he got up and went for me, watching him struggle to breathe, still surprised that it was working. Maybe he was surprised, too, because he didn't even make a move get up from the couch. He just sat there with the sweater tightly knotted over his head.

My backup plan, if the cat allergen-provoked asthma attack thing didn't work and he then went around accusing me of trying to kill him, was to just deny it. Like, who would do something that crazy? I even had some potential witnesses lined up to account for my whereabouts; I intended to leave straight from Jack's apartment to meet some of my fellow nursing students at a restaurant across town, where we would be spending the evening in a very public place eating and drinking and laughing.

But my plan did work. After Jack was dead, I pulled my sweater off his face, returned his rescue inhalers to where I'd found them in the bathroom, including the one I'd snatched away from him just before he was hit by the fatal asthma attack, and went off to meet my friends at the restaurant. We chatted about all the crazy stuff that goes on in the medical profession and had a really good time. One of the girls commented that I always seemed so chill. I just shrugged off the compliment and smiled sweetly at her.

****

Jerry could feel deep in his guts that he had a serious domestic problem blossoming up like a bank of dark, tropical storm clouds. He found himself chewing on all the possible scenarios and outcomes he could imagine whenever he wasn't focused on something at work that took his mind off his problems on the home front.

With Cassie, face it, he'd drawn one hell of a wild card. He might try to tell himself that it had just been a one-and-done thing with her, and, yes, although he had been unfaithful to Isabella, it wasn't going to keep happening. But he doubted that he was going to be able to stay away from Cassie, and he doubted that he would have any shot at keeping control over whatever was going to happen next. She was just too hot and too unpredictable. The thing with Cassie could easily go careening off in some unforeseen direction so fast that he would feel like he was in a motor vehicle spinning out on winter ice. Very thin ice. There was just something about her that made him feel like anything was possible.

But he had to see her again. And probably again and again after that. The sex had been unbelievable, without question the best of his life.

The quandary was that he really didn't want either to break up with Isabella right now or continue being unfaithful to her. And he was pretty sure, in any case, that Cassie wouldn't just quietly settle for being his side-chick.

He and Isabella saw eye to eye on most important things, like money and security. Their shared focus was on being hard-working and responsible members of their community. He could see a stable future with Isabella. They would save money, buy a nicer house than the one he had now, probably have kids someday, live a normal life. A life with Cassie would be none of that, at least not the normal part.

He guessed that was much of the attraction he felt toward Cassie. She was a little bit dangerous and a little bit wild. He loved that about her in bed, and he'd admired that about her when they'd been children, but he doubted that she could just compartmentalize that aspect of her personality and save it all just for him in the bedroom.

Maybe they could meet a few more times, and by then they would both have gotten all they wanted from each other. They were quite different people, so the thing with Cassie might just quickly burn itself out. Afterwards, they could go on peacefully living their lives apart, as they had before. Jerry recognized that he was lying to himself as soon as that train of thought bubbled up.

For one thing, if Isabella found out about Cassie before he and Cassie were finished with each other, all bets were off. Isabella was prone to being more than just a little bit over the top herself where jealousy was concerned. She came across as chill, but she always kept aware of little things, like changes in his work schedule or which guys he went out with for a drink after work. She was pretty subtle about it, but she knew the names of every woman he'd ever worked around and kept tabs on all of them through their social media. Sometimes, she'd even meet them for friendly lunches or girls' nights out, just to keep in the loop. And to make sure that they knew that she knew what was going on.

Cassie was the real wild card, though. She was hot as a pistol, but Jerry wasn't sure if Cassie was particularly concerned about his, or about anybody's, domestic stability. Would Cassie allow their relationship to remain a secret if they kept on seeing each other? If he dropped Cassie or slowly backed away from a relationship with her, now or in the future, would she just let it be or would she try to retaliate somehow?

And, if Isabella ever found out about Cassie, lots of things would start blowing up, pop, pop, pop, and the shrapnel would go flying in all directions. People would get hurt.

He couldn't begin to estimate the number of domestic calls he'd responded to as a law enforcement officer. He hated them, as did just about every cop he'd ever known. Aside from the expected ingredients of substance abuse and lots of yelling and screaming, there was also the very real danger of firearms at the scene in the hands of crazy people. Plus, all sorts of garden-variety derangement and volatility, stuff little kids should never have to witness. How do these people even find each other, he used to wonder. And why do they stay together and have kids?

Actually, he knew the answer to the last question, pretty much. Like all Florida cops, he was required to take periodic online training in domestic violence to maintain his certification.

As far as how the people in these situations found each other, well, the opinion of some experts was that the main abuser is pretty skilled at picking up the cues of vulnerable potential partners. Then, he goes about creating a web of financial or emotional dependency, and trains his partner in increments, day by day, to tolerate the abuse cycle. If the partner doesn't leave and stay gone after the very first incident or indicator, the abuser will normally apologize, sometimes profusely, and swear it will never happen again.

Next time, he'll just amp it up a little more, and, again, swear he's so sorry and beg her to give him another chance. But he'll continue to work on her, infiltrating and undermining her sense of self-worth with little not-compliments.

He'll probably tell her how much he needs her and get her to invest in him as a partner, emotionally and financially. Get her pregnant. Alienate her family and friends. Make it very difficult for her to work a steady job or to exit his sticky web without substantial external supports, supports which the abuser has been working overtime to remove as quickly as possible.

None of that was like anything Jerry had ever experienced in his own personal life. He'd never laid a hand on a woman he was involved with. He'd never made threats of any kind in a relationship. If she wanted to be there, and if they could work out any differences they might have, then great. If not…well, you go your way and I'll go mine, and peace be with you.

He couldn't even imagine being on the receiving side of the abuse equation. There was no question at all that he'd immediately cut ties and put a decisive, early end to things if anyone ever tried that kind of shit on him, verbal, physical, psychological, whatever.

His mom and dad had just been regular parents. That's how Jerry remembered them: birthday parties with a nice cake and candles, his father's scratchy face before he shaved in the mornings, pancakes for Sunday breakfast…a new baseball glove. Any spankings he'd ever gotten he could count on one hand, and that only happened if he'd done something really stupid. Like the time he and another eight-year-old from down the block went around letting the air out of all the neighbors' tires.

Then, his parents had died, and he'd been stunned into a numb emotional hibernation. He remembered pulling up to The Home, riding in the back seat of the car with a social worker from protective services. He didn't really understand at that point that he was going to be left there, and that the social worker was going to drive away without him.

There had been a flurry of activity at his arrival, warm greetings and introductions being made, all of which he heard through a gauzy, protective filter that muffled the input coming at him. He stood blankly in a small bedroom looking at the wool, army-green blankets on the bunk beds pushed up against three of the walls.

"You can pick either the upper bunk against the window, or the lower bed over by the closet," the lady from The Home said. He looked out the window. The car that had brought him was still parked down below. There was a young girl standing outside staring up at him.

"That's Cassie," someone said. "Her family died, too. Maybe you'll be friends."

Another thing Jerry clearly recalled about The Home was how sad most of the kids were when they first came to live there, because they missed their families so much. Even the kids who'd been taken away by Child Protective Services from horrible, abusive parents were sad. Jerry's parents had both died, so of course he was grieving, but all the kids in The Home were going through a kind of grief both for what they'd lost and for the fading hope that maybe things would get better at their house, and they could go back home.

No one at The Home was ever mean or disrespectful to the kids, not the staff anyhow, and most of the kids came around to feeling less sad after a while. A few never really seemed sad at all, even when they first arrived amid the disorienting flurry of attention from strangers. Young Cassie had been one of the kids like that. She'd seemed cheerful and really calm about living there.

After he'd left The Home and moved to Miami to live with his aunt and uncle, Jerry was sad again, this time for just a little while. It felt strange to be with relatives he didn't really know very well. They'd always sent him Christmas and birthday cards, but he didn't know his aunt and uncle yet on a personal, face-to-face basis. He missed the predictable routine of The Home, and he missed his friends there. Sister Margaret. Cassie. The boys he walked to school with. His Boy Scout troop. All of that.

Miami was so hot and humid compared to Up North. The bright Miami sun made Jerry's afternoon baseball practices, which he'd loved up north, feel like a sweaty chore. And it was so noisy. The traffic never stopped. There was music everywhere, thumping out of cars and floating in the air. Loud, happy-drunk backyard parties in the neighborhood spilled out on to the streets until late at night every weekend.

But eventually, Jerry's memories of his life in Massachusetts and his attachments there faded as he began to form new connections and involve himself with the kids in his new neighborhood. He'd never known there were so many people who spoke Spanish in America. And so many Spanish dialects. After his ears became familiar with the sounds, he started to pick up some of the language pretty quickly, at first mostly Cuban slang and cuss words.

Since he'd been reunited with Cassie, a surprising assortment of feelings and recollections from the various segments of his childhood had come flooding back. Cassie had been like a safe space for him when they'd been kids at The Home. He was pretty sure that he had also protected Cassie more than once from other kids' aggressions or from punishments from the staff that were coming her way. She'd been a feisty little rule-breaker, he realized. But back when they were children, he'd just thought of her as being braver and bolder than he was, a kid who was not at all afraid to take some liberties and to push the boundaries. He had admired her spunkiness.

She was still feisty now, in a much smoother, more sophisticated way. She was the one who had contacted him. She had taken the initiative to invite him back to her place, but maybe that part had been inevitable. The sex certainly wasn't her fault; he'd wanted it more than almost anything he'd ever wanted in his life. But he wasn't going to make the next move. He wasn't going to pursue her. What ever happened next was going to have to be mostly up to her.

It occurred to Jerry that he'd been handing all the choices over to Cassie right from the beginning. She'd been the one who had originally sought him out down here in Miami. She was the one who'd invited him to meet her at the restaurant. She had cast a spell on him during their lunch at the beach; he had felt himself being swept out to sea as their eyes locked across the table. Did that mean that his infidelity to Isabella wasn't quite as much his fault as it was Cassie's? Or did it just mean that he was being a pathetic liar to himself about who was responsible for what he'd said and done entirely of his own free will?

Some bad things were going to happen. He could almost smell the danger, like the first whiff of smoke you get as it curls beneath the bedroom door when your house is on fire. Jerry didn't know exactly what was going to happen; all he knew was that he wasn't ready yet to let go of Cassie.

Jerry's phone vibrated and he dug it out of his pocket. A text message from Cassie. The little jolt of excitement he felt told him that he was probably going to keep going down whatever road she had in mind for them.

****

The Home wasn't actually the first place I lived after my grandmother died. My grandfather said to me the day after her funeral that he was too old to raise a little girl. I stared up at him, tears spilling from my eyes. I thought he was telling me that he was going to have to go to the hospital, too, just like my grandmother had, and that he was going to die.

"No, no," he said. "I'm not dying, Cassie. But I can't take care of you by myself. My doctor says maybe I'm just too old to take care of a little girl."

I stared down at my shoes. It seemed like he was lying. He'd been taking care of me just fine without my grandmother for the two weeks she'd been away at the hospital, and all the time before that while she'd been sick at home, too sick to do much.

"But I've found a better place for you to live. It's a nice foster home just over past Oak Street. They keep two or three little girls there. You can walk to the same school you've been going to. You'll have the same friends. We can visit each other on special occasions, like at Christmas and on your birthday."

"I don't want to move over there," I said stubbornly. "I want to stay here."

On Saturday morning, my grandfather dropped me off at the place past Oak Street. He brought along a tattered suitcase, too, which held all my clothes and books, and some toys.

It was a big house, with a huge old oak tree planted right out front that was taller than the roof of the house. A girl with short, dark hair was looking down from a small third floor window. She waved at me. I didn't wave back.

The front room had high ceilings and heavy, dark wood furniture. It looked spooky to me.

My grandfather laughed a little when I said that. "Not spooky, Cassie. Just old-fashioned."

After my grandfather left me in the parlor with a man and a woman who said their names were Hank and Martha, they told me, "We'll be taking care of you from now on, Cassie." I asked where I was going to sleep.

"Upstairs," said Martha, "up on the same floor as the other girls. You'll even have your own room, all to yourself."

She brought me up the steep oak staircase, along with the small suitcase my grandfather had packed for me. It seemed like she was having a hard time carrying it, because she had to stop on each landing to catch her breath. She told me to unpack and to get ready for lunch.

I just stood there after she went back downstairs. I turned around and saw the dark-haired girl from the window standing at the doorway.

"Can I come in?" she asked.

I nodded.

She walked around the room. "Sarah used to be in this room," she said.

"Where did she go?" I asked. "Did her family take her back home?"

The dark-haired girl shook her head. "I think she died."

My eyes must have widened.

"You'll be okay if you remember to lock your door at night." She pointed to the latch. "And don't ever, ever stay inside the house all by yourself. When you come home from school, wait outside until Martha or one of the other kids gets home. Even if it's cold out and your legs are freezing."

I thought the dark-haired girl, Annie was her name, was just trying to scare me for some reason. I didn't believe her about Sarah dying.

"I'm not lying," she said, shaking her ponytail. "Don't let Hank trick you so you're all alone with him by yourself, or you'll be sorry."

But it turned out that I wasn't the sorry one.

At first, Hank just smiled at me, but he never bothered me at all. He spent most of his time down in the basement. I could hear his sad country music coming up through the floorboards. Then, maybe after I'd been there for about a month and the busy, over-worked social workers had all but stopped coming by to check on how the foster care placement was working out, he offered me a chocolate bar one Saturday. It was a Mars bar, one of my favorites. Martha was out grocery shopping. I remembered what Annie had said, and I shook my head and promptly went outside.

One day two weeks later, when I came home from school, no one else was there except for Hank.

"Martha took the other girls to get their teeth cleaned at the dentist. She didn't take you, because you don't need a dental examination yet."

"I do, too," I said, backing away as he came toward me, baring my teeth like a tiger. I turned to go back out the front door, intending to just wait on the front porch. But Hank grabbed my arm and told me I had to do what he said, because he was in charge when Martha wasn't there. But I wouldn't get in any trouble if I just went downstairs to the basement with him. He only wanted to take some pictures of me, he said, "just a few pictures with my camera. Then I'll give you a chocolate bar and you can go outside again and play."

Hank had a special room down in the basement, the dark room he called it. He led me down there and explained that it was called a dark room because that was where he developed all the pictures he took. It wouldn't really be dark, he said, not while I was down there. In fact, it would be very bright, because he was going to need to turn on some strong lights to make the pictures he was going to take of me.

"The room is only dark when I'm in here by myself, developing my pictures."

He showed me his setup, including his enlarger and his developer chemicals.

"People get their pictures made at the drug store," I said. I knew something bad was going to happen and that Hank was lying to me.

"Not these kinds of pictures," he said. "Now, Cassie, here's a glass of soda for you to drink, so you won't be thirsty."

I watched him pour the ginger ale from a can he popped open, straight into a glass. He handed me the glass and I saw some specks of white powder floating in it. I looked up at him.

"Go ahead," he said. "Drink it."

I shook my head.

"I'm not going to hurt you."

But he did. He hurt me, and he told me to shut up, and that no one could hear me and that no one would believe me.

Two weeks later, he was back down in the dark room again. No one else was home. I knew that sooner or later he was going to try to hurt me some more, or maybe one of the other girls, so I was ready. I'd brought some things inside from a shed in the backyard and had put them in the closet right near the top of the basement stairs, way in the back, where the wall slanted down.

I waited until I heard Hank's sad country music start floating up the basement stairs. That meant he'd probably been drinking his whiskey and was maybe lying down on the ratty old couch. I carefully opened the basement door so the hinges wouldn't squeak and peeked down the stairs. He had some pictures fanned out on a table and he was sitting on a stool, not lying on the couch, swaying from side to side. Now seemed like my best chance.

I quietly lifted the big, heavy can out from the closet near the stairs where I'd been hiding it and grabbed a box of wooden matches from Martha's junk drawer next to the old gas stove. I double-checked to see if anyone was back yet from shopping. Then, I carried the heavy gasoline can down the basement steps as quietly as I could.

Hank turned around when my foot scuffled as I reached the bottom step. He stared at me bleary-eyed. His almost empty whiskey bottle was sitting near him on the worktable.

"Cassie," was all he said before I swung the open can of gasoline, slopping the liquid all over him. Then I struck a wooden match and flicked it into the pool of gasoline that was quickly being soaked up by the dirty, old basement carpet.

Hank's mouth opened. The flames flared up tall with a loud *whoosh*, and I ran back up the stairs and bolted the basement door shut.

Then I jumped on my bike and rode away down to the park at the end of the street. I got on a swing, waiting to see if any fire trucks would come. I heard some sirens, but not until quite a few minutes later. I just hung around with a couple of other kids by the swings, listening. Then, when the fire trucks finally roared on to our street, a bunch of us rode our bikes up the hill to watch.

A few days later, some people came to talk with me, not just me, but with the other girls who lived at Hank and Martha's house, too. I shook my head, wide-eyed, and said I'd been at the park, you can ask anybody. The next day, the same people came back, helped me pack up my things, and brought me to The Home.

Did I ever feel bad about what happened to Hank? I don't know. I don't really remember, but I don't think so. Did Hank ever feel bad about what he'd been doing to the scared little girls who were supposed to be safe at his and Martha's foster home? I doubt it. Not until that day down in the basement, anyway.

CHAPTER 5

Not very long after Jerry and I had our reunion lunch at the beach and then hooked up back at my apartment, I got an interesting call related to my job. (I don't really like that term *hook up* and what it implies, but I'm feeling a little bit cynical right now, and maybe a bit disappointed in Jerry. More than disappointed. Actually, I'm kind of angry at him.)

The Irish mobster guy from Cranberry Pointe, the drug rehab where I was working right before I moved down to Miami, had found a way to get in touch with me. Danny said that he was doing great, just great, and that he was staying off everything except for an occasional drink with the boys. He implied that he'd gotten my number at my new job from some staff member at Cranberry Pointe, which was unethical on the part of the staff member, and a little bit worrisome for me. I didn't need South Boston hit men or anyone else from any of my previous lives showing up down here in Miami. I'm very big on letting the past stay back where it belongs.

I tried to sound calm and pleased to hear from Danny, but I really wasn't. The personal contact information of current and former staff members is never supposed to be released to patients for any reason, but someone at Cranberry Pointe had obviously screwed up. Who knows. It possibly could have been somebody down here in Miami, because I did have to give the personnel department at my current Miami job my Cranberry Pointe HR contact so they could check my job references during the hiring process. Whichever way it had happened didn't really matter now. A stone-cold killer from Boston had tracked me to my new life in Florida.

Anyway, Danny said he didn't want to bother me and that he'd mainly called to thank me once again for helping him to get sober, but that he felt an obligation was hanging over his head.

"You don't owe me anything, Danny," I said, quickly understanding what he was getting at. "If I helped you in any way at all, I'm so glad, but it was my job. And my pleasure. Drug rehab staff are supposed to do what they can for *all* their patients. And we get paid to do it. So, it's not a favor you need to repay. It's not like that at all."

"I know, Miss Cassandra, I know. But it's like you have a marker, that's what it feels like to me."

"Well," I said, "how about if I give you a call if I can think of anything?" I was trying to put him off politely. I knew what a marker was.

"Ok, sure, Miss Cassandra, but I'm only going to be in Miami for a few weeks. Maybe only for a few days. I just have some quick business down here."

I really didn't want to get mixed up with a former patient who was probably down here doing sketchy business as a member of some organized crime outfit from up in Boston. But the more I thought about it, I guessed I could probably come up with a job or two where Danny might be able to discharge his sense of obligation and maybe help me out in the process.

I wasn't sure what Danny's level of competence was, or what the other business was that he had in Miami. I didn't want to make things worse for myself by getting too involved, and, actually, not worse for

Danny, either, because if things went poorly for him, things could get ugly for me, too, and fast.

I thought for a long time that night during slow periods on my shift about whether I should give Danny the contact information I had for Isabella and just see what he could come up with. She was probably all alone for extended periods of time at open houses when there was no buyer traffic. Danny would need to know, of course, that Isabella's boyfriend was a Miami cop; Danny might decide that it wasn't really the right job for him because of that.

Or perhaps he'd like the challenge.

I brought that question to him when I called him back. Subtly, of course.

"Not really a problem," said Danny. "Miami used to be run by the Italians back in the day. People don't know that. They think it's all about the Colombians, the Medellin, that kind of thing, but they forget about the Trafficante family…I used to do some business…"

"No, no, no, Danny," I said, practically holding my hands over my ears. "Please don't tell me anything more about any of that. I don't need to know. I just have a simple issue."

"Well, maybe," he said, "but it won't be that simple since a cop is involved. Is he clean, the cop?"

"Yes, I'm sure he is."

"Ok, well, that definitely won't make it any easier. I'll have to look into it. I'll get back with you, Sweetheart." He ended the call. I could imagine him giving me a sly wink at the other end.

So. Now I had a guy who was a Boston contract killer thinking he could call me 'Sweetheart.' I wondered which of us really had the higher body count.

****

The Miami Night Nurse

It was a clear, blue Miami winter afternoon, seventy-two degrees and sunny. Best of all, the traffic hadn't been too bad on the drive over. Isabella leaned back on her park bench at South Pointe and admired the view of the water. It was still more than twenty minutes before she would be able to gain access the condominium apartment she was supposed to show to her prospective buyer. She checked her phone to see if there were any new messages pertaining to the showing.

She didn't know much about this buyer, yet. It was a woman she'd met at one of her open houses a couple of weeks ago, Gina Petracelli. The prospective had already cancelled the first showing Isabella had arranged, full of apologies about her work schedule. The condominium apartment she was showing her today was a whole new listing that Isabella had an exclusive on, so she was eager, at minimum, to bring some traffic through to show the seller that she was working hard to get a contract. Another prospective, one who'd recently cold-called her office, had said by message that he would "try" to come by this afternoon, too, but that he might have to leave for Boston before then.

Isabella shrugged to herself. She'd love to get a sale from either of them, but it wasn't a matter of life or death. Her bank account was healthy.

At the appointed time, Isabella took the glass and chrome elevator up to the listed apartment and quickly tapped in the entry code on the keypad. She turned the brass knob and opened the door.

The view took her breath away. She'd seen wide expanses of the Atlantic Ocean through the floor-to-ceiling windows of luxury apartments from plenty of angles over the course of her still-new real estate sales career, but this completely unobstructed vista was a knockout. She checked the listing sheet, confirming the square footage and the asking price. The unit was well-priced, and it would probably sell quickly. She hoped Gina Petracelli would love it.

At the top of the hour, the buzzer sounded, but the voice on the intercom was male, which surprised Isabella. The man said he'd already spoken with her office about the place, and that he had to fly out of Miami later today. Did she have time to show him the apartment right now?

Although Isabella was half-expecting some man to call her about this listing based on what her office assistant had mentioned, she didn't know anything about the guy downstairs and was very hesitant about meeting someone alone in a thoroughly sound-proofed apartment for the first time. There were stories about this kind of thing in the business, and it was only common sense to take some precautions. She opened the door to the unit to wait for the man to come up, half-thinking that maybe she would remain outside in the hall while he looked at the apartment.

She checked her text messages once more, pacing nervously. Gina Petracelli confirmed that yes, she was definitely coming, *really, I'll be there*, but that she was still running a little bit late, *sorry, CU in a while*.

Just then, the apartment door across the hall opened, and a fit-looking Cuban guy of about thirty stepped out.

"Hey," said Isabella in rapid Spanish, "could you possibly stay close by me for just a few minutes? I need some help. Please?"

The guy looked down at his phone and breathed out an exhale that was a cross between impatient and reluctant.

Isabella gave him one of her dazzling smiles and beckoned him inside just as she heard the elevator door open down the hallway.

"This will only take a minute," she whispered. "I don't feel completely comfortable showing this unit by myself." She looked up at him pleadingly. "Please, if you could just act like you are also interested in the place for maybe a couple of minutes…"

"Ok, I get it," the guy said. "You want me to act like your buyer's competition. Yeah, sure, I can do that for you. I'll go back into the bedroom, maybe be looking at the closet space, the view, something like that."

Isabella smiled her relief without bothering to correct her rescuer's take on the situation and prepared to greet her actual potential buyer.

She walked back out to the spacious living area. A tall, burly man was standing in the open doorway, blocking anyone from entering or exiting the apartment.

"Hey," he said in some kind of a New England accent. "I'm here to see the apartment. Are you Isabella?"

Isabella looked up at him and gave him as pleasant a smile as she could muster. "So pleased to meet you, Mr....?" she said, extending her hand. He took it, and she gasped as she felt his powerful, calloused hand pull her toward him.

"*Ay, Dios Mio!*" she said loudly, hoping her bodyguard guy would step up for her. There was no way she could defend herself against this powerful man. "Would you like to see the kitchen?" she croaked.

"The balcony first," he said. "I want to see the view."

"Over there," Isabella said. "There's one in the bedroom, too."

"Show me," he said, still firmly holding her hand. Isabella felt a curl of fear. Would this giant try to throw her off the balcony?

"This way." Isabella indicated the room where she prayed she would find her "buyer's competition" waiting and ready to intercede.

"Hey, my friend," Isabella said to her back-up guy in rapid Spanish. "I'm having some trouble with this one. Can you help me, please?"

The Cuban guy stood at least six inches shorter than the New England guy.

Isabella must have done a good job of communicating her fear; her spur of the moment bodyguard quickly thrust his hand under his jacket, pulled out a Glock 17, and stepped back out of the tall guy's reach.

"You can go, now," he said to the New England guy. "Or, not. Your choice." He pointed the semiautomatic weapon at the tall man's crotch.

"Jesus Fucking Christ," said the big guy in his heavy East Boston accent. "I'm just here to look at a condo. What's up with you fucking spics down here? Do you all carry?"

The Cuban guy smiled calmly and gestured with the Glock toward the door. "You've seen enough of this place for today, I think. Make an offer through the broker if you're interested. I understand the kitchen appliances here are all new. Pick up one of the cards from the table on your way out."

Isabella exhaled her relief as the door closed behind the scary Boston thug. "Thank you so much," she said to the Cuban man in Spanish. "I had such a bad feeling about him. I usually don't meet male buyers by myself unless I already know them. You were a lifesaver this afternoon, let me tell you."

"Are you through here for the day?" he asked. "I'm Carlos, by the way."

"Isabella," she said. "My knees are shaking, Carlos."

"May I buy you a drink, Isabella, if you are finished up here for right now?"

"I do have another appointment who should be here soon. My office said she was running a little bit late," Isabella said, handing him her business card. "Otherwise, I would be delighted. My personal cell number is this one," she said, pointing. "I'd love to meet you again soon, Carlos, but not today. You might have just saved my life, though, so thank you."

As she paced around the condo waiting for Gina Petracelli to show up, Isabella's knees were still trembling. *Should I tell Jerry about any of this?* she wondered. *If I do, he's going to worry about me every time I do a showing. I really don't want that. He might try to get me to quit doing showings by myself. No,* she thought. *I'll just ask some of the other girls how they handle these situations. I'm sure they are somewhat commonplace. Better for Jerry not to become too worried about me. Keep him out of the loop just this one time.*

Isabella sighed. She hated keeping secrets from Jerry, and she knew that he worried about her because he loved her. And also, because he knew what kinds of people were out there. *But things like this are just part of the real estate game. I'll just be more careful. I could start bringing along a rookie agent to give them experience, or something like that, if I don't know the buyer already. Maybe carry a gun in my briefcase.*

A full twenty minutes after her scheduled arrival time for the showing, Gina Petracelli called again, this time to cancel the day's appointment.

"I am so, so sorry, I just can't get there. I promise I'll call you back soon to reschedule."

Isabella suppressed her irritation with this unreliable Gina. On the way over to her next appointment through the thick cross-town traffic, Isabella wondered if Carlos would ever call her and what she would say to him if he did. He was pretty cute. Not gay, apparently, despite his meticulously put together outfit. His style was very different from Jerry's, who, like most off-duty cops in the area, dressed neatly but casually. Carlos was both slick and refined, in that way that some of the hot Miami Cuban guys had. Isabella smiled a little. Carlos…his lips were full. His smile was polite but with the hint of an offer.

Isabella shook her head. Nothing was ever going to happen with Carlos even if she did meet up with him. She was practically engaged to Jerry, right? Even though she still didn't have a ring. Besides, Carlos would be a very good contact to have in that nice condominium building, and who knows? Maybe someday she could sell him a new unit or get the listing on his place if he were to move out. Isabella smiled to herself. Maybe she could do both.

****

I looked down at my phone when I heard the swish of an incoming message.

It didn't go too well. She had company, and he was carrying. I guess I might have scared her, to be honest. I can't try again until the next time I'm in town. I'll keep in touch, though, Sweetheart.

"Well, Sweetheart," I said to no one but myself, "I guess it's on to Plan B."

CHAPTER 6

The private drug rehab in downtown Miami where I work is called New Dawn Alternatives, and is housed on the first five floors of a very nice high-rise building located a couple of blocks west of the Intracoastal. The actual ground floor is occupied by struggling retail shops that tend to come and go. Walk-in traffic isn't great in the immediate area, because it really isn't a retail destination, not one of the sections of town with lots of restaurants and bars or cool stores. So, I guess it can be hard for a small business located there to succeed.

One of the shops renting space right below the rehab which does do a very good business is a medical marijuana dispensary, so that's kind of hilarious, in a way. Although, frankly, drugs and alcohol are so easy to obtain in Miami that our patients might as well just learn how to keep on walking right by places like the High-Ho Shoppe straight from the day they are discharged. They can maybe have a laugh at the name of the business without succumbing to the urge to go inside to check it out. Assuming they intend to try to remain sober.

About a week ago, I made the acquaintance of another Miami cop, meaning someone other than Jerry, right in the parking lot outside the High-Ho Medical Marijuana Dispensary. She had apparently been responding to a call of some type, maybe a citizen dialing in a complaint, who knows, and she was just wrapping it up. I was on my lunch break, out to take a brisk walk because it was early February, and not too warm yet.

On a whim, I decided to introduce myself to the cop. Her name badge said Rodriquez.

We got to chatting, and I explained my job as an addictions nurse. We started talking about how so much of the crime in the area is in some way drug and alcohol related. I told her that I didn't drink at all, or very seldom. She said her grandfather had been an alcoholic and a coke addict. He'd died in his late sixties from his addiction, and the whole family still missed him.

Apparently, he had been a great guy, other than when he got trashed and spent the rent money on hookers and cocaine.

I wondered if I should ask if she knew Jerry. There were pros and cons to that, and I didn't want to raise any trouble, at least not yet, for either Jerry or for his relationship with his girlfriend. Instead, I asked Officer Sofia Rodriquez if she would like to have lunch with me some time, so she could help me gain more insight into the drug scene in Miami.

We continued chatting as we stood outdoors on that sunny day, and finally my curiosity got the better of me, so I did ask her if she knew Jerry. I told her he was the only cop besides her that I'd met so far in Miami.

"Yeah, sure, I know Jerry. How do you two know each other?"

"Well, Sofia," I said calmly, having had time to mentally rehearse for the question, "Jerry and I actually went to the same elementary school up in Massachusetts a long, long time ago." I didn't say anything about The Home, because I didn't know if Sofia knew about that part of Jerry's life. My delivery was very matter-of-fact. I knew what her next question would be.

"Do you know Isabella?"

"No, not really," I said. "Do you?"

"Yeah, I've met her. She's okay. I think she's good for Jerry. He's been a lot happier since he met her."

I looked at Sofia questioningly.

"You know," she said. "After his former girlfriend broke it off with him, he was kind of a mess…"

"Yeah, I guess so," I said, even though I didn't. "Is she still around, the Ex?" I asked.

"Nah, I heard she took off for California or somewhere like that. I didn't know her."

I wondered if that meant that Isabella was a rebound for Jerry, so I decided to ask.

Sofia shrugged. "Maybe. But they seem to be doing okay. I think they're in the process of moving in together, or maybe they already have. They've been together for a while now, a couple of years. I'm pretty sure Isabella was hoping for an engagement ring for Christmas, but it didn't happen, so now she has her heart set on Valentine's Day at the latest. I'm not sure where Jerry is with that plan, though. I don't want to get too far into their business, because I have to work with him."

I didn't ask anything more about it, because I didn't want to seem to be anything other than mildly curious. Sofia was a cop, so she knew how to read people. I wondered if she would mention to Jerry that she'd met me, and how he would handle it. I sort of shrugged to myself. I hadn't lied to Sofia, unless you consider lies of omission a big deal. I would discuss the engagement ring business directly with Jerry. I wasn't about to let that slide.

Sofia was nice. She seemed intelligent, honest, and appeared to know how to interact normally with civilians. If she weren't a cop, especially a cop so closely associated with Jerry, I would think about befriending her.

One of the many people I would never befriend under any circumstances is a woman I sometimes have to work with when I do an evening shift at New Dawn Alternatives. Sharon Cowlitz, BSN, RN is frequently on the schedule as Evening Charge Nurse, which is fine with me. It keeps her busy and mostly off the floor.

There is quite a bit more to Sharon than meets the eye. She is blond, thin, almost anorexically so, and is fairly good-looking. I heard her tell someone that she used to be fat in high school. She interacts with other staff members like she is just totally exhausted by their incompetence and professional shortcomings. She used to be married to some doctor, I don't know who. She merely refers to him as "The Doc," with an air of detached bemusement. She doesn't seem to miss being married to him.

Sharon associates mainly with one of the other of the nurses who sometimes works evening shifts on our floor. Carolyn is tall, friendly, married, and kind of husky. I know that word isn't normally applied to women but hear me out.

One evening, I was in a hurry, and I kind of flung open the door to the room that holds the nursing supplies. There was big Carolyn, sitting on a desk chair inside this little room, holding Sharon on her lap in an embrace.

Sharon reacted with embarrassed exasperation, like it was somehow my fault that I was busily doing my job while those two were having at it. I don't care what people do, but don't give me attitude. Back at the rehab up in Massachusetts, Doug and I at least would lock the supply room door when we were doing the deed.

I decided to pretend that I hadn't seen a thing and had drawn no conclusions at all, but Sharon persisted in approaching me.

"You should knock," she said, like I was somehow supposed assume that the nursing supplies room was used routinely for private meetings. I guess it was.

I just looked at her with a neutral expression on my face and shrugged, like none of it was a big deal to me. Which it wasn't. I don't care who screws who on the evening shift, as long as the patients don't figure it out and start gossiping about it. Taking the focus off themselves and their recovery journey is too tempting for some of them as it is, and they are paying a lot of money to get top-notch treatment at New Dawn.

Plus, I don't want Sharon to get started with me and to try to bully me out of my job.

But I don't really think that Sharon would try to make a power play like that. She's just worried right now that I might spill the beans about her on-the-job trysts with Carolyn, but once a little bit of time passes, she'll realize that I don't intend to rat her out or gossip about what I saw. We have always had, and I hope we will continue to have, a distantly cordial relationship. We will never become close friends, and that's how I want it. We'll be fine. I think.

The one person at work who I suspect will for sure try to give me some real shit at some point is Melissa Canfield.

Missy, as she likes to be called, is one of the drug and alcohol counselors on the day shift, so I don't normally need to spend too much time around her, which is how I like it. And I never call her *Missy*. What a dumb name for a forty-something year-old woman.

She's a Certified Drug and Alcohol Counselor, meaning her qualifications don't necessarily imply an advanced degree; rather, she is a trained specialist in addictions and recovery. I've sat in on a few group therapy sessions with her and saw that she is really very good at what she does. She is very perceptive. Perhaps 'savvy' is the better word. She really understands the emotional damage that so many addicts carry. I was initially quite willing to befriend her, even admire her, until I realized that she had taken an almost instant dislike to me. I really don't know why.

But it was very stupid of her to be so open about it. She has no idea who she will be going up against if she ever tries anything with me.

****

I asked Jerry to attend a casual party with me that one of the doctors at work had invited me to. It was scheduled for the coming Saturday night at the doctor's super luxe high-rise off Collins Avenue. The apartment where the get-together was going to take place wasn't up in the actual penthouse, but it was just a couple of floors down from it.

The main part of this high-rise was a redesign of a historic Art Deco building. A surprisingly tasteful glass tower structure was just kind of pasted on to the south side of it. The tower was where the party was being held. The Deco apartments all had big, graceful curving balconies with full ocean views. The tower balconies mainly had the killer city views. Speaking of which, I imagine Jerry's real estate dilettante of a girlfriend would probably be willing to kill just to get a listing in there.

Jerry said he couldn't make it to the party, and that he hoped I would understand.

I pushed him a little bit, assuming that he just didn't want to come with me because of something he had going on with his short little girlfriend. He denied that anything related to Isabella was the reason. I thought about mentioning what I'd heard about the engagement ring business from Sofia, but I didn't. I'd save that for another time, or maybe not bring it up at all. But, for sure, Jerry was definitely not going to be getting married to Isabella.

"That building where you're going to the party is notoriously full of drug dealers," Jerry finally said after I'd nudged him a little more, "plus lots of Russians who are over here to launder money. A cop can't hang around a place like that. It would be a very bad look for me and for the Department."

"Just wear your civvies, gel up your hair, and put on some cool shades. You'll fit right in," I pushed. "You'll be the best-looking guy there, with the hottest-looking date," I cooed with what I hoped was a convincing little smile.

"For sure you'll be the sexiest woman there, or anywhere," he said, giving me a kiss on my forehead, "but I really can't do it."

"Please?" I begged. "I don't think there'll be any drug dealers; someone I work with at *the rehab* told me about the party. There probably won't be any drugs there at all, just alcohol, totally legal alcohol."

It wasn't that I couldn't have a good time at a party without Jerry. I just really wanted to win. I wanted him to come out on a public date with me, let me show him off to some of the people I work with on my shifts, assuming that any of them were there, and screw his stuffy principles. And, most importantly, I wanted to see if I could pry him away from Isabella.

"No can do," Jerry said firmly. "You go ahead and have a good time. And, please, don't ask me to do something like this again. It makes me feel bad."

The look on his face really was more pained than angry. I could tell he was upset, so I didn't say anything more.

Besides, I was already getting some good ideas about how I could make him feel sorry that he had turned me down.

The night of the party, I took a Mercedes ride-share out to the Art Deco building. On the way up in the elevator, a tall, fit Black guy and a woman in a shiny silver dress stood silently. I asked the guy if he was a Miami Dolphins player. It came out a little more flirtatiously than I had intended.

"Oh, he's a player, all right," said his date snippily.

I just smiled and shook my head a little, to let her know she wouldn't have any problems from me. No one has problems from me unless they cross me deliberately. But I did swing my ass a little as I exited the elevator, just because I could.

As it turned out, I met someone at the party that night who would soon become very important to me. His name was Maury Levitt, he told me. His wife, Evelyn, was at home taking care of their little grandkids who were visiting from New Jersey. He was a lawyer who had gone to the University of Miami for his undergraduate work, he said, and that's how he knew the doctor whose apartment this was, from way back in school.

Maury was kind of a short, dumpy little guy, but he obviously had brains, and he had some seriously sharp, funny repartee. I told him a little about my job at the rehab, and he told me with a casual shrug that he was representing a guy on a variety of past and current drug charges who was supplying the cocaine for tonight's party. I liked Maury straight off.

I guess I was wrong, though, when I'd told Jerry that there wouldn't be any drugs at the party. It was a good thing he hadn't come; he would have been so pissed off at me.

"Does the doctor whose apartment this is know anything about the coke?" I asked. I didn't really know that particular Doc well, but, of course, I'd seen him around the rehab.

Maury shrugged. "I would assume so. But the Doc isn't even here right now. He had to go make a run out to the airport. I have no idea when or if he'll get back here."

Maury nodded at a tall white man who was maybe in his late thirties and was wearing a red Hawaiian print shirt. "I guess he was a frat brother of the Doc," Maury said to me quietly. "Now he deals coke."

The cocaine-guy's facial hair made him look like one of the Eagles, circa 1980, one of the good-looking ones.

"I think I'll go talk to a few more people," I said to Maury.

"Here," said Maury, handing me one of his business cards. "I was just now on my way out. You might find you need this someday," he said with a wink. "Just give me a buzz if you ever want my help. Seriously, for any reason at all. Or even if you just want to run something by me. I'd be more than happy to do a consultation, no charge."

I didn't know for sure what that all meant, but I slid Maury's card into my wallet, right next to the one reminding me of a dental appointment I had in Brickell the next week. I gave him a daughterly air-kiss at the doorway.

I was still thinking about Jerry, wishing I were here with him instead of with all these people I didn't know. I'd prefer to be out with Jerry anywhere, really. But he was no doubt loving up his little Cuban girlfriend this very minute. So, I strolled over to the tall coke dealer.

"I was hoping you'd come over to say 'hi'," he said.

"Hi," I said.

"Don't tell me your name," he said.

"I wasn't going to," I lied.

He took my hand and led me to one of the white marble bathrooms and locked the door. He laid out two fat lines of cocaine on a shiny black business card from some area Mercedes dealership. Then he handed me a short plastic straw.

I very rarely use drugs, but I just impulsively huffed up both the lines, one for each nostril.

"Hey, hey, hey!" he said. "What about me?"

"Be my guest," I said flirtatiously, handing him back the straw. He stuck the tip in his mouth and sucked off the white residue. Then, he pulled up my skirt, picked me up, and set my naked buttocks down on top of the cold, hard vanity. We tore in to each other with our mouths and our hands. We shed some more of our clothes, piled a big heap of soft, white towels onto the cold tile floor, and ignored all the knocking on the bathroom door. When he slid it inside me, I thought I was going to die, he was so big.

I don't know if it was the cocaine or his cock, or the combination, but I wasn't thinking about Jerry or about the people just outside the door or the people at work or about anything at all except what the ride was feeling like.

When it was over for both of us, I realized he hadn't used a condom. I sat on the tile floor looking up at him.

He dressed quickly and pulled on a light jacket. "I need to talk to someone here, and then I have to go right back out to make a quick run," he said. "We're almost out of party favors."

"Shit," I said. "You didn't use a rubber."

"Aren't you on the pill, or something, Babe?" he asked, pulling out his phone.

"I meant for like HIV. Or VD."

The coke guy grinned. "I'm not dripping."

"You said it, not me," I snapped, straightening my clothes.

If I catch anything, I'll be really pissed, I thought. "I'm out of here, too," I said coldly, gathering up my things.

He just shrugged and said, "Maybe we'll run into each other again sometime," and turned his attention to the call he was making.

I didn't realize how angry I was at the drug dealer for not using a condom, or for not even at least asking about it beforehand, until I was already standing outside.

It was cloudy and more than a little bit breezy up this high. There was barely any moon. Instead of ordering a rideshare right away and getting into the elevator, I looked down over the outside corridor railing. The apartment was on the sixth floor, so maybe eight-five feet to the ground? I took out my phone, turned on the flashlight app, and shone it around, looking for door camera lenses. I didn't find any in the corridor, which was kind of surprising, but kind of good. So, I waited off in the shadows, pretty close to the elevator, breathing calmly, gathering my strength.

A few minutes later, the coke dealer I'd just fucked came outside. He was alone, still talking on his phone. What little I could hear sounded like he was negotiating prices. I swear I didn't plan it, but he leaned way out over the rail like he was looking for something or at someone down in the parking lot, and I just quietly speed-walked over to him, crouched down, and flipped his long legs up and over. I stood there, shocked that I had managed to shove this big, tall guy over the railing in some kind of adrenaline-fueled rage, or maybe it was all the cocaine I'd just snorted. He never made a sound, except to quietly say, "Oh, fuck," as he started to go over.

Then I turned my head, looking all around, my heart pounding in my chest. Shit! What if someone had seen me? Things looked clear, though. I took a deep breath, trying not to get paranoid, and hurriedly took the elevator to the ground level. A taxi was waiting for someone over near the main entrance to the building. I just acted like the cab was there for me and gave the driver an address in my general neighborhood.

"I thought you was just going over to The Flamingo Club," he said, as he pulled away from the condo tower.

"I changed my mind," I said.

"That will be maybe another six *tarro*," he said, wheeling on to Brickell Ave.

"Fine," I said. Then I shut up and looked down at my phone to see if there were any messages. Work wanted to know if I could come in tomorrow, well, today by now, and sub for the Sunday medication nurse until noon. I shrugged to myself. I hadn't had any alcohol, but I was still kind of hopped up on the coke. *Sure*, I typed. *See you at 6:45*. I just hoped that bitchy counselor Melissa wasn't scheduled to be there, too. I didn't need her eyes on me. She might infer that I was still a little bit high. But, even if she did come in, it probably wouldn't be before noon.

I got in to bed, but I doubted that I would be able to catch any sleep and still get up in time for my shift. I was pretty wound up, but I made sure to set the alarm, just in case. I lay back on my nice pillows and soon was breathing calmly.

Did I really need to kill the coke dealer-guy just because he didn't use a condom? No. But I definitely needed to kill someone right about then, someone who deserved it, and he was the closest fit. I needed to relieve the pressure that was building and building inside me, pressure to go after Isabella. It wasn't time for her, yet. So, I did the next best thing.

Hopefully, when Danny gets back down to Miami someday, he will take care of Isabella for me. He still owes me. I'll keep track of her for him until then.

In the meantime, I figured I'd give my new friend Maury Levitt a call soon. It was never wrong to be friends with a good lawyer. Maury seemed like he could be a real shark if there was ever a need. I felt I could trust him, too. I don't know why.

CHAPTER 7

On the Sundays when Isabella accompanied her grandfather to Mass, Jerry usually went for an early morning run and then hit the gym for a couple of hours. He liked to go through his whole workout series: glutes, back, chest, biceps, tri's, legs, and so forth all before the gym got crowded. Then, he'd ride his bike or jog back home and fix himself a snack, usually just a protein shake.

Today, he ran into Sofia, just north of the park, who was also out and about on this lovely sunny morning. He suggested that they go get something to eat. An egg white omelet sounded good to him about now. He'd really pushed himself at the gym.

"Ok," she said, "but just a quick bite for me. I need to get back to take Ollie out for a run. I should have brought him with me, but I had to drop something off for my auntie, and she really doesn't like big dogs." Sofia sighed. "It's so hard to please people. My Ollie is such a sweetheart."

Ollie was a black labrador retriever which Sofia had adopted after Ollie flunked out of doggy drug-detection school. *Too friendly, and he alerts to everything*, was the verdict. "Too stupid, you mean," Sofia had said, rubbing the top of Ollie's head near his ears. "No," the trainer had said. "He's smart. But he thinks he's pleasing us if he alerts. He just wants to make everyone happy."

"I'm finding out that's definitely impossible," Jerry said. "Making everyone happy…"

"You mean Isabella or the other one?" Sofia asked.

Jerry shot her a look. He was tempted to tell her that there was no other one, but Sofia would know he was lying and think he was a douche for trying to deny it. The thing with Sofia was, she seldom took people at face value. She needed time to figure out who exactly they really were. Her skepticism had its good and bad points. Once she was good with you, though, you were probably going to be friends for life. Until then, you were on probation.

"It isn't that simple," he told Sofia. "I knew her when we were both just little kids at an orphanage. We didn't really have anyone else besides each other. We needed each other. She was my best friend. I protected her, and she helped me not to be so sad all the time."

"Yeah, I'll bet," Sofia said. "I met her."

"How?" Jerry asked. "Why didn't you tell me?"

"It was a work call. Larceny from a building. It was near where she works, and I just ran into her. We started talking and she told me she knew you, and that she had been friends with you when you were both up north. I never knew you'd been in an orphanage."

Jerry stood with his hands in his pockets. "It was after my parents were killed in a car accident. Her parents had died, too, and she'd been shuffled around in foster care. Later, my aunt and uncle got me out of there when they found out where I was and brought me down here to Miami."

"I'm so sorry, Jerry. I had no idea…"

"I don't really talk about it very much. The place was ok, really, and it was a long time ago now. My aunt and uncle gave me a good life."

He paused. "I think Cassie had a pretty hard time after I left. She didn't have any family and got bounced around from place to place. But she landed on her feet. She has a good career."

"And she's gorgeous, let's not forget. That will get a woman a leg up in most situations."

"She's educated and she has a professional career, Sofia. I'm surprised to hear you say that, about a woman's appearance, considering that you know what a hard time a woman can have, let's say just in law enforcement alone, proving her worth."

"I only meant that she has the advantage of being very attractive. My Social Psychology of Police Work instructor at the college had us do a whole section on the various advantages attractive people—men, women, even kids, even criminals---have just because of their looks. Juries will tend to go easier on a good-looking defendant, for instance. And they will tend to associate credibility—or not— with a witness's appearance."

"I guess that's true. But Cassie has worked hard for everything she has. It's not easy to go from where she started to where she is now."

Sofia gave Jerry a little peck on his cheek. "I'm sure you're right. See you later, Bro. Gotta go take care of Ollie." And I might just dig a little deeper into Cassie's past, she thought. Get my girl in IT to take a long look into her, completely off the record.

Sofia was well aware of the laws and policies pertaining to police doing a background check on a non-suspect and what kind of disciplinary action she might be subject to if she were caught.

"But I have a bad feeling about this," she told her work friend, Angela.

"Give me what you have. I can't really do much in my position, but I can ask someone," she said, smiling like the cat who swallowed the canary.

"Not Suarez! Are you kidding me?"

"We went out a couple of times. Now he's eager to please, shall we say. I'll find out for you what I can."

On Wednesday afternoon, Angela asked Sofia if she were free for maybe a drink after work. They went to a place where cops didn't usually hang out and ordered margaritas and chips with salsa.

"Ok, girl, here's what I know. Ready?"

Sofia nodded.

"This Cassandra chick is from Massachusetts. Went to school up there in New England and is a fully credentialed registered nurse with a Bachelor of Science degree in nursing. She worked for quite a while at a drug rehab place south of Boston after she was done with school and before she moved down here to Miami. Now she's employed at a high-end rehab where some of the patients can be pretty rich and famous, and they maybe pay for their treatment mainly with cash. A significant minority of the people they get there come up from South America--Columbia, Venezuela, and like that. Medical tourism. Those definitely pay cash.

"She was briefly married up in Massachusetts but get this: the guy died. No kids. No other marriages. No arrest record."

"What did the husband die from?"

"Natural causes. Asthma attack. They were divorced by then."

"Ok. Anything else?"

Angela shrugged. "I could ask my guy to check for juvenile records, but I would definitely need a solid court order for that."

Sofia shook her head. "She was in some orphanage, but I think those were all eventually closed down by the state way back when they deinstitutionalized to a foster care system. So, if there were any records on her from then, they probably weren't electronic and may not even exist anymore, except for maybe as papers in a moldy box in some basement. No red flags, though, right?"

Angela shrugged. "Apparently not."

****

Maury Levitt had long ago lost track of how many years he had been married to Evelyn. She dropped hints when their wedding anniversary was approaching so he could do the appropriate thing on the appropriate date.

They had two grown children, three grandkids, and a fourth grandchild on the way. He'd never been with another woman after he'd met Evelyn, which was in September of his first year in law school. But neither was he immune to the charms of the women around him: cute, bespectacled law clerks, legal secretaries without whom he would be truly lost, women on Collins Avenue strutting their stuff for the guys in Ferraris—he loved them all. At least to look at.

Miss Cassandra was well on her way to becoming his latest fantasy crush. He liked her long, lean legs and her reddish-blond hair and her smart mouth. He liked the way she didn't feel the need to say everything that was on her mind. Also, there was something little bit dangerous in her smile. If he'd been younger, she would have been way out of his league, but now he was at an age where she probably felt safe enough around him to be her true, unguarded self.

Maury hoped she would call him and use his legal expertise. He wanted to know a lot more about her; he'd love to sit for an hour or two over a cup of coffee, maybe in his office, just chatting, maybe helping her with any problems she might have. A woman like her was never far from circumstances requiring prudent legal advice.

Maury did understand that it would be the smart thing to put Cassie out of his mind; nothing was ever going to happen with her, romance-wise, in real life. So, partly to dampen the little touch of guilt he was feeling, he asked his wife if she'd like to spend a nice, long weekend with him down in the Keys. We could just get away from everything going on in Miami, he'd said. He didn't tell her that, for him, this little getaway would represent the start of his resolve to firmly tamp down his budding infatuation with Cassie.

He showed Evelyn the website photos of a mid-priced motel right on the water just south of the Seven Mile Bridge. It had a pool, but the main attraction was that it was set on a quiet lagoon on the bay side and offered pontoon boat rentals at below-market prices to vacationers staying at the motel.

"I thought you hated driving all the way down there on weekends," Evelyn reminded him. "The traffic, you said, is terrible, and by the time you get there, Saturday is half over."

"Monday is a holiday, and I have nothing on deck for Friday. We could leave early."

"Okay," Evelyn said. "Let's do it."

Maury was pleased she didn't bring up anything about the grandchildren. A weekend of passionate romance might be too much to ask at this point in their marriage, but they could at least eat grilled Mahi sandwiches and have drinks at a restaurant on the water while they peacefully watched the sun go down. Maybe they could even talk about something other than the same conversational topics they always rotated through: the grandchildren's doings, should they sell the summer house they owned in Maine because they hadn't been up there in three years, and how much would their various insurances go up this year.

Around eight o'clock, after they'd checked in to their motel and had an okay but expensive dinner, they watched some people doing what Maury considered a piss-poor job of bringing a 17' rental boat up alongside the wooden dock. After gaping at the clown show involving an obviously intoxicated guy banging the boat around and finally sort of tying it off, Maury asked Evelyn if she would like to accompany him down to a shopping center on Big Pine Key to buy some booze for the weekend.

"Okay," said Evelyn. "I'll come along. I can get us some snacks at the supermarket while you're in the liquor store. I'm thinking chips and salsa, just snack foods like that. Maybe some ice cream to put in that little freezer we have in our room, assuming it works. Chocolate okay with you? Or butter pecan?"

The Miami Night Nurse

By the time they arrived down in Big Pine Key, it was late. All the businesses except for the supermarket and a nearby bar that stayed open until 4 a.m. were already closed for the night. Maury said he would hurry over to the liquor store attached to the supermarket while Evelyn shopped for the snacks and groceries on her list.

As Maury walked over to the place that sold the liquor, he noted that some of the lights were out on the tall poles illuminating the almost empty parking lot. There were thick areas of darkness under the trees at the perimeter of the shopping center. It was difficult to determine whether the remaining parked vehicles were empty or if someone was inside of them. Very few customers were still in the parking lot with their shopping carts, just a guy loading cases of beer into the back of a ratty-looking SUV. Maury caught a glimpse of a few of the Keys' famous wild chickens still straggling into the landscape shrubbery to roost for the night.

Maury walked up the concrete steps and pushed open the electronic door to the liquor store. It was brightly lit inside with flickering fluorescent tubes. He picked out his purchases and set them on the checkout counter.

The middle-aged liquor store clerk was blond, moderately overweight, and had some serious undereye bags. She looked like she couldn't wait to get off work so she could go home and start some real drinking. Maybe she already had. No one shopping at this time of night would care how much she drank on the job as long as she was standing upright and gave them the correct change.

She did seem like she was putting in the effort to be nice to Maury, so he took the time to be friendly.

He could see all the cash piled in her drawer when she opened it.

"Don't you ever worry about getting robbed in here at night? It seems so dark and deserted out there in the parking lot."

"Nope," she said, shaking her head. "Never."

"Why not?" Maury asked.

"Because there's a hundred miles of road down here with nowhere to go except the one way out. And I've got the cops on speed dial. The people that come in, they all know that."

Maury looked at her more closely. There was a spark of savvy humor in her rheumy eyes. He decided not to ask how any of what she'd just said would help her if someone walked in, immediately shot her in the face, grabbed the cash sitting in the drawer, and just drove calmly away. The next customers who came in might call the crime in to the cops or to the paramedics unless they decided, instead, to scoop up as many free bottles of booze as they could carry through the door while the clerk bled out on the floor.

"I guess you're right," he said agreeably. "Unlike up in Miami, where you can board a plane out to Bogota or London three times a day if you have the right passport."

"Yeah, well, it's nothing like Miami down here, and that's how we prefer it." She looked at the bottle of vodka he had set on the counter. "That brand won't rot your guts too fast, and it's as good as the more expensive stuff. Good choice."

Maury just nodded as he fought off the impulse to make a clever quip about her probable level of expertise in the assessment of liquor quality. She really did look like she'd been guzzling cheap swill for too long to have done her liver or her brain any good. But that was no reason to be unpleasant when someone was just trying to get through their day. Besides, she knew way more about liquor brands, the liquor business, and how things worked down here in the Keys than he did.

"Just because you're a lawyer doesn't mean you're an expert in everything," Evelyn would say to him whenever she thought he needed the reminder.

Later that evening, while he was sitting peacefully outside by the water with Evelyn, watching how the light breeze ruffled the trail of moonlight spreading across the otherwise flat surface of the ocean, the spark of an erotic thought flickered up into Maury's consciousness.

The Miami Night Nurse

At first, he assumed he was just feeling a little bit aroused because he was sitting outside in the soft, tropical air with a drink in his hand and that his thoughts had, quite naturally, settled on the image of a beautiful woman. But as the face in his imagination shifted in to focus, he realized it was Cassandra. He brushed her away from his thoughts like a cobweb from the corner of a ceiling. What did he even know about this woman, someone young enough to be his daughter, younger, in fact, than his actual daughter?

It doesn't mean I'm a lech if I just want to find out more about her, does it? Maury thought. People look up all kinds of things online about the people they meet, mainly out of curiosity more than a need to know. It doesn't really hurt anything, does it? Besides, doing background checks is a normal, necessary, and routine part of my job. My clerk does it for me on my clients all the time.

While Evelyn was occupied with one of her favorite television police dramas, Maury got to work on his laptop, accessing his preferred legal search engine. Then, he sent a few text messages to colleagues in Boston and Nashua, New Hampshire. He wanted to dig deeper and find out more than just the basics about Cassandra.

So much for tamping down my obsession, he thought. He finished his drink and poured himself another one.

He'd managed to sneak a look at Cassie's driver's license, so he knew her birth date. Thus, he was able to do an online search himself for her Florida driving record. It turned up clean. So did her nursing license. She was up to date on all the continuing education requirements for her professional licensure and had chosen to meet most of the required hours for each renewal period by taking online courses, all approved by the state board, of course.

Maury took note of his relief when he discovered that Cassie's driving record was spotless. He hadn't expected anything in particular to show up. Still, something annoyingly persistent, just a cautious, lawyer-like need to ferret out the details, he supposed, was tickling away at the back of his mind. He decided he would go ahead and do an even deeper dive, although he was a little bit ashamed of using his skills and connections to go digging around in Cassie's past. It made him feel like a dirty old man, violating her, in a sense, by weaseling his way into her life history without her knowledge or consent.

Nonetheless, once he and Evelyn were back home in Miami, Maury asked one of his Massachusetts state records sources to email him a copy of Cassie's birth certificate. A few days later, after he had received the document, he looked up what information he could find about her parents. According to the data bases he accessed, both had died on the same day in a motor vehicle accident, so he ordered a copy of their death certificates. He would also be able to easily obtain a copy of Cassie's marriage license, but he realized that what he really wanted to get his hands on was a copy of Cassie's ex-husband's death certificate. He asked a law school buddy up in Massachusetts put in a request for that, too, with the appropriate town clerk.

Pretty soon, Maury thought, I'll know everything there is to know about her.

"Pretty soon" turned out to be several weeks before Maury received the copy of Cassie's ex-husband's death certificate. All he really learned from it was that the guy was at home and unattended when he died of an asthma attack. Her ex had a history of severe asthma and the medical examiner who was called to the scene, apparently two or three days after the guy had died alone in his residence, hadn't flagged anything officially.

Someone from law enforcement could reasonably call and see if there was any more information about Cassie's ex-husband's death, but Maury really could not. Besides, he felt quite satisfied, at least for now, that after all his digging around, Cassie was exactly what she seemed to be: a woman in her late twenties supporting herself as an RN and living a fairly typical life for the times. He did wonder, though, how Cassie had managed to transition so easily from being a tragically orphaned child to becoming an educated, professionally employed young woman brimming with self-confidence.

"How do you know it was easy?" asked Maury's wife. "I'll bet she had to work really hard. Losing your parents so young…awful. How did they die? Car accident?"

"Maybe," said Maury. "They did both die on the same day, in a motor vehicle, but it wasn't called a motor vehicle accident. The wording in the documents…death by misadventure…implies it was something more complicated than just a car crash."

"Oh, my god!" said Evelyn. "That's horrible! Was Cassie able to tell you any of the details?"

Maury shook his head. "It's possible she doesn't even know. She was very young, so any details about her parents' deaths, other than that it was a motor vehicle accident, may have been withheld from her. It would be interesting to learn more."

"Well, Maury," said Evelyn. "It's nice you're trying to help that poor girl. Should we invite her over to dinner some night when we get back to Miami?"

"That's not a bad idea. I think she works evenings or nights mostly, but we might be able to schedule something with her. I really do want to find some ways to help her. Perhaps a lunch?" Maury paused. "I am also curious about what she really knows about her parents' deaths. Maybe very little, since she was so young."

"Maybe you should just leave well enough alone, then, as far as her parents." Evelyn said. "Stop digging around in something that definitely doesn't concern you."

Instead, Maury called to schedule a meeting with Cassie in his downtown office at a time she said was convenient for her. He was surprised but delighted that she was so willing to agree to a meeting with him.

"No, no," she said. "No problem at all. I really was thinking about calling you to set something up." After a pause, she said, "Did you hear about what happened that night at the party, after you left?"

"What?" Maury asked.

"One of the guys who was there died, apparently. He fell off a balcony or something. It was in the *Herald*."

"No, I hadn't heard that," said Maury, alert now. "What happened?"

"I don't know anything besides what I told you. I'd already left to go home. I had to go in to work early in the morning."

"I'll call my friend who owns the place. He must be devasted. The poor guy wasn't even there at the time, but an interested party could conceivably try to press civil charges against him. Fortunately, I can't think of any criminal charges that would stick in a case like this."

I can, thought Cassie.

But she didn't say anything more about anything, including that she knew the guy who had fallen over the railing was, in fact, a client of Maury's. There was no reason at all she should have remembered that tiny bit of information. Maury would discover that for himself when he checked in with the doctor who owned the place.

Maury was so shocked by Cassie's news that he forgot what it was he had called her about, and he hung up.

CHAPTER 8

I liked having Maury for, well, something like a surrogate father. He was helpful and kind and he seemed delighted with me. I also sensed that he was developing a little crush on me. So, I tried to make sure that I carefully filtered any information about myself that I revealed to him. I very much wanted Maury to keep on liking me, and to think of me as just an ordinary young woman leading an ordinary life. If he ever found out about all the stuff I keep private from everyone, he probably wouldn't think too highly of me anymore. He might even try to have me arrested.

So, I will never, ever allow him to know too much about me, because I would hate to be forced to put some kind of an end to our friendship.

Maury does know that I spent time in an orphanage and that my parents died in car accident, and, of course, that I am a registered nurse. I had told him all that. I also understood that he was capable of doing a very thorough background check on me if he ever really wanted to, but I doubted that very much would turn up. No matter how deep anyone ever tries to dig, all they would hit would be various dead ends.

When I was a child, I didn't have any control over who recorded what about me in their little progress notes and in their psychosocial evaluations, but on the plus side, health and human services organizations back then were very late to the party as far as using computerized data bases. It was mostly all hand-written notes and evaluations when I was a kid, paper files, in other words, that were never computerized.

And my understanding is that juvenile records were supposed to be kept permanently sealed anyway unless extraordinary circumstances required a judge to rule otherwise. So, any orphanage or foster care or juvenile detention files that might still exist on me are, or were, pretty carefully gate-kept. It would take special legal permission to access them, assuming they even still exist.

Most important, I doubt that anyone inside or outside the system would ever have the time or the resources to locate and to go through boxes and boxes of moldy, handwritten papers to try to find something out about me.

Let's consider the first foster family I stayed with before I was sent to The Home, that place where there was the fire. I never saw my foster mother ever write anything down except the medical and social work appointments for all the girls. She kept them listed on a big calendar in the kitchen. As for The Home, that was closed down years and years ago, and I know for a fact that there were no computers at all in at that loosey-goosey orphanage back when I was there. The nuns were pretty old-school. They were very big on things like three-drawer filing cabinets and hand-written notes on yellow legal pads. Paper gets moldy and crumbles with time if it isn't carefully preserved. So, I was willing to roll the dice on that one.

More problematic *might* be the New Hampshire juvenile facility where I attended high school. That place was called The Southern New Hampshire Academy, and my high school transcript from there intentionally looks like it came from a private prep school, rather than from a detention center. That was a choice on the parts of both the Academy and the state, in order to give young graduates a fresh start if, like me, they were capable of making it to college or, perhaps, to the military. The idea was to let promising students' pasts remain in the past, a philosophy to which I, too, firmly adhere.

In summary, I'm not worried about my deep past coming to light, and after I became an adult, I've been very careful to cover my tracks. I guess I was a little impulsive recently about the coke dealer, though.

Maury called me again just a few weeks after that party, the one where we'd met and where the coke dealer fell to his death. I was pretty happy when he invited me over to have dinner with him and his wife. I explained my work schedule, so we agreed on an evening when I didn't have to go in to work at the treatment center.

Maury's wife Evelyn was a delight, and a very good cook. I let Evelyn explain her recipes to me, even though I barely get more complicated at home than making coffee and putting together a salad. I take most of my meals at the treatment center. I don't mind institutional food, and I can say with assurance that it has gotten so much better than it ever used to be. New Dawn Alternatives' patients probably wouldn't pay the big money to get treatment there if the place didn't have a chef and a menu worthy of some of Miami's nicer restaurants.

I did not expect, though, that it would be Evelyn who started to really question me about my past. She didn't seem to have any particular agenda other than to get to know me and to maybe to satisfy her curiosity. I don't know how she got me to do it, but we hadn't even finished the main course of the delicious meal she had prepared, Florida Keys lobster tails, wild rice, and some kind of a spicey mango sauce, before I was telling her and Maury all about Jerry.

I confided, now that Jerry and I had reconnected, that I had hoped the two of us could be together. Maybe even get married and start a family. I don't know why I said that last part; maybe there really is such a thing as a woman's biological clock ticking away, influencing her on some molecular level to want to have a baby. So, I told them that I would love to have a family.

"That sounds wonderful," Evelyn said.

"Well, it really would be," I said. "But he has a girlfriend and he's living with her. I've heard through friends that she wants to get engaged. He hasn't given her a ring, yet, but Valentine's Day is coming up..."

Evelyn made an appropriately sad face.

"I'd always dreamed that I'd find him again someday and that we'd be together, maybe even as husband and wife."

I really had no idea why I was laying it on so thick with them, even though all of it was true.

"And I was so happy when I finally did reconnect with him, and he seemed so happy, too. We've spent some wonderful dates together. Unfortunately …he has that other girlfriend."

I made another very sad face.

At this, Maury chimed in. "Cassandra, surely you must have ways to charm him, to maybe…"

Evelyn shot him a look. Maury was out of his depth on this one.

I demurred, lowering my eyes. "He's pretty loyal to her…just like he was pretty loyal to me when we were little kids. I love that about him, but…"

"Maybe you could just be honest with him," Maury suggested. Evelyn and I looked at each other and kind of rolled our eyes. Men have no idea what we have to go through.

"Maybe I'll take your advice," I said politely, and then, thankfully, we moved on to other topics.

Still, what did I have to lose? So, a couple of days later, I texted Jerry and said that I wished we could get together for lunch or a drink to catch up.

Jerry responded pretty much right away and said that he would like that. He didn't suggest a specific place or date, so I told him I was off work on Tuesday and Wednesday of the next week and would be working the night shift on the other days.

He asked if he could come over to my apartment on Wednesday afternoon. I happened to know that his girlfriend was going to be busy showing a house out in Kendall at that time. I don't literally stalk her, but I do follow her agency's listings to keep aware. I have no idea if Jerry even realized that day was also Valentine's Day. I'm quite sure his girlfriend knew.

Before Jerry arrived for our little Valentine's Day date, I wasn't entirely certain how I would feel when I saw him. I had originally expected that by now we would be living together or even married. He's certainly been a little disappointing as far as how fast he's been willing to move forward in our relationship. I am prone to holding some grudges, yes, but I have such a soft spot in my heart for Jerry that as soon as I saw him again, I melted into his arms. I didn't say anything at all about Valentine's Day, but I was wearing a deep red lacy pushup bra and a matching thong under my dress. And red lipstick.

We didn't start out in bed, but pretty soon we were on my white leather couch with some of our clothes off, kissing passionately. He groaned when I slid my hand down his jeans to his crotch to feel how things were progressing for him.

"I can't lie," I breathed. "I can't stop thinking about you." I took his hand in mine and brought it up to my red lace bra. I shrugged one of the straps off my shoulder and he slipped his hand inside the embroidered cup and squeezed my nipple with his fingertips.

"I'm so jealous that it's not me in bed with you every single night," I breathed. "I'd be kissing you all over."

Actually, I frequently work nights, but he got the idea.

"I think about you, too, Cassie, all the time."

And then he kissed his way down my body and buried his face between my legs. I refuse to talk about very intimate details, but I will say that it was some of the best oral sex I had ever had. We were just so perfectly in sync with each other, it was like we were twin hearts that had been separated long ago but now we were joined again. Jerry didn't say very much, but his groan when he came inside me sounded like it was torn from his soul. We stayed wrapped together and fell asleep.

Later, I fixed us some snack food. We still didn't talk much, but things felt easy between us. I knew he was falling in love with me. I knew we would be together forever and ever, very soon.

As he was leaving to go home, I said cheerfully, "Happy Valentine's Day!"

The startled look on his face made it clear that he had totally forgotten what day this was. Maybe his girlfriend had arranged a surprise for him, or maybe he had made a promise that he had forgotten. I could imagine him rushing out to pick up a random card and some chocolates in a heart-shaped box from the leftovers at the drug store on his way over to try to fix things with Isabella.

I hoped she would smell the scent of our sex all over him as soon as he walked in the door.

****

Jerry and Isabella sat outside on their concrete patio late on Valentine's Day evening, eating the Cuban takeout that Jerry had brought home, and drinking a bottle of cold champagne. Isabella had set the patio table with a nice white tablecloth and red candles in jars as soon as she realized they would be staying home. The candle flames flickered under the patio umbrella and sent up curls of smoke. She should have trimmed the wicks before she lit the candles, Isabella realized, but now it was too late.

"I didn't make reservations at a restaurant because they are so crowded and overpriced on Valentine's Day," Jerry said quietly. "I hope you don't mind. We'll go out to some place nice this weekend."

Isabella nodded. Jerry was right. He had brought her a sweet card and some flowers that looked a little picked over. Better than what some guys do, she thought with a mental shrug, and at least she hadn't had to remind him of the occasion. But her hoped-for engagement ring didn't seem like it was going to materialize tonight.

At bedtime, she put on a sexy black silk night gown from Victoria's Secret. Jerry smiled appreciatively, hugged her close to him, and buried his face in her hair. Then, he fell asleep.

So much for all that, Isabella thought. She examined her hurt feelings while Jerry snored quietly next to her. Did he want to marry her? Was she wasting her time being with him? She felt a little embarrassed that she had confided in a couple of her friends at work that she was hoping for a Valentine's Day proposal.

She sighed. Men are so clueless. It takes such a little bit effort to please the women in their lives, just something to reassure them they are special and have the main place in your heart.

Maybe that was the problem. Maybe Jerry just didn't love her as much as she loved him.

Or maybe he has commitment issues. That's the covers-all-the-bases diagnosis that women tend to use when the guy just isn't ready to settle down, Isabella thought. She had her doubts about that explanation. She'd known several friends over the years who'd broken up with a guy over his so-called inability to commit. Then he'd married the very next woman he started dating.

Maybe Jerry just didn't want to marry *her*. Maybe there was already someone else. Isabella quickly shook her head. No, not possible, not her Jerry.

Isabella next considered whether there was perhaps some big problem at work that had Jerry so preoccupied. He hadn't talked about anything in particular that was going on that might be affecting him, though, and her girlfriends who worked with him downtown hadn't mentioned anything about a new or intensified stressor in their precinct.

Isabella sighed. She would just have to give Jerry some more time to sort things out for himself. And maybe engage in a little detective work to ease her worries.

What if he was seeing someone else? What would she do?

All the next week, Jerry was polite, preoccupied, and distant. Isabella asked if something was wrong once or twice and did he want to talk about it? He would shake his head. Isabella thought he looked sad, like he had lost something he valued. She caught him looking at her sometimes, and then he would drop his eyes down to his phone or his tablet or whatever he was holding in his hand. She still wanted to hope that he was just having problems at work, but her girlfriends at his job had firmly said, nope, nothing was going on there, just the usual.

Isabella wondered if they were lying to her or hiding something from her. Maybe Jerry was having an affair with a woman at work and his people knew about it and no one wanted to tell her the bad news. But if he was seeing someone, he wasn't gone very often and not for very long.

Was he thinking that he wanted to break up and he just didn't know how to tell her?

****

Jerry knew he wasn't being fair to Isabella. She kept trying to understand what was going on with him, variously leaving him alone, being extra sweet, or trying to get him to tell her what, if anything, was troubling him. It killed him when she'd asked if it was her, if she was doing something wrong.

"Maybe I should just tell her that I've been seeing someone else, and that I'm so sorry that I've been hurting her?"

"Are you fucking out of your mind?" his old pal Jo-Jo from over at the next precinct asked. "Are you really ready for World War III?"

"I'm not going to fight with her. What are you talking about? I just want to be honest. I don't want to hurt her."

"Oh, I know *you* don't, but Isabella might have different ideas about this. She could go after you, or go after your little side piece, with all her claws out, hell bent on destroying you for screwing around on her."

Jerry shook his head. "Nope. That's not Isabella. She'd be quiet about it until she decided what she was going to do."

"Is she being quiet now?"

"Actually, yes," Jerry said.

"Okay, then. She knows."

"She doesn't know," Jerry said.

"Yeah, well, you just wait and see. She's still in the deciding what she's going to do next phase; I'd bet on it."

What Isabella had decided was that she was going to call Carlos, the *rico suave* guy who'd saved her from nearly being assaulted when she was showing the Boston-accent guy a condo by herself up in one of the high-rises over by the Intracoastal.

After a short hesitation, Carlos said, "Oh, yes, yes, yes, of course I remember you, Isabella, I had to pull my gun on that *matón*. How are you, *mi amor*?"

"I'm good, Carlos. I'm calling to invite you to meet me for a drink, maybe in Wynwood? I keep thinking about how much you helped me with the situation in that condo…"

"Okay, when? I'm free tonight, but then I'm flying to Venezuela for business for just a few days."

Isabella took a deep breath. "Tonight's good, Carlos."

"What time should I pick you up? Is seven okay?"

"Could I meet you somewhere?"

"How about El Patio?"

"On NW 23? That's a fun place. Ok, see you there."

Isabella slipped on her red, freshly laundered Valentine's Day bra and panties, used red lipstick to make her lips full and pouty, and slid into a silky black dress. She stepped in to her highest heels and left a note for Jerry on the kitchen counter.

Meeting a friend downtown. See you later tonight. Love, Isabella

She texted Carlos when she was almost there, and when she arrived, he was waiting for her out front. When he saw her, he took her hand and kissed it.

"I don't think this is the right place for tonight, not for someone who looks as beautiful as you."

Instead of going inside the restaurant, Carlos waved down a cab and they headed over to Cocoanut Grove, to a stylish and expensive rooftop joint with a view. He ordered them an excellent bottle of champagne, and a large plate of the house specialty appetizers.

"We'll see what we are hungry for after we finish this," he said with a seductive smile.

As the cold champagne warmed her stomach, Isabella felt herself relaxing. She leaned into Carlos slightly on the banquette. He smiled at her and placed his hand on her knee. He rubbed the inside of her thigh with his thumb.

"Are you ready to tell me what you want?" he asked, indicating the menu.

Isabella raised her eyes to his. It was hard to pull away from his intense study of her face. She looked at his lips and imagined them on hers. "I'm not sure," she said. "Why don't you decide for us?"

After another glass of the excellent champagne and a plate of tasty small bites, Isabelle asked how he liked his condominium, the new one he had purchased for himself in a different building from the one where they had met.

"Would you like to see it?" Carlos asked. "It has a fantastic view. And beautiful modern bathrooms and kitchen."

Isabella hesitated. Carlos waited.

"Yes," she said, "I think I would like that very much. But not tonight."

"I'll call you when I get back, then," Carlos said.

Outside, Carlos took Isabella in his arms and kissed her like she hadn't been kissed in years. Maybe ever.

"I'll call you when I'm in town again," he repeated softly. Isabella stared up at his handsome face, and didn't take her hands from his shoulders until he signaled that he really needed to go.

If I told Jerry about tonight, would he even care? Isabella wondered as she pulled into their driveway.

The house was dark, lit up only by the porch light which she had turned on when she'd left. Isabella wondered if Jerry had gone out. Inside, she found him sitting in their bedroom, scrolling on his phone. The lamp on the nightstand on his side of the bed was the only light on in the whole house.

"Hi," she said. "Did you get something to eat?"

He looked up, smiled faintly, and nodded. "Did you have a good time?" he asked.

"Yes, a very good time." Isabella decided not to offer any more information unless Jerry could show that he was interested enough in her evening to ask her more about it. "Sure I can't make you something to eat?" she asked.

He shook his head. "I ate a big bowl of cereal with strawberries. And walnuts. I'm all set."

Maybe if I make him jealous, he might start paying attention to me again, Isabelle thought, maybe even finally propose. She considered telling Jerry exactly where she had been and with whom, but she decided against it. There was no rush. She hadn't done anything wrong, just a drink with a friend. She could keep her secrets if he could keep his.

Isabella stood for a moment staring down at Jerry as he scrolled on his phone. I wonder what I would find, she thought, if I looked at his messages.

CHAPTER 9

Maury leaned back in his comfortable brown leather chair. His home office setup, with its flood of natural light and its views of his lush Coconut Grove garden through two floor-to-ceiling windows, suited him very well. He often spent hours inside the room with the door to the rest of the house closed and the large, screened windows wide open.

Lovey, a tortoise shell cat that used to belong to a neighbor until Lovey decided she preferred living with Maury and Evelyn, sat outside on the patio watching the breeze ruffle the big leaves of the banana trees. Lovey was always alert, looking for the little chameleons which hunted insects in the yard. She loved to pounce on them and then bring them inside. Maury or Evelyn would have to rescue the tiny reptiles; Lovey had a soft mouth, so they usually survived their encounter with the cat. Then, after the little lizard had been released back outdoors, Lovey would howl inconsolably at the unfair loss of her prey until something else rustling in the breeze distracted her or she felt the drowsy need to take another nap in the sun.

Maury look down at her. Lovey was a well-loved cat living the good life. He and Evelyn agreed that fate deals such different hands to each of the creatures on our planet. Who or what decides which child, or which pet, will be loved and nurtured and which will be left to fend for itself against the unkindness of people or the draw of a bad hand in life's deadly serious game of survival?

Maury's thoughts settled on Cassie. She was a beautiful, intelligent woman who had made a good life for herself, despite her bad beginnings. He clicked open the email from one of his research associates and read it and the attached documents once again.

The information was devastating, or it would be, Maury was sure, if Cassie were to ever learn the details outlined in the documents. He didn't want to tell her if she didn't already know; if she did have the information, she obviously didn't care to discuss it with him, or she would have brought it up herself. He decided to ask for Evelyn's opinion.

He invited her into his office; she brought a glass of iced tea for him and a glass of cold rosé for herself.

"I would like to run something by you. I don't know what to do with some of the research I've been doing on Cassie's early life."

"Ok," Evelyn said, making herself comfortable. "Sounds serious."

"Cassie has told me that her parents were killed in an automobile accident when she was very young," Maury said. Evelyn nodded. "Her mother's parents took her in to raise, but then the grandmother died, and she had to go to a foster care situation. Later, she was moved to an orphanage-type group home that was run by a religious order but licensed by the state."

"I don't know if I'd heard the part about the grandmother," said Evelyn. "That poor girl."

"Well, it gets worse," said Maury. "My researchers in Massachusetts were able to dig around and they accessed some documents pertaining to Cassie's parents' deaths."

"Oh, dear," said Evelyn.

"They died in a motor vehicle accident."

"I think we knew that, didn't we? And Cassie knows that, too, I thought."

"But it wasn't actually an accident, according to my sources."

"Well, what was it, then?"

"It was suspected to be a murder-suicide. Or a double suicide."

"Oh, my gosh," said Evelyn. "That's horrible. How did Cassie react when you told her?"

"I haven't told her. That's why I'm telling you now. I don't know what to do with the information. I don't just want to drop something like that on her."

"It seems to me like you would want more clarification before you would do anything," Evelyn said.

"You mean motives. Details. Circumstances."

Evelyn shrugged. "Do you know Cassie's birth date?" she asked. "If you do know it, I can probably find out some things from the genealogy website I use to do all our family tree research. It would be even better if you could also get me a DNA sample."

"Like a mouth swab?"

"The companies that I know of mail you a small tube that you have to spit into multiple time until you have a certain number of milliliters of saliva in the tube. Then you send it away and they eventually email you a report."

"Well, that wouldn't work in this case. You can't just ask someone to spit and spit and spit into a tube without their awareness of what it's for."

"No," Evelyn agreed. "I guess you'll have to find some other way to satisfy your curiosity."

Actually, it's becoming an obsession with you, Maury, but she didn't say that part out loud.

"Just ask her about her birthdate. Maybe you could say that your wife is interested in astrology and that I'd like to do her chart?"

Maury turned back to his computer, and Evelyn left the room, shaking her head. Maury next focused on trying to trace down the police officer listed on Cassie's parents' accident report. The guy would probably be retired now. Maury also sifted through newspaper death notices, looking for information about possible relatives of the deceased.

Eventually, with the help of a genealogy website, Maury was able locate a cousin of Cassie's father who was still alive. Her name was Rosamund Korhonen, she was eighty-two years old, and she was living in Central Massachusetts in the town of Fitchburg.

"What are you going to say to that poor old woman?" Evelyn asked. "Hi, you don't know me, but I was wondering if you could tell me anything about what happened with your cousin who died tragically, leaving a young child? We have met his daughter, Cassandra Couri, and we were just idly curious."

"I don't think I would put it quite that way, Evie, but maybe something along those lines."

"Well, I think you should just leave it alone. And I think you are getting too emotionally entangled with Cassie. I hope you don't get disappointed."

****

Melissa Canfield tends to really get on my nerves. She's one of the counselors at work. I've mentioned her briefly in the past. I have absolutely no idea why she has taken such an active dislike to me and why she acts like such a condescending bitch towards me.

She does things like roll her eyes in an exaggerated manner in staff meetings when I am providing evaluative feedback on a patient. There is rarely any direct eye contact between us. When her eyes do pass over my face, they don't stop, and her expression remains blank. She seldom reacts affirmatively when I provide information or observations about one of our patients unless it is strictly medical data: blood pressures, medication dosages, medication allergies, and so forth. Then, she might nod her head. If I offer a bit of insight into their psychosocial background and how it seems to be affecting their progress in treatment, I might as well just be moving my lips with no sound coming out for all the reaction she gives.

When staff members are discussing a patient's progress in these treatment team meetings, it is normal for the other people present to at least nod, or to add something to what has been said about a patient's current functioning, or to offer reasoned disagreements. Melissa does all that when anyone else is talking; with me, she looks up at the ceiling or maybe nods with her face totally blank when something I've just said is indisputable. I think her attitude toward me is becoming obvious to everyone.

I like my job. I like the money, and I like the benefits. The treatment facility is great, the kinds of patients we have are interesting and mostly committed to their recovery journey, and I enjoy working with almost all of the other staff members. I tend to be chummier with the doctors than I am with the patient treatment staff. That's simply because the doctors drop in and out of the unit, whereas I feel I need to keep a bit of a protective distance from the psychotherapy staff with whom I regularly see every shift for many hours at a time. That's one of the reasons I take as many overnights as I do: no counselors around except briefly at the two changes of shifts.

There are a couple of sweet patient care orderlies, gay Dominican guys, who I love to joke around with, but I stay cautious with the counselors. I intentionally keep them at an arm's length. I don't need them getting too close a read on me. Normally, this has never been a problem, because the counselors aren't very interested in what the nursing staff has to say unless they need some medical information or want us to make sure to pass something on to a doctor.

I figured, though, the way things were going, that this Melissa bitch might really start to get to me at some point. Her pitch-black eyes lack any emotion as they look past me. It's as if I'm as invisible as a ghost.

That's a little uncomfortable, but I could live with it. It's not like I'm seeking validation from her. And it's not like I'm worried that she has some special therapist capability that can see into my soul and figure me out. Although, frankly, she is an excellent diagnostician.

Still, I know at this point she has no idea who I am and what I am really capable of.

What concerns me about the situation is that other people can and do observe her reactions to me: the patients and the other staff members. I just don't like having lots people looking too closely at me day after day while they go about building some kind of a behavioral dossier on me in their minds. So, although I would hate to have to do it, I just may have to change jobs; quit this one while I'm ahead, so to speak.

Or, maybe Melissa will have to quit.

One evening I arrived at work and learned at shift report that one of our new admissions was Melissa's husband, Angelo. He had been admitted for a medical detox from alcohol and cocaine and was currently stable and snoring away in his bed in the detox wing.

I had been aware that both Melissa and her husband Angelo were in recovery themselves, Melissa for many years. She was apparently a leading light in the local AA sober community. I hadn't known much about her husband Angelo other than that he ran a scooter rental concession out at the beach and that he kind of looked like a little gigolo. I'm not being mean; Melissa had proudly shown us pictures of him literally dressed in tight black pants, a white shirt open at the chest and tied at his waist, and wearing an unnecessarily pimpish-looking hat. Like she thought he looked handsome in that get-up. And, no, I don't think it was a costume for a party.

Now, here he was snoring away in one of our patient beds after his latest coke run, detoxing along with the rest of the alcoholics and addicts.

There were other facilities in the greater Miami-Ft. Lauderdale area where this douche could have gone for a detox. That he came here seemed weird to me, like maybe he was trying to publicly rub something about their marital dysfunction in his wife's face. Possibly he was trying to get back at her for some specific reason. My guess was that she had cut him off financially because of his cocaine binges.

Also unfortunate for their family finances, I learned that Melissa had been forced to take a leave of absence from her job at the treatment center as soon as her husband was admitted. Ethically, she couldn't keep running her group therapy sessions on the same unit where a family member was a patient.

I'm sure that most of the other staff members felt sorry for Melissa, except, perhaps, for the doctor who had agreed to admit pimp-boy. That doctor could have just as easily turned the guy away; like I said, there are plenty of other places in the Miami area where Melissa's husband could have gone for treatment.

I heard through the grapevine that the doctor had deliberately admitted him to get back at Melissa for some nasty things she'd said at a staff meeting about his competence. The doctor is a gay man from Argentina, and he really knows how to hold a grudge. So, Melissa ended up having to take a leave of absence from the hospital. I heard she was going to be running her husband's scooter rental concession out at the beach for the duration of pimp-boy's treatment.

I was glad to have her off the unit for a while, but I wasn't glad to have to interact with her husband. He was such a little prick.

So, I started cutting way back on his detox meds, but, of course, I recorded every dose as if he had been given it as prescribed. When pimp-boy started saying he needed more drugs to feel "comfortable," I immediately shot a message to the doctor, who said he was at the correct dosage. I entered that conversation as a note in scooter-boy's patient chart.

The Miami Night Nurse

It wasn't too much longer, meaning only a couple of hours, before he bounced, meaning he left our facility against medical advice. I have no doubt at all that his first stop was the ATM on the ground floor of the hospital.

When Melissa came back to work, she was sullen. Fortunately for me, she assumed the doctor was somehow to blame for her husband leaving our facility AMA and then immediately going on a cocaine and alcohol binge with money he withdrew from her bank account.

If you try to fuck with me, I'll fuck with you right back, I wanted to say to her. But I didn't have to, because actions speak louder than words.

I could also have said that she must be a moron to not have changed the PIN number on her bank account.

****

Maury got off a long phone call from Massachusetts and sat back in his chair. Twenty minutes later, he was still sitting there looking out into the garden with a blank expression on his face when his wife came in to check on him.

"I was calling you from the other room," Evelyn said. "Are you okay?"

"No, I don't think I am," Maury said.

"What's the matter?" she asked.

"I'm trying to figure something out, something about Cassie's family."

"What's going on? Can you tell me?"

"I've discovered something that's really hit me hard."

"What, Maury? What is it?"

"Well, you know that Cassie's parents died in a car crash, right?"

"Right," said Evelyn.

"The so-called car accident they died in was not an accident, it was intentional, almost certainly a double suicide. I'd thought there was some hint of that implied in the original accident report. But I've now read the full coroner's report. Both her parents had massive overdoses of painkillers in their systems when the car the father was driving slammed at high speed into a concrete abutment at a highway overpass."

Evelyn stared at Maury, taking in the stunned look on his face. "Why didn't they just take the overdose at home if they wanted to die so badly?" she asked. "Why bother staging it as an accident? That's what someone would do if they were trying to cover up a murder, or something, isn't it? Seems like either the car crash or the overdose would have sufficed."

Maury nodded. "Possibly. But maybe they just didn't want Cassie to know. Maybe they didn't want her to have to live with the fact that her own parents were so desperate to die that they killed themselves. So, my interpretation is that they were trying to spare her the burden of knowing that they died on purpose. They must have loved her very much."

"Poor Cassie," Evelyn said, shaking her head. "It's phenomenally rare, practically unheard of, for both parents of a child to kill themselves without also killing the child. It's actually much more common to kill the child, or all the children, at the same time, rather than to leave them unattended. In fact, I can't believe there isn't some other explanation. Or something we're missing. What are we going to do with this information, Maury?"

"We don't have to do anything, yet. I think we should try to learn a little bit more about the circumstances before we even think of dropping something like that on Cassie. That poor, poor girl."

Maury called up to Massachusetts again and was able to reach a woman named Rosamund Korhonen, a relative of Cassie's mother that he'd previously tracked down. Maury introduced himself and explained the reason for his call. Mrs. Korhonen said she didn't want to talk with any one about the family, and that her daughter, Elsa, who was at school teaching third graders, wouldn't be home until much later. And that this Elsa was unlikely to be willing to talk, either.

"May I please leave my telephone number with you?" Maury asked.

"You can leave it, but it won't do you any good. I won't ever call you back. And my daughter is too busy, she's got kids and a job, so please don't bother her."

"Well, Mrs. Korhonen, how about if you could give me just a minute now. I've been talking to Cassandra Couri," Maury pressed. "Do you know who that is?"

"Of course I do. I'm not senile. She's my second cousin once removed. What about her? Is she dead?"

"No, she's a friend of my wife and mine down here in Florida, and I have her permission to try to find out some information about her parents. Now that she's grown up, she has some questions," Maury lied.

"Why didn't she call us herself if she has questions?" Mrs. Korhonen asked.

"She's very busy at work. She's a nurse. And I'm her lawyer."

"A lawyer," Mrs. Korhonen said flatly. "Well, if you're trying to track down the inheritance they left for her, it's much too late for that. My rotten ex-husband stole the money her parents put in trust for her college education. I have no idea where he is, or else he'd be in jail. I haven't heard anything about him in over thirty years. Maybe he's dead. I certainly hope so. But I can guarantee you there's nothing left of the money."

"I'm very sorry about the accident," Maury said, trying to prolong the conversation.

"What accident?" Mrs. Korhonen asked.

"The accident where Cassandra's parents died."

"It wasn't an accident."

"What do you mean?" Maury asked. "I read the accident report."

"Doesn't matter what the police wrote down. I had a talk with Cassandra's mother, not too long before they died. She was a sweet, sweet woman. She made me promise with my hand on a Bible, our old family Bible, that I would take care of Cassie if anything ever happened to them. I said I would, just to set their minds at ease, because she seemed so intent on getting me to agree to act as Cassandra's guardian. Of course, I had no expectation of ever needing to do that. I never imagined they were planning to go so soon and to just leave Cassandra with me. That would never have worked out."

"Why not? Wouldn't her trust fund have covered expenses for her upbringing, not just for college?"

"Money wasn't the issue."

"What was the problem?" Maury asked gently, but he was getting annoyed that pulling answers from this woman was so difficult.

Mrs. Korhonen took a deep breath. "Are you really sure you want to hear this?"

"Yes."

"Ok, but you better not call me a liar or question me like I'm spreading gossip. I've never told anyone, not my ex-husband who told me not to get involved, and not my own daughter."

"Okay," Maury said. "I promise."

"Her mother and father went for a drive in their old Buick, popped a bunch of pills, and then, at some point, deliberately drove the car in to a concrete bridge wall at eighty or ninety miles an hour. They killed themselves. On purpose."

Maury was silent. He let the information settle for a moment. It was horrible, but it fit with the coroner's report.

"You still there?" Mrs. Korhonen asked after a minute.

"Yes," Maury nodded.

"You want my opinion?"

"Okay."

"They should have taken Cassandra with them. In the car."

"Why do you say that?"

"Do you know her very well? Cassandra?"

"Yes. I do know her, and so does my wife."

"Well, if she's anything like she was as a little girl, I would advise you to watch your backs. She must have gotten it from Elmer, who was her grandfather on her father's side. That's all I'm going to say."

"What do you mean? What was the situation with Elmer?"

Mrs. Korhonen was silent, but she didn't hang up. Maury waited.

"Can you look up old newspaper articles?" she asked.

"Yes, I have a paid subscription service, so I can find quite a few old news articles."

"Okay, then. Look up these names from forty, fifty, sixty years ago." She listed them off and gave her best guess as to how they were spelled. "I think you'll be able to figure most things out for yourself. And do not ever tell Cassandra that you spoke with me. I don't trust her, or any of the rest of them from that line. If she ever shows up at my door, I'll know you're to blame."

Maury was silent and waited to see if Mrs. Korhonen would add anything else. After a moment, she continued.

"Elmer, Cassandra's father's father was…not normal. He lacked something. He was so handsome when he was young, and he was wonderfully bright. People assumed he would become a lawyer like his father and his uncle. But there was something wrong about Elmer. The family knew it, and talked about it, but other people might not see it right away. He was tall and blond and so well-spoken that maybe no one wanted to look past that. I think when Cassandra's father was born, and he was such a sweet little boy and then he grew up to be a hard-working and kind-hearted man that everyone was relieved. Cassandra's grandfather, Elmer, left the family when her father was just starting in elementary school, which was probably fortunate for the little boy."

She took a deep breath. "That's definitely all I have to say. Good luck."

And she hung up the telephone.

Maury imagined Mrs. Korhonen standing in an old-fashioned kitchen with a sheet vinyl floor, Formica countertops, and a wall telephone with a long, coiled cord. She would maybe go over and start emptying the dishwasher to push the disturbing memories about her family to the back of her mind while she went through the routine of straightening up the kitchen.

Or maybe she would sit down with a stiff drink while she entertained those memories for a while before she finally nudged them back to where she tried to keep them locked up.

Maybe that's what Cassie did, too.

CHAPTER 10

Maury had been sitting alone for several hours in the comfortable tan leather chair in his home office, absorbed in his reading. He'd downloaded several articles by authorities on antisocial personality disorder. An earlier label, sometimes still in modern use, was psychopath. Maury liked that term the better, though, and that's the one he normally used in his thinking and speaking. He skimmed the biographies of Ted Bundy, Charles Manson, Jeffrey Dahmer, and John Wayne Gacy, plus a few more of the serial killers of the modern era. Then, of course, there was Maudsley, the inspiration for the fictional Hannibal Lector character.

None of these serial killers ever came close to topping the numbers of Josef Mengele, though, who was called the Angel of Death. Mengele was a main architect for the murders of the millions of innocent people in the Nazi death camps. He specialized in devising tortuous and scientifically useless medical experiments which he then inflicted on thousands of helpless prisoners; he escaped to South America, never facing society's justice.

Maury shook his head. Those killers were evil and remorseless; their crimes were incomprehensible. He couldn't, by any stretch, imagine ever wanting to be in their company. It was unthinkable that he and Evelyn would bring any one of them into their peaceful South Florida home. He envisioned a Ted Bundy, someone who looked very presentable, someone who would sit pleasantly with them while making polite, intelligent conversation at their dinner table and manage to inspire their affection. His skin crawled at the thought.

He went on with his reading. Psychopaths often have a normal, or even delightful, personality on the surface. Many can hold responsible jobs in business and professional settings. A smaller percentage even have families and a circle of friends, although managing to maintain these close relationships over time is far less common than having only superficial, temporary associations.

Underneath their so-called "mask of sanity," though, lives a person very different from most of us. They carry a profound sense of entitlement, evidently stemming from an underlying rage. That rage is close to the surface, and when it bubbles up, they feel it is their right to act out in whatever manner they choose. Nothing is off-limits for them.

More sophisticated and intelligent psychopaths will have cultivated an attractive, polished exterior. They may be handsome or beautiful, and dress and groom themselves in ways that attract admiration and attention from others. They may hold professional jobs and function quite well in them. Beneath that shiny exterior, though, is a hidden self who feels entitled to win, win, win at any cost, without regard to others.

Maury read that between one and four percent of adults in the United States would qualify for a diagnosis of sociopathic personality disorder. My god, there can't really be that many of them, he thought. That would mean there are four million of them in just the United States at this time, living their lives among us. And that would be the bare minimum, if the actual incidence of the disorder is only one percent, which is the low end of the estimate.

Maury skipped through the rest of the statistics in the article he was reading and jumped down to the section on causes of the sociopathic cluster of disorders. Over half of the risk factor is genetic, he read. Meaning, people with sociopathic personality disorder usually have one or more close relatives, a parent or a grandparent, who is also sociopathic to one degree or another.

In other words, people seem to inherit at least the predisposition for becoming a psychopath. The biology of the disorder appears to stem from the effect of having lower than normal brain levels of the neurotransmitter serotonin. Serotonin helps all of us control and manage our feelings of aggression in socially acceptable ways. Studies with people and animals suggest that poorly controlled impulses and aggressive behaviors, two of the primary characteristics of sociopaths, are strongly associated with abnormally low serotonin.

Maury continued reading a section about high-functioning psychopaths and the destruction they wreak when they become our elected politicians or business leaders. Threats, intimidation, and ruthless competition are their hallmark strategies. Entire civilizations have been brought down when psychopathic leaders are elevated to positions of great power and influence. Their indifference to the harm caused to innocent people as they pursue their self-centered agendas, and their callousness to others' suffering, is just the normal way they function in society as they walk among us.

"What have you been studying, Maury?" Evelyn asked, coming into his home office with a small plate of cheese and crackers and a glass of his favorite merlot.

"Sociopaths. Psychopaths."

"Oh, that must make for some fun reading. Any particular reason you're on to that subject?"

Maury shook his head. He didn't really want Evelyn to know where his thoughts had been heading concerning Cassie.

"Does this relate in some way to Cassie's parents' deaths? Like we were talking about earlier?" she asked.

"I'm just not sure, not yet," Maury said, hedging. "I'll run it by you when I've worked it out in my mind." He took a sip of his wine. "Oh, this is good. Did you get it at the grocery store?"

"Yes. It was on half-price sale. So, I got two bottles."

Maury nodded and went back to his reading.

I just wish there were some way I could help Cassie, he thought, before something really bad happens to her.

****

Late the next Wednesday afternoon, staff members from all the shifts at the treatment center, including nurses, counselors, and patient care attendants, gathered for one of the facility's monthly in-service educational presentations. Cassie and the other staff who worked evening and overnight shifts were asked to come in early so they could be present. Day shift staff stayed late. Midnight shift patient care workers' attendance was hit and miss.

"Nope, not coming in," many would say. "I'm asleep then. Not unless they pay me triple time for the next three days, until I get my sleep cycle back right."

Nurses and therapists who attended received at no cost some of the continuing education credits required for maintaining their state or national professional licensure. That was the carrot part of the carrot and the stick approach to mandatory participation. The stick part was that non-attendance at very many of these education presentations might show up on staff members' annual performance reviews.

Cassie didn't feel particularly comfortable mixing with so many mental health professionals all at the same time in a large group. She doubled down on making sure that everything about her appearance was both professional and boring. She normally wore very little makeup at work and tied her hair up in a messy bun. She dressed in pale green or blue nurses' scrubs when she could get away with it, particularly if she worked a late evening or an overnight shift and there weren't any administrators or visitors around. She dialed down her charm, saving it for when she really needed to lay it on someone. She was chummiest with the orderlies and the nursing assistants, staff members who she assumed wouldn't be too analytical about any quirks or verbal non-sequiturs that bypassed her vigilant self-monitoring.

It's really not a bad way to live, Cassie thought. I can be friendly with whomever I want outside of work. Here, I just need to stay somewhat superficial, making sure that I stay socially appropriate. It's not like I care about any of these people, anyway.

Jerry is the only person I really want or need. It's been that way since I was eight years old, and I guess that's how it's always going to be. I think about him all the time, and I imagine how he would want me to be, and then, most of the time, that's what I do, something that he would think is right.

The topic of the current month's educational in-service program was *Approaches to Treating Substance Abuse In-Patients with Personality Disorders*.

Cassie knew the basic answer to that. In a nutshell, it could be quite a bit more difficult for patients who are dually diagnosed with both a personality disorder and a substance abuse problem to successfully maintain sobriety within traditional 12 Step recovery aftercare programs.

Out of all the personality disorders, individuals with borderline personality disorder, antisocial personality disorder, and, perhaps, histrionic personality disorder, tended to be the ones most likely to have a co-occurring substance abuse disorder right out of the gate, so the speaker focused her presentation on those three.

During the question-and-answer period after the main part of the lecture, Cassie's current work-nemesis, Melissa, raised her hand.

"What about people who don't have a substance abuse disorder? What are their most common personality disorders?"

"Most studies suggest obsessive-compulsive personality and narcissistic personality are the personality disorders most prevalent in the general population," the speaker responded

Cassie turned slightly in her chair and stared at Melissa for a few seconds. She kept her expression pleasantly blank. Melissa knew that Cassie wasn't a recovering addict, unlike the case of many of the other staff who worked on their treatment unit. Cassie suspected that Melissa might be trying to publicly bait her for some reason, but her effort fell flat because Melissa didn't get the answer she was hoping for from the speaker.

I will definitely have that bitch taken care of someday, Cassie thought.

But Melissa wasn't finished. "Could someone with antisocial personality disorder ever work as a therapist or as a medical professional?" she asked.

The speaker shrugged. "I think we are all aware of cases involving famous or infamous guru-types who started out with some professional degree or experience and who later became, let's say, a charismatic cult leader. Often these men, and they are most often men, are primarily narcissists with some antisocial elements to their personality structure. Charles Manson certainly comes to mind. Some have even said that a recent contemporary president seems to fit the category."

Again, not an answer Melissa was looking for, Cassie bet. Cassie's expression remained neutral, but she pushed out her lower lip slightly. Cassie knew she looked particularly beautiful and angelic when she emphasized her lovely mouth.

Cassie also understood perfectly well that she might qualify for a diagnosis of antisocial personality disorder.

She'd studied the Diagnostic and Statistical Manual of Mental Disorders in nursing school and during her psych rotation. Medical and nursing students were always comparing their own symptoms to what they were learning in their classes and practicums, whether it was acute inflammation, schizophrenia, herniated discs, or whatever. Cassie had read the section of the book detailing characteristics of the various personality disorders and wondered if some of the diagnostic criteria could fit her.

Cassie shrugged. *So, what if I might have a little bit of that? Like our speaker said, plenty of people have some of the characteristics or symptoms of a mild version of a personality disorder. I have a good career and enough money. I live a normal life, for the most part. If it's true, I don't really seem to have let it become a problem for me.*

****

Elmer Couri, Cassie's paternal grandfather, was born in the small mill town of East Millinocket, Maine. He was taken in to be cared for by his own paternal grandparents after Elmer's father killed his wife and then himself in what the local newspaper described as *a most horrible crime unlike any other seen Down East in anyone's memory.*

No one told six-year-old Elmer what had happened, but he had seen his mother's carved, bloody corpse crumpled in the back of the barn the morning after she had died. He had awakened early to run down to see the new-born baby pigs. Little Elmer had pushed open the barn door and rushed over to where the old sow was nursing her eight piglets. His mother's body lay nearby on the barn floor, stretched out flat on her back in a pool of dark, congealing blood. Elmer stood staring at her blood-streaked face. Her eyes were open, but one of them was oozing out of its broken socket.

He turned to race back to the house so his father could call the doctor to come over from across the river to fix his mother's eye. His head smacked into the toe of one of his father's boots. Elmer looked up and saw his father's red, bloated face staring down through the slits of his eyes. A noose encircled his neck. The cold wind that had driven its way in through the open door had set his body swaying gently as it dangled from a barn rafter.

A few weeks later, during that same cold winter with its waves of arctic winds sweeping down from Canada and penetrating the crevasses of the house, Elmer's grandmother died of pneumonia. The ground was by now frozen too deeply to bury her in the churchyard, so her wrapped body was laid out stiffly behind the barn until the ground would soften in the Spring.

Elmer, who was not yet seven, was sent by his grandfather to live at the Maine Home for Orphan Boys. The day he arrived, bundled up in the back of a wagon, he was told by a tall nun in a dark wool habit that he would learn to work hard and to serve God. Little Elmer stared up at her. She had a French accent and an unlined face.

The nuns at the Maine Home walked about serenely with calm expressions. Elmer was tutored in reading and writing and was taught to recite the prayers of the Order of Sisters Immaculata who ran the home. When he was older, he was taught to cut and measure lumber. He was sent out to work at one of Maine's largest paper mills when he was almost fourteen.

When he was nineteen, Elmer moved down to Boston, vowing never to return to the State of Maine. He quickly found employment at the historic Charlestown Navy Yard, building and repairing ships. He met a lovely young woman, the sister of one of his fellow ship's carpenters, and they were married. After a few years, he began to believe that he was far enough away from the trauma of his childhood so that it could never reach him or his growing family.

It did find him again, although gradually, much too slowly for Elmer Couri to even feel the first touches of its creeping darkness.

Prohibition had long been repealed, and there didn't appear to be any reason at all why a hard-working man couldn't enjoy some whiskey and conversation with his friends at the ale houses and taverns down at the waterfront after his day was done. After all, he had a secure job, a well-tended home, and a happy family. His son, who would one day become Cassie's father, was almost grown.

Once Elmer picked up the first glass of whiskey, the family's darkness began to take hold of him, too. He never felt it or recognized it for what it was. Cassie's father, however, became very familiar with the pain that Elmer's darkness caused other people. Serving as his father's most handy target, he became an unwilling expert in its prodromal symptoms.

****

Maury concluded that his next move should be to inform Cassie about what he had learned from researching her deep family history. His hope was that, if he warned Cassie soon enough, and if he emphasized the importance of her getting a thorough psychological evaluation and some preventive therapeutic treatment for herself, she might be able to learn to recognize and manage any emerging symptoms and behaviors before they caused her or anyone else any harm. Treatments such as cognitive behavioral therapy for antisocial personality disorder do exist, he'd read. Unfortunately, psychopaths rarely begin treatment voluntarily, mainly because the people with the disorder aren't usually the ones who are most troubled by it: the people around them are.

When he'd told Evelyn what his thinking was, she told him he was no psychiatrist and shouldn't be digging into Cassie's background without her knowledge or consent.

"I want to help her," Maury insisted. "I just want to warn her…"

"What makes you think she doesn't know?" Evelyn asked. "She has certainly had medical education courses and mental health practicums addressing the whole range of psychological disorders."

"But what if she doesn't recognize it in herself? People hardly ever see themselves objectively. You know all those sayings about professionals… like, any doctor who treats himself has a fool for a patient, right?"

"Oh, come on, Maury. Of course, I've heard that expression, only the version I know substitutes 'lawyer' for 'doctor'."

"This isn't a time for jokes, Evelyn. Do you want to know what I think?"

"Yes, of course, dear," she said, trying hard to keep sarcasm and impatience out of her voice.

"Ok. Listen to this. I think it is entirely possible that Cassie's parents knew what Cassie was, and that, in their despair, they killed themselves in that car accident, rather than continuing to live with the knowledge that she was a psychopath. They chose death, rather than having to watch her develop into some kind of a monster."

Evelyn grew quiet. After a moment, she said, "If Cassie really was a child psychopath, and her parents recognized it, why didn't they just put her in the car with them? And go ahead and kill her along with themselves. Wouldn't that really make more sense, Maury?"

Maury dropped his chin. "It would, Evelyn. And maybe they even thought about doing that. But, maybe, like most parents, they loved her too much, and they just couldn't bring themselves to end her life."

"Please, Maury, let's just leave this one alone," Evelyn said. "Nothing good can ever come of it. I would suggest, instead, that we gently cut all our ties with that girl. No more dinner invitations. She's beautiful and intelligent, so I think I can understand your interest in her. But I'd like to go back to living what's left of our lives without all this drama and obsession."

Maury nodded. The one last thing he would do, he thought, would be to tell Cassie what he had found out about her family history, and give her the names of some experts in the area who offered psychotherapeutic treatment to people like her.

****

Maury invited me out to breakfast one morning after I was coming off an overnight shift. I was tired and cranky, because we'd had three admissions on my shift whereas normally, we have none. There was all the extra paperwork that goes with an admission, plus dealing with the on-call doctor, and, of course, helping the patients get medicated and settled down on the unit.

One patient was brought in by his hysterical mother at 3:30 am. She was frantically yelling that we needed to give her baby boy special treatment. In the next breath, she wanted us to punish him for having been such a terrible son who kept breaking his promises and stealing from his own mother.

"You know what he does with my money? He gives it to a drug dealer, that's what he does with it!"

"Duh!" the orderly whispered to me as he wheeled the patient into his detox room.

By the time I met Maury at the breakfast joint he had suggested, I was irritable and already wired up on the high-test coffee I'd been drinking all night. The only thing I wanted was to wind down somehow and get ready to sleep. I had to be back to work at 2:45 pm for a full evening shift. Thank God I was going to be off for four straight days after that.

When I walked in the door to the restaurant, Maury was already sitting at a table with a sober expression on his face. I greeted him with a peck on his cheek, like I sometimes did. This time, he recoiled, or perhaps that's an exaggeration. Let's say he definitely flinched.

I sat down and picked up the menu. More coffee sounded just awful. Instead, I ordered a tall glass of orange juice with ice. I asked the server if she could get me a shot of vodka from the bar, which was technically closed until noon, so I could put it in the juice. She gave me a wink and said she thought she probably could.

"I thought you didn't drink," Maury said.

"I don't very often," I said as politely as I could. "But I absolutely have to get some sleep today. I need to be back at work mid-afternoon."

"Maybe this isn't the best time to talk," he said.

"Spill it," I responded. I was trying to do something to my mouth to make it look like a cute grin, but it wasn't working.

"Ok," he said. "Cassie, you know I care about you. So does Evelyn."

I nodded. Next was going to be some kind of lecture. I could feel it, and I could see it in his body language. I took a deep breath. God, I wanted nothing more than to take a shower and get in to bed. I probably shouldn't have come.

"You know what, Maury, you're right, this really isn't a good time. I don't feel up to any kind of a serious discussion this morning. I'm exhausted and irritable. I desperately need to go to sleep." I stood up, finished off my drink, and put some money down on the table. "I'll call you or Evelyn soon, and we can get together when I'm in better shape. I'm so sorry."

Then I left and went home. I had no idea what Maury wanted to discuss, but it would have to wait.

The next day, one of my days off, after I showered and had my coffee, I called Evelyn back. She'd left a message on my phone yesterday sometime after I'd blown off Maury. She asked if I'd like to come over for lunch. I hesitated.

"Maury won't be here," she said, reading my mind.

"Ok," I said, "but I have a busy afternoon." I didn't tell her what I had going on, because I didn't have anything planned. I was just trying to set some boundaries with her. Both of them were starting to get way too far into my business.

As I was driving over to their place, I got a text from Jerry, saying that he'd like to get together again so we could talk some more. I was so excited that I almost called him back from the car. Then I thought better of it. I didn't want to be his puppet. He could wait.

When I arrived at Evelyn and Maury's house, I knocked on the door, and was greeted by Evelyn, graciously as always.

"Maury's in his office. I'll show you back there."

So, I thought. Evelyn lied to me about Maury not being here in order to get me to come over. Bad news. I contemplated just walking back out the door, but I didn't.

I sat on the couch, and he swiveled his chair around to face me. I didn't like the look on his face. It was anxious and determined at the same time. Like how I imagine someone would look if they had to tell you that you were fired or that they wanted to break up with you.

"What's going on?" I asked a little coldly. "It must be something important if you thought you had to get Evelyn to lie to get me over here so you could tell me."

What he had to say concerned the results of all the digging he had been doing into my family history. I didn't really know that he'd been spending so much time on this research, and I was shocked at all the things he now knew about my grandparents and great grandparents, things I'd never heard, and in such peculiar and specific detail. But he hadn't invited me over merely to review my family tree.

It turns out he wanted to talk about my genetics, to warn me about the genes, *the bad seed* he said, that I might be carrying.

The "bad seed" phrase comes from the title of an old novel that was made into a movie back in the 1950's, about a little girl whose mother gradually discovers terrible things in her own family background, including the family basis for the psychopathic characteristics that her cute, conscienceless little daughter has apparently inherited. She decides to kill the child and herself, but only she dies. The child is saved. *Dot dot dot.*

Shit, I thought. That's way too close to home, if that's where Maury is going with this. And, he must have told all this to Evelyn.

My choices right now were few, I thought, as I faced Maury. I could sit and nod and say very little. I could be insulted and tell him he had no right to dig into my family history, to which he would probably respond that he was only trying to help me. I could totally blow up at him, leave, and end our friendship. I opted for the choice of saying little, plus looking appealingly beautiful.

"Go ahead," I said calmly. "Cut to the chase."

He nodded. Then, he proceeded to sketch out my intergenerational family history of murder, suicide, and general craziness, ending with him begging me to get psychiatric help with a specialist who treats psychopaths.

I stared at him. At that moment, I honestly felt like slitting his throat. Instead, I softened my face and said, "Okay. I guess I'll need to take some time to think about everything you've told me, Maury. Do you have a card for that psychiatrist?"

His relief that I wasn't going to make a scene was palpable.

I just smiled at him and took the business card he handed me. I didn't recognize the name. It was for some shrink in North Miami Beach.

Then, as if on cue, Evelyn tapped on the door to Maury's home office and asked if we were ready for lunch. I wanted to get out of their house so badly at that point that I could taste it, but I got up and joined the two of them for a pretty delicious tuna salad on rye with a pickle. And some good potato salad. We made small talk at lunch while their gardener puttered around outside near the patio.

I left after about forty-five minutes, which was longer than I had wanted to stay. As soon as I turned my car on to Coral Way, I jumped on my phone and called Danny up in Boston. Turns out I did have a job for him, I said, if he was still interested in discharging the debt he'd felt he had, considering that the thing with Isabella that time up in the condo she was trying to sell had never panned out.

CHAPTER 11

Maury and Evelyn died at home one evening while I was working my normal shift at the treatment center. I found out about it when Danny left a message on my phone thanking me again for my help and telling me that he now felt satisfied that everything was wrapped up between the two of us. I took that to mean that if I ever wanted his services for anything in the future, I would have to pay cash up front, just like everyone else.

A big, lurid story appeared in the news a couple of days later, after someone found the bodies and left an anonymous tip for the police. I would assume the tipster had been Maury and Evelyn's housecleaner, or maybe their gardener. Both those employees were probably undocumented, so I doubted they would want to reveal their identities or sit for a full interview with or without an attorney present. By this point, they would have simply stopped showing up for work and would have faded back into their community.

All I know for certain is that it wasn't me who called the cops. My plan for now was just to keep my head down and stay busy at my job.

After things calm down, though, I will need to get back to dealing with the problem that is Jerry's girlfriend, Isabella. Also, I have to admit that I still am harboring a growing resentment against Melissa, that snide, skinny bitch at work. But let's be real. I can't just keep killing anyone who is in my way or who annoys me. I guess.

At this point, despite my frankness in discussing my life, and my honesty in revealing all my thoughts and the motives for my actions, you might still be wondering about my story. Is she telling the truth? What kind of a whacko does those things? Who even thinks those kinds of thoughts? And why isn't she locked up yet?

The reason I'm not locked up in prison is because I've never been arrested or even pulled over for a speeding ticket. Okay, sure, you might think, but it's just a matter of time, right? No, that's flat-out wrong. Roughly ten thousand homicides a year go unsolved in this country. The odds of a careful, controlled killer being apprehended are really not that high. Strangers commit only a minority of murders...maybe ten, fifteen, twenty percent, and at the beginning, I killed mostly strangers. Well, maybe not right at the *very* beginning. Still, I feel pretty confident I'll be okay if I stay careful.

As for the kind of whacko I am, if you insist on applying some kind of a dismissive, derogatory term like that to me, is, well, a psychopath. I would be a considered a psychopath. Not actually a sociopath, although people do mix up those terms all the time. This is based on my understanding of the parsing of the various diagnostic possibilities as they are used in contemporary psychological assessment. I'm pretty controlled and methodical. I blend in well to society, what with my education and my professional career and my social skills.

I don't feel bad about what I do, in case you're wondering. The people either had it coming, or I needed them to not turn me over to the law enforcement system. Or, I just had a building urge that I needed to safely discharge and they were handy and, in my opinion, of no real benefit to society. I do know the difference between right and wrong, but I mostly don't factor that into my decisions.

The Miami Night Nurse

Which brings us to Isabella. If she weren't in the picture, would Jerry and I be together? Of that, I have absolutely no doubt. We would get married. He would always be there for me, making me feel better after a tough day at work, helping me to decide what to do when I felt confused about how to handle a problem I was having with other people. And he would always, always protect me from the people who might try to hurt me.

I love the fact that he's a cop, serving and protecting the public. He knows how to de-escalate a situation. He's been trained to take control of tense confrontations. He knows where the lines are between what some people might want to do and what's legal. He's honorable. I think I love that about him the most.

And, what's also important to me, but what I would never, ever tell him, is that I believe just being with him would help me keep a lid on some of my more questionable responses to the kinds of situations that get me pissed off. I know he had a very helpful effect on me back when we were children. I never got into any kind of trouble at the Home while he was there with me. Only after he left.

For a more recent example of Jerry's potential good influence on me, if only he had come to that party with me, I'd never have done any part of what I ended up doing with that hot, horny jerk of a cocaine dealer. And, I'd probably not have spent as much time there as I did talking with Maury, who was the coke dealer's lawyer, at least not enough time chit-chatting to have begun a friendship. So, all three of them, the coke dealer and Maury and his wife, would still be alive, for better or for worse.

Also, I wouldn't know about all the very upsetting things Maury found once he started digging around in my family tree. So, I'd probably just be living a peaceful, normal, happy domestic life with Jerry, assuming his chunky little girlfriend was out of the picture.

I guess I need to get back on track and deal with her. It won't be easy removing her from my life, since Jerry is a cop. It would be great if I could find someone else to take care of that problem for me.

****

Jerry pulled his personal vehicle into a spot behind Julio's Tire and Auto, back where the employees parked. A hot wind was blowing around the dry dirt layered on the alleyway. Its gusts twisted up tiny dust devils.

Inside, someone was grinding metal in one of the repair bays. The high-pitched, rasping whine was like fingernails on a chalk board times one thousand. An old boombox perched on one of the shelves was blasting *Radio Mambi*.

The grinding stopped and the guy looked up.

"*Necesitas un cabo?*"

"I was looking for Julio," Jerry yelled over the radio.

The grinder guy indicated the front of shop, where the sales office was. Jerry nodded and circled around some stacked boxes of muffler parts on his way to the office door. He stepped inside, and as he closed the door behind him, the grinding resumed, but at much lower decibels. Jerry found Julio sitting at his desk, examining a stack of receipts. It was near the end of the month, and he was no doubt preparing to close the books. The room smelled like cigarette smoke with a hint of oxyacetylene.

"Hey," said Jerry.

Julio looked up and flashed Jerry a grin. He stood up, and gave Jerry a quick, one-armed hug.

"*Que bolá?*"

"I have some things I'd like to run by you," Jerry said.

"Okay, good, but let's go across the street, get away from this noise. He'll be starting back there with the impact wrench pretty soon."

Julio was only a few years older than Jerry, but when he'd been a kid, Jerry had looked up to Julio as a kind of father-figure. He'd started hanging around the repair shop after school, and Julio had put him to work cleaning up, learning to return tools to their proper places, and finally, he started paying Jerry to help him change tires once he turned fourteen. Jerry reflected on how, in so many ways, Julio had been more of a father to him than the uncle who took him in after his parents died. Not to say that he didn't appreciate all his aunt and uncle had done for him, but Julio had taught him much more about how to understand the world.

They sat on a bench under a tree in a small, neighborhood park by one of the city's many drainage canals. White ibises with long, curved beaks stalked the banks. A couple of kids, maybe ten years old, were standing on a muddy slope of the canal, looking for alligators. That's what I would have been doing at that age, anyway, Jerry reflected.

Julio was a former member of a slightly notorious motorcycle club, and he had guided Jerry's first purchase of a motorcycle, a very old Ducati that Julio had acquired somehow and had restored. He taught Jerry motorcycle safety and car repair basics, although the work Jerry did for him was primarily tire changing and muffler replacements.

Jerry understood, once he grew up, that what Julio Acosta had mainly taught him was how to be a man. How to tell the truth, and why you shouldn't be afraid to find out if something you believe is incorrect. On a more practical note, Julio had explained to Jerry, when Jerry was sixteen and dating Jenny Perez, how to purchase and correctly put on a condom. He'd used a big Costa Rican banana for demonstration and practice purposes.

Back when Jerry was first thinking about joining the police force, he had consulted with Julio. Julio had smoked half a cigarette before he said anything. Finally, he nodded.

"I think that would be good for you. You're a straight-arrow kid. Just don't be disappointed. Not all cops are good cops. You can be one of the good ones, but if you're too good, the ones who aren't so good might start to think that you're not on the same team."

On this sunny afternoon, Jerry wasn't too concerned about the contradictions of his job.

"Julio, I'm here because I have woman problems."

Julio shot him a look. "No such thing. You have problems with yourself."

"I don't know what to do."

"Yes, that's definitely a you-problem. *Qué pasa?* You have something going on with Isabella?"

"Yes and no. There's someone else, too."

"Another girlfriend?"

"Yes. Someone I knew when I was a little kid, before I moved down here."

Julio didn't say anything. He lit another cigarette and stared across the street at the park.

"What should I do? I know Isabella wants to get married someday soon. I feel bad."

"What do you want?"

"I don't want to hurt Isabella, but I want to keep seeing the other one."

"How is all this lying and cheating feeling so far?"

"It feels amazing to be with Cassie. Like we were always meant to come back together again," Jerry said.

"And with Isabella?"

"It's hard to look her in the eye when she asks if anything is wrong. I worry about my text messages, about her getting my phone and reading them. And I don't really want to have sex with her very much anymore."

"Isabella is a good woman, and she has been good for you."

"Don't you think I know that?"

"So, what does this other little *chica* have for you?"

Jerry didn't reply.

After a while, Julio said, "*Una candela* doesn't last forever, as far as I know. As the months and years pass, what does this other one bring to the partnership?"

Jerry shrugged. "We were little kids. She was my friend, and I protected her. She was so small, and her parents had died. Then, I moved down here, so I had to leave her. Things were very tough for her after I went away."

Julio sighed. "You feel sorry for her. Her life hasn't been going too great."

Jerry shook his head. "That's not it at all. She has a really good career, and I assume she makes good money. She grew up to be poised and beautiful, like a model, or something."

"Playboy or runway?"

"What? Fashion, I guess. Or, Playboy, but not with huge tits."

Julio chucked. "Tits can be over-rated."

"I don't want to talk about her like this."

"Well, little Jerry, I can't tell you what to do. Yet, your *chica* knows all about Isabella, but Isabella doesn't know anything yet about the other girl, am I right?"

Jerry nodded.

"That doesn't really seem so fair, does it?"

Jerry was silent.

"I bet Isabella knows something is wrong. Maybe she thinks it's her fault. Maybe it's making her crazy, wondering. Do you think you should tell her, so she knows it's not her, that she's not imagining the things?"

"I don't want to hurt her like that."

"Do you maybe like to think that you're going to just keep seeing the other one on the side until you feel finished with her, and then go back and continue with Isabella like it never even happened?"

Jerry shrugged.

"That's chicken shit. *Mierda de pollo.* Someone is definitely going to be hurt here, maybe two somebodies or three somebodies. It's what always happens."

"So, what can I do?"

"Your only good choices are to break up with Isabella, break up with the other one, or maybe you just move out of town and leave them both before someone shoots someone else." Julio slapped the tops of his legs, amused at his own hilarity.

****

Late one weekday evening, after I got off work just before midnight, I drove over to Kendall. I was feeling restless. I slowly passed by Jerry's house a few times. His police cruiser was parked there, as well as his personal vehicle. So was Isabella's. I was tempted to just pull up out front, knock on the door, and then, when Jerry or someone else answered, push my way inside and have it out, just the three of us. I wanted to tell her—and him—that I love him, and she had about ten minutes to pack up any of her stuff she'd been leaving over there and to clear out before I found a way to make her life very tragic.

Instead, I decided to creep slowly around the block just one more time and then go check out an interesting-looking night club that I'd seen on some of my late-night drives. Maybe I'd get a drink, relax, and take some time to review my options more calmly.

The reason that particular night spot had caught my eye in the first place was because it had pink and aqua neon signage, like back in the 1980's, or perhaps the 1930's even before that. There was a hot-looking Cuban door attendant dressed in tight black pants and a fitted white cotton shirt just sort of standing around out front, smoking a cigarette. The joint didn't look that crowded. In fact, I saw only women, and maybe one guy, enter the place. Maybe it was Ladies' Night.

I decided to check it out, mostly just to distract myself.

Normally, I wore my coppery-blond hair long and straight, except at work, where I would keep it tied back or piled on top my head. Tonight, though, I guess as part of the prowling-the-city mood I was in, I had pulled on a short, pixie-cut brunette wig from my small stash of fashion wigs and hairpieces. I had on a short, black, knit dress and no jewelry except for simple earrings and a gold bracelet. I had no idea how the people inside the club were dressed, but judging from the door guy, I assumed pretty nice.

The first things I noticed when I walked in were that the place wasn't crowded at all, the music was lively 1980's, and the décor was faux art deco, like the exterior. I slipped my tight little ass on to a chrome and black fake leather bar stool and ordered a Cosmo. I have no idea why I picked that drink, except maybe to go along with the theme of the place, although I do like them. Normally at a bar I might order one glass of white wine or a shot of straight vodka on ice. Or just a sparkling water with a lime wedge.

After a while, a woman sitting across from me on the other side of the bar got up and came around and sat down one seat away from me.

I looked at her. She had long, straight dark hair, was very slender, and dressed like she could be a high-fashion model. She was drinking something in a stemmed glass, too. I didn't say anything.

After a while, the dark-haired woman said, "Hi, I'm Ashley."

Ashley. The name sounded so fake to me, but who knows?

"Connie," I replied. I could go with a fake name, too.

"What do you do?" she asked.

"I'm a paralegal," I lied. "I work for an attorney in Miami. He specializes in drunk driver cases."

She looked pointedly at my Cosmo.

"What?" I asked, a little irritably. "One drink. I'm not going to end up in the newspapers."

"I bet you could do some reconnaissance around here for potential new clients for the law firm, though. People go stumbling out to the parking lot…you could follow them, and if they get pulled over by the cops, jump out and offer them your card."

"I'm off the job. I'm just taking a break, having a drink. Don't even want to think about work," I said, a little coldly. I didn't feel up to discussing a fake job with her. I'd just picked the paralegal thing out of thin air, and now I was on the verge of thinking about Maury and Evelyn. Which I did not want to do.

"So, what do you do?" I asked. I didn't care. I just wanted to change the subject without seeming rude.

"Various things. Last thing I did was help my boyfriend fence car parts that he jacked."

"Very classy," I said.

"He's in jail now."

I raised my eyebrows.

"I testified at his trial and helped put him there."

"In exchange for you getting off?"

"No, just because. I was sick of his shit."

I nodded. "I need to pry my guy away from his soon-to-be ex."

"What does she do?"

"Real estate, I guess."

"What's her name?"

"Isabella something. She's with East Everglades Home Sales."

"What does he do?"

"He works… in security."

"Is he a good fuck?"

"I wouldn't put up with all the drama if he wasn't."

Ashley, or whatever her real name was, nodded. "You ever been with a woman?"

So, that's what this was about.

"No."

"I was thinking that maybe you could just join them if you can't get her out of the picture."

"No. Not what I was thinking."

"What were you thinking?"

"Eliminate her completely from the picture, forever."

"Wouldn't you be a suspect, Connie?"

"Yes, probably."

"So. You need help."

I shrugged. Now I for sure didn't know where this was going, but it wasn't quite off the rails. Yet.

"And…I need money."

"Why?" I asked, although I didn't really care and was about to get up and leave this crazy place. I didn't want to hear what I thought she might be hinting at.

"To start over. He's getting out in a couple months. Good behavior, over-crowding, like that."

"Did you want to start over before or after he gets out?"

She looked at me like I was nuts. "Before, obviously. He's going to come after me for putting him away."

I shrugged. "I didn't know. I'm not a mind reader. People are into some weird shit. For all I knew, you two might have this love-hate cycle you go through with each other."

After a pause in the conversation, I asked, "What's the going rate for doing someone who has no security around?"

"But you just said the boyfriend was in security. Right?"

This conversation really was getting too weird, even for me. I thought I should leave, so I picked up my pocketbook and signaled for my check.

"Come back tomorrow," she said.

"I have to work late tomorrow."

"When, then?"

"I'm not sure."

"You're trying to blow me off, and I get it. You don't know me, so you don't trust me. But maybe I could do something that would let you know I'm totally for real. Give me the address and the details on her car."

"I wouldn't want anything to happen while she's at his place. It could come back to me."

"Then where does she work? That real estate place you just said, right?"

I nodded.

"Oh, easy. I'll just go see her at an open house. Here," she said, and slid her phone over to me. "Put your number in. I'll call you if I come up with any ideas."

I don't know why I did it, but I typed in my real number, and my fake Connie name. I guess I didn't think any harm could come of it. I mean, you can always just block someone. It did occur to me, though, that this Ashley chick, if that was even her name, might not be totally sane.

"I guarantee you'll never be sorry."

I stood up to leave.

"We'll see. Nice talking with you," I said, and I left the place as fast as I could without sprinting.

That was so nuts, I thought, as my tires spun, kicking up gravel on the way out of the parking lot. Who had I just been talking with? Did I just imagine what she was implying? How long would it be before I had to block her number? I wished I hadn't given her mine.

I decided to drive by Jerry's house again instead of going straight home, just because I wanted to feel close to him. I rolled by on the dark street and stopped my car a few houses down.

Amazingly, I had just turned off my lights when Isabella and Jerry came outside together. A ride share vehicle was pulling up. Isabella kissed Jerry on the lips and the driver took her bag and put it put in the back. The car drove off in the night with Isabella in it while Jerry stood there waving. Then he started back up the front walkway and went inside the house.

I parked in a dark, shadowed spot away from the streetlight, walked over to Jerry's house, cut across the front grass, and rang the doorbell. Jerry answered, cautiously I thought, standing defensively off to one side, as if whoever were at his door this late at night might turn out to have a weapon pointed at him.

"Cassie!" he said when he realized it was me. "What are you doing here? What did you do to your hair?"

There were a lot of ways I could respond to all that, so I just said, "I was missing you."

He opened the screen door to let me come inside, so I took that to mean his girlfriend was definitely gone, at least for the night. He gave me a light kiss on the forehead. I'm sure I smelled good because I was wearing plenty of Chanel. I know I looked good because I had dressed up for the bar.

Jerry, on the other hand, had rumpled hair, was wearing not-so-clean underwear and a ratty blue cotton robe, and his breath didn't smell great. I didn't care.

"I need to get some sleep," I said. I took his hand and led him back to his bedroom. I touched one of the pillows. At least the sheets felt clean, like they'd been recently changed. I pulled off my dress, unpinned my brunette wig, and took his toothbrush into the shower.

When I came out, he was standing near the bed with the night-stand lamp on, waiting for me. He'd combed his hair, splashed on some cologne, and, I assumed, brushed his teeth. Although, since I had his toothbrush, maybe not.

"Where were you tonight?" he asked.

I told him the name of the nightclub.

"That place has a lot of coke dealers who hang out in there."

He seems awfully fixated on cocaine dealers, I thought. "I didn't see any," I said. "I was talking with a woman I met in the bar. We talked about men. Then, I drove over here."

"Were you drinking?" It was like he was trying to figure out what, on this particular night, had motivated me to drop over unannounced.

"I had one Cosmo. So, yes. But that's not why I decided to come here."

I put my arms around his neck, pressed my clean, naked body against his, and took his hand and put it on my breast. He squeezed me a little roughly and brought his mouth down hard on mine. Then, he pushed me down on to the bed and started kissing his way down my body. I knew I was going to come almost immediately if he started with his tongue down there, so I pushed his face aside, and whispered, "Wait. Wait."

Then, the doorbell rang, and right away the knocking started. I doubted it was Isabella coming back, or she would have just used her key, and it probably was not a job thing, or they would have called Jerry's phone. Jerry got up, pulled on his shorts, and took his service weapon out of the nightstand drawer.

He stood off to the side of the door, and said loudly, "Who's there?"

"Emilio from down the corner. Some bros are taking a car." He described my vehicle.

"Fuck!" Jerry said. "*Mil gracias*. And stay safe, Emilio. I've got it."

I plopped back on the bed, figuring my night with Jerry was over. And my car had gotten jacked. On the plus side, Isabella was still in the dark and would remain so, because I don't think the neighborhood boys had seen me or connected my stolen car to a visitor at Jerry's place.

I decided to just get dressed and was wondering about calling a ride share for myself, but then Jerry came back inside.

"All set," he said. "I know the kids who tried to take your vehicle. It's parked back outside now, but in front of the house and under a streetlight. It doesn't seem damaged. I have to say, the kid who started it knew what he was doing. I made him drive it to the front, here, and park it. He didn't even scrape the tires on the curb."

"What happened to the kids?"

"I let them off with a warning."

"Really? That's all you do for grand theft auto?"

Jerry sighed. "The car was recovered right away, undamaged. I didn't want to call it in, because then you'd have to make a statement, and all that."

I understood that Jerry would most likely have known the officer who took the call and showed up here, and that person would probably also know Isabella, or at least know that Jerry had a girlfriend, but she wouldn't be here, and I would, and all that.

I shrugged to myself. Fuck it. I could let it go. It had been a crazy evening. I wondered if the moon was full, or something. So, I just put my arms around Jerry's neck and invited him to continue where we had left off.

CHAPTER 12

Isabella's plane touched down in Miami at eight o'clock in the evening, a day sooner than she had told Jerry she would be getting in. Things had wrapped up early at the real estate sales training convention, and she thought it would be fun to surprise him. She picked up a good bottle of merlot from the wine store where they usually shopped, and, in case he hadn't made a recent run to the grocery store, some tasty sandwiches from the deli next door.

As she was headed up the walk, a kid from down the street approached her.

"Hi, Emilio," she said. "*Qué pasa?*"

"Not much, Miss Isabella. Did you hear about someone stealing a car around here the other night? Officer Jerry took care of it."

"No, I didn't hear. Everything okay?"

Emilio nodded.

"Okay, then," Isabella smiled. "You take care of yourself, you hear? Say 'hi' to your mama for me. And don't stay out too late!"

She tapped on the front door, inserted her key, and opened it. Jerry was standing in the kitchen, still in his uniform.

"Babe!" he said. "I thought you were coming back tomorrow! Sorry, I didn't get the grocery shopping done."

"It's okay. I brought some food home for tonight. There's coffee for tomorrow, though, right?"

"Right." Jerry enveloped her in a hug. "You didn't call me to let me know."

"I figured I'd surprise you. I didn't find out myself until this morning." Isabella stepped out of her heels and poured herself a glass of wine. "What did Emilio mean about someone stealing a car?"

"Oh," Jerry lied. "It was nothing much. Some kids tried, but they didn't get away with it. Emilio and I stopped them." After a second, he asked, "Did he say anything else?"

"Not really, but he seemed excited about it."

Jerry smiled. "Maybe he'll decide to join the force when he grows up. If he doesn't start hanging around the wrong kids and jacking cars himself."

"Did you ever do that? Hang around with the wrong kids?"

Jerry shook his head. "I was set on becoming a cop. And playing baseball. Plus, I had a little job at a muffler shop after school."

"Oh yeah? I didn't know that."

"Yeah, I worked for a guy named Julio. Over near Le Jeune Road. He's still got the shop there."

"Oh, I think I know that place. Down an alley?"

"Yup. I went to see him the other day just to say 'hi' and to talk about old times."

"You want to invite him over for dinner some night? Or a barbeque out back?"

"Maybe," Jerry said. "I'll think about it." But…it would be very awkward for both Julio and me to have him over, Jerry thought, since he had told Julio about Cassie.

After the dinner dishes were cleaned up, Isabella took a shower, put on just a little makeup and did her hair. She put on pale blue silk lingerie and joined Jerry in front of the TV. He sniffed her hair.

"Perfume?" he asked.

"And a little hair spray," Isabella said. She cuddled close to Jerry and put her head on his shoulder. "You want to go in the bedroom?"

"The TV out here is better," he said. God, that was so pathetic, Jerry thought as soon as the words were out of his mouth.

Isabella sat very quietly, her eyes on the screen. She rested her head on Jerry's shoulder. It seemed like the heat had been leaking slowly out of their relationship like a party balloon going soft. Was their relationship dying? Tomorrow, if she still felt like it, maybe she would get back in touch with Carlos. She wanted to feel that heat again. Her lips parted slightly as she imagined his mouth on hers.

The next morning, Jerry left for work early, earlier than normal for his scheduled shift. Isabella picked up her phone and texted Carlos, the guy who'd saved me from the Boston thug.

Hi, if you are in town, would you like to get together again soon? Maybe lunch this week? My treat.

Carlos called her back right away.

"I'm so happy you reached out to me. I was just thinking of calling. How are you, *mi hermosa novia*?"

Isabella inhaled. His beautiful girl…she would call the salon, get her hair and nails done, and maybe even do a Brazilian…

"I'm good, Carlos. I'd love to see you…"

"Definitely. How about somewhere different than last time? Would that be okay? Is tomorrow too soon? Not lunch, but an early dinner. But, definitely, my treat. I have someplace very special in mind."

"Tomorrow is perfect," Isabella said. Jerry would be working an evening shift. She might not even say anything about going somewhere to meet a friend.

Isabella showed up at the restaurant early the next evening waxed, buffed, and spray-tanned, and wearing a sparkly black cocktail dress and her highest heels. Carlos was standing near the entrance to the terrace dining area. He gave a low whistle, took her hand, and kissed it.

The maître d' showed them to a table with an exquisite view of the city as the sinking sun lit the glass towers of the office buildings with a rosy-orange glow. Off farther to the east, storm clouds hung in dark layers over the Atlantic Ocean.

As they were finishing their light and delicious dinner, Carlos and Isabella ordered another drink. They took their drinks and stood outside on the terrace, looking out over the whole city. There was no breeze, even up this high. Carlos put his arm around Isabella and pulled her close. He kissed her lips gently, and when she responded by inching herself more snuggly into his arms, he pulled her into his hips and slid his hand down and beneath her short dress. Carlos knew exactly what to do with his fingers, to give her a foretaste of what she could expect.

"Are you married, Carlos?" she breathed, her body pressed tight against his.

"No," he smiled. "But my mind is open on that subject. Come back to my new place, okay? Please?"

"Okay," she said. "But only for a drink."

When Isabella left Carlos just before 10 pm, after more than one drink, her whole body, but especially between her legs, still felt deliciously hot and swollen. Carlos was a smooth, sensitive lover. As much as she hated to make comparisons, she'd had nothing like what Carlos did for her since early in her relationship with Jerry. Isabella understood there was no fair comparison between the excitement of being with a new, skilled lover and the satisfactions of a comfortable, established relationship, and she also knew that the hot, early excitement eventually settles down if it doesn't fade away entirely.

Still, she said yes when Carlos asked her out to dinner again for Friday evening. She didn't even care about the dinner. She just wanted more of his exquisite, intense lovemaking.

****

Jerry had been asked to work a double shift. The second one would be a desk shift, usually an easier but a more boring assignment. It was late afternoon. Sofia was working, too. She'd kept looking up at him from her computer terminal; every time he glanced her way, she seemed to have her eyes on him.

"Okay," he said. "What's up? What's going on?"

"I don't want to talk about it in here."

"In the break room?"

She shook her head. "Outside."

"What's it about?"

Sofia hesitated. "A cold case, I'd guess you'd say."

"An urgent cold case?"

"You could say that."

It was just past sunset when they took their lunches out to a bench on the quiet side of the building. There was enough of a breeze so that they wouldn't immediately attract the mosquitos from the drainage canal across the road.

"So," Jerry said. "Something's on your mind about a cold case?"

"Yeah, well, I was doing some background checks, and I ran across something that you should know about."

"What's that?"

"A supposedly accidental death up in Massachusetts about ten, twelve years ago."

"Okay. Does it pertain to a case down here?"

"Depends on how you define *case*, I guess."

"Just tell me, Sofia."

She took a deep breath. She was fairly sure Jerry wouldn't believe her.

"First, I need you to promise to think about this carefully, and, no matter what, absolutely do not tell that girl you've been fucking that I was the one who gave you the information."

Jerry gave her a cold look. "I wish you wouldn't talk like that."

"Who are you, my fucking father and I'm fifteen? You need to hear this."

Jerry sighed. "Okay, Sofia. Spill it."

"Cassandra Couri was married to a guy named John Hartford aka Jack up in Massachusetts when they were both in their late teens or very early twenties. College age. They weren't married long at all. He died of an asthma attack."

"She never mentioned anything like that," Jerry said.

"Yeah, well, there's more. The family, his very *rich* family by the way, tried to have the medical examiner take another look at the death."

"Because…"

"They thought that his death wasn't accidental."

"What was the result?"

"Same. Asthma attack."

"And Cassie was married to him?"

"Not at the time. They'd gotten divorced a few months or maybe just a few weeks before he died."

"Okay."

"He was the one who filed for the divorce."

"Based on what?"

Sofia shrugged. "A no-fault state. So, who knows."

Jerry sighed. "So, what you're saying is, Cassie had a short marriage when she was much younger, up in Massachusetts where we are both from. They got divorced, and then he died of an asthma attack. It was reinvestigated, with the same result for cause of death."

He looked over at Sofia. "Like I said, I did not know any of this. But why are you telling me now?"

"Because I think there is more to her than meets the eye. Or, at least, more than meets *your* pussy-blinded eyes. I met her once, too, remember. I know she's hot. But I'd hate to see you lose a nice girl like Isabella and get mixed up with someone who you might not know as much about as you should."

Jerry stood up. "I've known her since we were small children."

"A lot can change, Jerry."

"I'll talk with her about it, find out some more about it." More about *her*, he thought.

"Well, just leave me out of it, okay? Do not bring up my name. Not for any reason whatsoever. None. Nada. Never. I don't trust her. And I don't think you should, either."

"I think I can handle myself in an interrogation."

Sofia coughed and sprayed a little coffee from between her lips. "What?!"

"I was thinking about that scene in the *Basic Instinct* psycho-killer movie, the one where all the cops are interviewing Sharon Stone. She's sitting there cool as a cucumber, crossing and uncrossing her legs, and the interrogators, who are way, way out of their league, get all tongue-tied as she flashes them beaver shots. So…take that for what it's worth."

****

Sunday afternoon, Isabella was hosting an open house for one of her co-worker's listings out in The Crossings as a favor to her friend at their agency. It was a 1,700 square foot ranch, three bedrooms and two baths. The layout of the rooms was good, although just standard for the area. The back yard featured a large, caged pool with average but fairly nice landscaping. The driveway still desperately needed to be power washed, even though Isabella knew the owners had been told to do so by the listing agent.

Isabella didn't think the house was going to show as well as it could. Aside from the filthy driveway and some scraggly foundation plantings, the bathrooms needed to be updated, and the owners had left way too much personal décor up on the walls throughout the home. Still, it was priced reasonably, and it was in a good neighborhood, so it would sell eventually to the right buyer.

Around 2:30 pm, after a brief flurry of traffic, a slender, dark-haired woman walked quietly into the kitchen where Isabella was sitting scrolling on her phone. She was wearing sunglasses, shorts, and a ratty t-shirt.

"Oh, my gosh," said Isabella, standing. "I didn't hear you come in."

The woman nodded, and walked around, looking at the rooms. Isabella followed and handed her a listing sheet.

"Three bedrooms, two baths, well-priced for the neighborhood. Are you looking for yourself?"

The woman shrugged. "Maybe."

"I'm Isabella, and this listing belongs to an agent I work with. The place has so much potential and is in a great neighborhood."

The woman nodded.

"Would you like to sign in?" Isabella invited, sliding the sheet across the kitchen island.

The woman glanced at it. "I don't think so. I don't want to be on some mailing list, or anything. I'm just casual about all this for now."

Isabella shrugged and said, "Sure…and what was your name?"

"Ashley. You can call me Ashley."

"Do you work around here, Ashley?" Isabella asked, writing down the name on the sign-in sheet herself.

"Not really. I was wondering, though…do you have anything maybe farther out west, with more land?"

"Well, can you tell me your budget, Ashley?" Isabella asked politely.

"About four hundred thousand."

"Ooh, I'm not sure, with that budget. I could get you some land for that, but not with a house out there, or maybe just a tear-down. Could I call you if I find something you might like?"

"Better if I call you," Ashley said, picking up one of Isabella's business cards.

"No problem, no pressure," said Isabella. "But my agency kind of insists we get contact information. I guess to show I'm doing my job out here at the open houses I do."

Ashley reluctantly wrote down a number. "Actually, I'm sort of looking for something for a girlfriend more than for myself. She doesn't have any time to spend looking for places right now, but she needs to move. I'll tell her what you said and maybe get back in touch." She put Isabella's card in her purse.

Isabella shrugged, and watched Ashley walk away down the scarred driveway toward an older compact car. A new, white Escalade cruised slowly by, but didn't stop.

Then, Ashley paused, turned around, and walked determinedly back toward the house, her head down. Maybe she left something? Isabella thought.

"Hey," said Ashley. "I need to tell you something, but you're not going to like it. You seem like you can take it, though."

"Is it something about the house, something I need to tell the sellers?" Isabella asked.

"No. It's something about you. Someone might be trying to have you killed."

"What?" Isabella asked. "Who?"

"Some woman I met in a bar the other night. She wants your husband."

"I don't have a husband. I have a boyfriend who's a cop."

"Him, then, I guess. I just wanted to let you know to watch your back. You seem like a nice, upstanding person. That's all I wanted to say. So, be extra careful. There are more crazy people out there than you might think."

"Wait," Isabelle called after her.

But Ashley pulled out, made a U turn, and was down the street before Isabella managed to get the license plate number.

Wow, Isabella thought, that was a crazy one. The first person she thought about calling was Carlos and had already hit his number before she realized she'd chosen him over Jerry.

"How much longer are you supposed to be there today?" Carlos asked.

Isabella told him. Carlos said, "Stay inside, lock the doors, and wait for me. I'm leaving right now."

****

I really don't like undependable people, and lately, they have been everywhere around me.

Ashley called to say she'd decided she might want to wait and think a bit before she did anything more about the possible job we'd discussed involving Isabella. In fact, she said I might not be hearing from her again for a while, because she was going to be "busy, but good luck."

Apparently, she'd driven out to one of Isabella's open houses to assess things, talked with Isabella some, did some thinking, and decided not to continue. I wasn't at all upset over her change of heart, because, unless I am remembering things wrong, it was her idea to begin with.

"I'll call you again when I get freed up," she said.

I naturally thought of Danny next. I sent a message to his number, and of course he remembered me. He said he was currently out in Las Vegas "for work, not for fun." I didn't care what he was out there for, but to be polite, I asked how he was doing.

"I'm fine, Miss Cassandra, just fine."

"Are you staying sober?" I asked.

"For the most part, I am," he said, "thanks to you. Once in a while, I do have a little drink, but I only do it as a social thing, to fit in. I haven't done any cocaine at all. But I guess I have kind of burned out some priests, here and there."

"I could be wrong, Danny," I said, "but I don't think that the rite of absolution clears the deck so you can just start back doing the same things all over."

"No," he agreed. "What it is, is that I bring up different things each time I go."

"A fresh batch," I asked, "or more from the past?"

"Mostly more from the past. I have sort of a backlog."

I admitted to him that I had been thinking of another job or two down here in Florida. "You did such smooth, professional work for me," I said, referring to Maury and his wife, "that it's almost like they aren't gone. Every once in a while, I find myself thinking that I might call them to see if I can inveigle a dinner invitation, and then I remember."

"I'm glad you're pleased with the work," he said. "I try to do a pro job every time."

"Danny, I think that maybe we should talk business," I pressed. "I'd like to offer you some more work."

"Well, Miss Cassandra, that could be possible, but anything else I might do for you would have to be at full retail, and I might decide to sub it out to another pro. I don't go to work, you know, just because I don't like someone or for anything personal. It's strictly to accomplish a job I'm contracted for."

"I can understand your business model. I am mostly capable of doing my own work, but sometimes I do need help."

I expected Danny to ask for details (I was thinking of a job involving the removal of Isabella, of course), but, instead, he actually turned me down, which surprised me.

"Miss Cassandra, I feel I need to offer you some advice, and you can take it or not, your choice."

"And what is that?" I asked. I was no longer really interested once I understood we weren't going to be "doing business," as Danny called getting paid to kill people.

"Once you do some business, unless it's strictly in self-defense, or unless it's in a war or maybe if you're a cop or something, then you're in the club. Even if you hire someone to do the job for you, you're still in the club. You might have an easier time pretending to yourself that your own hands are clean if someone does it for you, but they're not.

"So, as soon as you have crossed over that bridge, your personal support system becomes people like me, people who have killed other people. You might think you can still socialize like before with normal people, but you'll find that you are not ever going to be real friends with them anymore. You might try to maybe have a drink with them, or go over to their homes for dinner, discuss their kids and jobs and the weather, but that's all on a very superficial level. You know they couldn't truly relate to you if they knew what you've done, what you do. Because you're not normal. You're in a special club. You're a killer."

I listened politely and thanked Danny for sharing his thoughts and I wished him well. I didn't bother telling him that I've never felt normal, and that I didn't want to be in any stupid club.

Plus, I was pissed off that he was turning out to be just another undependable, judgmental asshole. I get so tired of having to do everything by myself.

****

Carlos pulled up to the curb in a conservative, dark blue Mercedes sedan. He flashed his lights and Isabella waved. She was already outside, standing near the front door, stacking up the signs for the open house, preparing to load them into the back of her vehicle. She opened her lift-gate with her remote and carried the signs over to her car. Carlos hopped out and helped her position the signs so their metal pieces wouldn't scrape the interior of her vehicle. Then he took her in his arms and gave her a tight hug.

"I'm so very happy you called me, Isabella. Are you available to come out to dinner with me? I want to hear all about this situation. I must say, I never once considered that real estate showings could carry as much risk as yours seem to. I want to hear all about this."

"I'm not really dressed for any place nice, Carlos. Is it possible we could just go to your place, maybe for a drink?"

He nodded, got on his phone, and placed a delivery order from a nice Italian restaurant. "I have an excellent bottle of a red blend that will go well with our dinner. The food should be delivered soon after we get home. Alright if you follow me there?"

Isabella nodded. She would give him the details about her day after they ate.

Carlos listened carefully, a glass of the very good wine in his hand. When Isabella was finished telling him about the woman and what she had said, he sat silently and rubbed his hands on his knees. Finally, he said, "It was a man you had never seen before up in that apartment on the first day we met."

Isabella nodded.

"And this was a woman you never before saw?"

"Yes."

"Did the man say anything that one time?"

"Just a few questions about the apartment, like a buyer might, only I felt very uncomfortable about him right as soon as I saw him. The woman today was fairly chatty. It seemed like a totally normal showing, although she was a little bit evasive about where she lived, and she didn't want to sign the registry that I keep for my contact list. Then, right as she was leaving, she told me that I seemed nice, so she wanted to tell me that someone was trying to get me killed."

"And you believed her?"

Isabella nodded. "It was like she was apologizing."

"It might have been her, sent to do a hit on you," Carlos said. "But she changed her mind for some reason."

Tears welled up and began to spill down Isabella's cheeks. "She said she was telling me because I seemed like a nice person. I *am* a nice person, Carlos. Why do these people want to kill me?"

Carlos took Isabella in his arms protectively and kissed her hair. "The reason could be because they want something you have, and you are standing in their way."

"I really don't have very much," Isabella said. "My car, my real estate license, a little money in the bank, that's all right now. Who would be so interested?"

"What about your man?"

"Jerry? He has just a little house, and, I guess, average money." She shrugged her shoulders.

"I meant, my dear Isabella, does someone else want to be with him? To take you out of that picture?"

"Oh, I don't think so..." she said quickly. "I never thought..."

Carlos looked at her. "Sometimes, when a beautiful woman such as yourself is out meeting someone," and he gave a self-deprecating little shrug, "it can happen because she knows something isn't right at home."

"It's..."

"...not like that?" Carlos asked. "I think it could be."

Isabella shook her head. "No," she said firmly, and she stood up. "Thank you for coming to save me again today," she said, "but now I think I should go home."

"If you wish, of course. You understand, though, that today you called me to come help you. You didn't call your man. Please think about why that was."

"I *know* why it was, Carlos. I don't want him to worry. Because of his job, he always thinks something terrible is going to happen."

Carlos shrugged. "That could be part of it. It could also be because your heart is telling you something very important."

Isabella was quiet.

"You have options right now. I can offer you a different life. My *mamá* is coming to visit soon. I would be pleased if you would agree to meet her."

"Why?"

"You know how our mothers are. She would like me to settle down and have a family with a nice girl. Grandchildren for her."

Isabella laughed. "Carlos, you are so handsome, and rich, too, I guess. I know you have had so many choices. Why me? Is it maybe because I already have a man, and you know I will say 'no' and then you can tell your mama that you are trying? And keep on being a happy *hombre soltero*? A *rompecorazones*?"

She thought he might be angry at the slight insult, but Carlos merely shrugged and said, "That would have been a fair assessment of me when I was younger. I'm finished with those days now."

"Have you ever said that exact same sentence to another woman, Carlos?"

He smiled. "You know me too well, Isabella. When I was younger and not a serious man, perhaps so. Not lately."

She laughed. "Let's just see how it goes, Carlos."

"That will be fine for now, Isabella." His face went serious. "But don't forget about what happened today. I think you need a bodyguard. Would you like to move in with me for a while?"

Isabella shook her head.

"Then I will just give you a key. Come here any time, in the middle of the night or in the middle of the day, if you don't feel safe. You know the front door code?"

Isabella shook her head again. Carlos put his hand out for her phone and entered the passcode below his name.

"Just come. Any time."

"What if you have company?"

"Isabella, I'm not seeing another woman at this time. If I have company, it would only be friends or family I would be pleased for you to meet."

CHAPTER 13

I've explained, I think, about this woman I often have the misfortune of working with on the drug and alcohol treatment unit. Her name, in case you forgot, is Melissa Canfield. I consider her an enemy, based solely on her behavior toward me.

She is a counselor, so you'd think she'd know better, but she is showing no indications that she plans to dump the loser she is married to, a guy I consider to be a total sleazebag.

After her husband left our treatment unit AMA a while back, he emptied their joint bank account and then, predictably enough, went on a massive coke run. Although I haven't given Melissa much thought lately with so much else on my mind, I have noticed, when I've seen her at work, that she has been more subdued, and she hasn't been aiming her little barbs at me in staff meetings. I think, or I'd like to think, that having had the experience of her choice of a husband staying on the unit as a patient, displaying himself to all her coworkers as the low-life little douchebag that he is, must have been humiliating for her. I mean, she obviously chose to marry him. She proudly carried around a picture of him in her wallet in which he was dressed like a pimp. At least that's what my impression was when she was showing people the photo.

I don't like to think of myself as the type of person who enjoys someone else's public humiliation, but I guess that's who I am in this case.

For a few weeks after Melissa's husband walked off the unit against medical advice and went roaring away on his next coke run, Melissa continued to just go quietly about her duties at work. I heard that she finally got the husband admitted to another facility farther up the coast. I don't know how things with that admission are turning out, but Melissa herself has continued to come in to work her scheduled shifts and I heard through the grapevine that she has redoubled her attendance at the AA meetings in town.

If I had any kind of a personal relationship with her, I certainly would suggest she also add an Al-Anon meeting or two to her schedule. Al-Anon, in case you don't know, is a 12-Step support group for people in a relationship with an addict or alcoholic: a parent, spouse, friend, son or daughter, and so forth.

The primary goal of Al-Anon is *not* to learn how to help the addict, even though everyone around an addict typically wishes they could somehow control that person's drinking and drugging and stop them from causing so much damage and chaos. But it's impossible to control someone else's addiction. So, instead, Al-Anon is aimed at helping you examine and modify your own unhealthy responses to the difficult situation of living with or being in a relationship with an active alcoholic or addict. That is apparently much harder than it sounds.

Unfortunately, it didn't really take too long after her husband left our treatment facility before Melissa was once again acting pretty snotty towards me. I cannot emphasize enough that I have never said an unkind word to that woman, and, initially, I actually hoped we would be friends. I thought I could learn so much from her about conducting group therapy just by sitting in on the morning sessions she runs when I worked a day shift.

But once I had heard from a reliable source, one of my friends who usually just works on-call shifts, that Melissa wanted to get me fired, I'd had all I was willing to take from her. It wasn't that I was worried about getting fired. She was in no way popular enough with the unit manager to be able to influence his personnel decisions. Plus, he is very much a by-the-book type guy, and I always follow the rules and procedures, am on time for work, volunteer to cover shifts when needed, and all that. Plus, of all the people I work with, Melissa is the only one I have a problem with.

Now, to be totally fair, I will say that most people like her. I mean, I did, too, when I first started here at the treatment center. So, it isn't like her job is hanging by a thread.

Which means that, in order for me to get her out of my work life, I was going to have to spring a trap of some kind so that her job *was* hanging by a thread. A thread that just suddenly snaps.

I decided that her douche-bag husband's drug problem might provide me with some kind of an opportunity if I kept my eyes and ears open. Everyone knew about his outrageous behavior when he was using. Many people had heard that he'd run though Melissa's money and had maxed out her credit cards. Pretty standard cocaine addict behavior, truth be told, but no fun at all when it's your money and you still have to find a way to pay the rent, the electric bill, the car payment, and all that.

What, then, might be a straightforward way in South Florida to make some quick money when you're Melissa and you're feeling cornered, and the bill collectors are circling like vultures? Well, selling drugs is pretty much the gold standard down here. So, that's what I decided she should do: Melissa would sell drugs. And get caught stealing the drugs she intended to sell from our treatment unit's locked and carefully monitored drug cabinets and mini refrigerators.

That scenario was not going to be easy to set up. For one thing, counselors have no access to the drugs, except for maybe once or twice a shift if a busy nurse just rushes off during an otherwise quiet period to attend to a patient and fails to lock up as she should. But that's an opportunity window of only a few minutes with no way of predicting when it might occur. Days can pass with no chance of that, and, besides, any discrepancy in the unit's medication inventory would be detected almost immediately at the next change of shift when the meds are counted.

Another method would be to form a partnership with the medication nurse. That way, the two of you could plan it out and figure out how to cover your tracks. But *I'm* the medication nurse when I'm on the same shift as Melissa, so that's definitely out. There is no way in hell I would ever enter into a criminal partnership like that with anyone, let alone her, because I would never risk my nursing license and my career. Or trust anyone who would be dishonest enough to steal patient medications.

Someone might be able to get around the treatment unit's drug-stealing obstacles entirely by figuring out how to snag the drugs directly from Central Supply. In this facility, Central Supply is located on the lower level, meaning it's in the basement, where the hospital laundry is also located. There is a convenient door to the parking garage nearby, plus a bunch of storage and housekeeping supply rooms. However, getting drugs out of Central Supply would definitely have to involve a partnership between a supervisor in Central Supply and the person who was hoping to access the drugs to sell on the street. So, yes, difficult, but not out of the question.

I thought about all this for a while and decided to befriend one of the two guys who usually works down there. One of the men is named Hughie, and he is very tanned and fit, but none too bright. In fact, he reminds me a little bit of the blond orderly I used to know back up north in Massachusetts at the treatment center where I worked nights, the one near the spooky cranberry bogs.

The other guy, Juan Martinez-Cordero, always smiles at me, and sometimes he just sort of sneakily appears around our treatment unit when he doesn't really need to be there. I think he could be dating the unit secretary, which might make him ideal for my purposes. Although he might not think that if he knew what I have in mind.

The important thing, though, is that Juan has already put in his two-week notice at work. The really good part is that he is then going to be moving back to Puerto Rico right away because his father is very sick, and the family wants him down there to take over the father's car repair business for the near future. I don't know if our unit secretary will be joining him in Puerto Rico at some point or not.

I could go on and on about my plotting and planning, but the main things I was mostly interested in were quick results and not getting caught.

So, what I did first was to get the maintenance guy, Juan, to make me a copy of the medication room door key.

I didn't tell him what the key was to, but I sort of implied that it was for a lock at my house. He looked a little skeptical, probably because he'd seen a lot of similar keys around the facility. But, since he was on his way out, he didn't really bother to investigate the matter. I didn't think he would. I can be very charming and flattering when I want to be, and most straight men are total suckers for a good-looking woman. I also had him copy the key to the controlled substances cabinet located inside the medication room. The lock for that cabinet is sturdy enough, but nothing that you couldn't find in a hardware store. I tried out both my new keys several times up on the unit to make sure they worked smoothly.

Then, I simply thanked Juan and offered him a nice cash tip for his quick work, which he accepted without question. I waited calmly for the two and a half weeks to pass until Juan had left his job at our hospital and had gone back to Puerto Rico.

Next, I waited a little more time until one of those days when Melissa and I were both scheduled to work the same shift. Then, while we were going about our business on the unit, I snagged a little diazepam, some lorazepam, and quite a bit of methadone from the securely locked unit medication room. I selected those drugs to steal because, at the time, we had a good supply of them of them up on the floor, but very few patients at present were being prescribed them for their detoxes. I wouldn't want to short any of our patients, even temporarily.

Next, I flushed all those drugs I'd removed from the medication room right down the toilet, and slipped the keys that I'd had Juan Carlos make into the back of Melissa's top desk drawer in her counseling office. Finally, I made myself quite visible around the unit a few times, on each occasion leaving both the nursing office and the medication room vacant while I interacted with patients.

The big show occurred immediately at shift change when I had to count the medications with the nurse coming on duty. Guess what? Some drugs were missing.

I was totally prepared to be the one to come under immediate suspicion, and, indeed, I was. But I cooperated fully and was aided by the fact that the missing medications were treated, at least at first, as a hush-hush affair.

The unit supervisor organized a sweep of the unit and of all staff members' and patients' personal belongings. I appeared to be as surprised as anyone when keys to both the nursing office and to the drug cabinet were found in Melissa's office desk drawer. They were clearly copies, not the originals. I could have said to the nursing supervisor how relieved I was that the matter had been resolved, but I decided to keep my mouth shut and just go with looking surprised. Why lay it on thick when things are going well?

Melissa screamed bloody murder and had to be escorted off the unit by hospital security. I watched from down the hall with a mildly sympathetic expression. The unit director informed the staff that, while he understood how much stress Melissa had been under with her addict husband, her employment would most likely be terminated following an investigation.

I knew I would probably have to give an accounting for all the times during the particular shift when the medications went missing when I wasn't working inside the medication room, but I wasn't worried about that. Part of my job was to interact therapeutically with patients out on the unit, so it was fine and even encouraged that I get out on the floor when I had free time. I think I did a particularly good job of explaining what I had done at what times during the shift in question. And, of course, I emphasized how I had definitely secured the medication room each time I was out on the floor and kept my set of keys with me, attached to a lanyard.

Juan was really the only one who could throw me under the bus, and he was long gone from the area.

In the immediate aftermath of Melissa's departure, I felt rather sorry for a while that I hadn't decided just to kill her. It would have been a lot less work, involved a lot fewer people, and, if need be, I probably could have easily enough cast suspicion on her husband. That was my thinking at the time, anyway. Not too long after Melissa left her employment at the treatment center, though, I found out something that make me very glad that things had gone down as they had.

One of the orderlies who I like to hang out and gossip with on our breaks told me that Melissa had said to him a while back that she was afraid that I might try to do something to her.

"*Do* something?" I asked, genuinely surprised. *She* was the one who was trying to get *me* fired, I thought. "Like what?"

He shrugged. "Kill her, maybe."

I stared at him, my mouth open.

"Yeah, I know. Crazy, huh?"

"Very crazy," I said. "I knew she was under a lot of stress, but…"

He shook his head. "You just never know about people, do you?"

"I know I was surprised," was all I said. Mainly, I was surprised that Melissa had figured me out better than I had realized.

But thinking back to that time when we had the in-service presentation and she kept publicly asking those obnoxious questions, I guess it makes sense. If she'd kept her mouth shut back then, probably none of this would have ever happened. I didn't like her, and she didn't like me, but I could have lived with that if she weren't a pain in the ass about it. But she just had to keep poking at me and so what happened, happened.

Now, she had no job and certainly wouldn't be getting a good reference from her former supervisor at our treatment center. I shrugged to myself. People who steal drugs really shouldn't be working around them.

You might still be wondering why I didn't try harder to find a way to just kill Melissa, given what a bitch she was to me, instead of going through all the difficulty of setting her up the way I did. I don't have a satisfactory answer for that, other than that sometimes I just don't feel like it. Plus, I really can't think of a time when I've killed another woman, not unless you want to count when it happened by proxy, like with Maury's wife Evelyn. I don't think I have some kind of real reluctance about it, though.

I guess we'll find out more about that if it turns out I need to personally eliminate Jerry's little real estate salesgirl. No one seems to be coming through for me on that matter.

****

Jerry called Cassie while he was at the station. She said she was getting dressed for work, because she had an evening shift, but that she got off at eleven pm. Would he like to come over then?

"I would like to, very much," he replied. "There are a few things I need to talk about with you."

There was silence on Cassie's end for a moment. Then she replied, cautiously, he thought. "Sounds serious."

"I just have some questions is all," he said.

"When somebody like a cop or a lawyer or an auditor for the IRS uses those words, it sounds really serious," she replied. "But I'll be home by about eleven-twenty, and I look forward to seeing you."

After he ended the call nicely, Jerry stood up and went to look for Sofia. He found her outside, smoking a cigarette.

"I thought you had quit those," he said.

"I went back, but it'll just be for a little while. I'm having a tough time over something."

"Over what? That asshole in Internal Affairs?"

"No, no, nothing like that. I broke up with him. It was just a short little fling."

"Well, that's too bad, I guess."

"You just called him an asshole. So how is it too bad?"

"I wasn't thinking. I'm in sort of a quandary."

"Ah, so your fucked-up love triangle is still a fucked-up love triangle?"

He ignored Sofia's jab. "It's about Cassie. You know how a while back you said you did a background check on her, and you briefed me about what you'd found?"

"Yeah, well, apparently it wasn't enough to get you to quit her. But enough to make any sane guy take a minute to think about it."

"Well, I've been thinking about it."

"Great. Let me be the first to know when you dump her. I'll throw you a party. And even buy the alcohol. You're drinking what kind of booze these days?"

"I'm not dumping her."

"You moron. Don't tell me you're dumping Isabella. I'll punch you in the face if you say that."

"I honestly don't know what to do. I love them both. But in different ways."

"That's so lame. It's the lamest thing I've heard all day. No, wait, that moron Luis said something even stupider about an hour ago, but he's a regular fountain of idiotic remarks."

"I'm trying to figure out what to do. Don't keep busting my balls."

"It's what I do with guys like you. You screwed around on a nice girl, fucked a not-so-nice girl, and now you don't know what to do." Sofia waited, and then said, "Do you really want me to tell you what to do?"

"I'd like to hear a serious suggestion or two, yes."

"You can start by digging much deeper than you have into your side-piece's past. I gave it a shot a while ago and didn't come up with too much that you didn't already know about her besides a divorce followed by a dead ex and a bad feeling. I still have the bad feeling."

"Sofia, you haven't tried to make any personal contact with her, have you?"

Sofia shook her head. "Nope. Never. And if you were smart, you wouldn't either."

Jerry stood up. "I think I'm going to talk to her about all that stuff again. Get her to tell me her life story. Ask her some questions."

"Would you like a suggestion?"

"I guess…" Jerry waited, watching Sofia's smirk spread into a grin.

"Ask her gentle questions that you already know the answers to, maybe while you're cuddled together during one of your trysts. Get her talking, like you would with any reluctant suspect. You know how you try to get them relaxed and chatting away and then you drop the hammer? And how then they sometimes tell you what they didn't want to tell you?"

Jerry nodded.

"Do that. Only, be sure to watch your back, afterwards. Or your balls, as the case may be."

Jerry arrived at Cassie's apartment just before midnight holding a simple bouquet of white carnations from the supermarket and a bottle of a good California sauvignon blanc.

Jerry had told Isabella that he was going out for a drive to collect his thoughts about an issue he was having at work. She'd nodded and said, "I hope everything will be alright, Jerry," and had then turned right back to the book she was reading on her tablet. He'd hesitated for a beat and then walked over to where she was sitting and kissed her on the cheek. She'd given him a tight smile back.

Cassie was wearing a short, pale green dress and espadrilles. He was dressed casually in clean clothes. She had set the table with an array of snack plates and bottles of cold soda water. The curtains and the slider were open. He could see the lights of the city, and then beyond those to the empty darkness of the Atlantic Ocean.

Cassie greeted him with a light kiss and then stepped back. She didn't seem either cold or particularly excited to see him. The word he would use was watchful, like an unconcerned wild animal simply measuring your approach.

"You look beautiful," Jerry said. He looked around. "I envy your view up here. I never really considered living anywhere in Miami besides where I do, I guess because that's where I grew up after I left Massachusetts. I just stayed in basically the same area where my aunt and uncle raised me. But I love seeing the ocean."

"Yeah," said Cassie, turning to look at the dark sea. "The colors change every day. I like it smooth, the way it is in the summer. When it's windy, like now, it's one roller after another. I guess it's fun for the tourists at the beach, though."

"Maybe less fun for the lifeguards," Jerry said.

We could chat superficially like this all night, he thought. It would be easy and pleasant. If I bring up what I came here to say, it might change everything between us forever. Would she ever let him hold her in his arms again? Would they even still be friends?

"Do you want a glass of wine?" Cassie asked.

He nodded and watched her open the bottle and fill their glasses. She set his on a fancy napkin decorated with an embossed palm leaf.

"Very nice," he said, nodding at the napkin.

"Yeah, I ordered them online. I like a few luxuries. Life is short."

Jerry thought that sounded like her opening salvo. He took a sip of his wine and began.

"We're both so far from where we were as kids. Back in Massachusetts, I would never have imagined that any of what we have now was possible. I was just living from one day to the next."

"I definitely recall that you wanted to be a cop, though," Cassie said. "You told me you wanted to be like Crockett and Tubbs, remember? We would all sit in the TV room and watch reruns of that show, and that's what you said."

"Did I? You remembered that?"

"I remember almost everything from back then," Cassie said. "I remember with perfect clarity the day you left The Home to move away to Florida."

"My aunt and uncle gave me a life I would never have had if they hadn't taken me. I hope I thanked them enough."

"I'm sure they knew," Cassie said. She paused. "I remember standing outside watching their car drive away with you inside. It was worst thing that had ever happened to me."

"I was so excited to be going to Florida," Jerry said. "I didn't really think about what I was leaving behind."

"I stood and waved, but I couldn't see through the rear window to tell if you turned around to look."

"I don't remember if I did," Jerry said. "I might not have. I guess I was just looking ahead."

"Things were pretty tough for me after you left."

"But you survived," Jerry said.

****

It seemed to me that he was just placating me, like he didn't want to get too deep tonight into reminiscing about The Home. I started to wonder what his actual agenda was for coming over. He didn't seem to be here for sex, as I had assumed and hoped. I decided to wait until he showed more of his hand.

"More wine?" I asked, indicating the open bottle.

He shook his head. "I'm good," he said.

We'll see about that, I thought. I smiled, waiting for him to get to what he was really here for.

"You've done so well with your career, and everything," he said. "How did you decide to go into the medical field?"

I thought about what to say.

"I think it was sometime during my later high school years. I started to realize that I was actually going to need to support myself, you know, get a job and all that, and the medical field seemed like it had a lot of flexibility in terms of the kinds of jobs and the types of job settings. So, once I was in college, I decided to try for a BSN. Then, when I graduated, I took the National Nursing Exam right away, like you need to in order to become a registered nurse.

"Overall, it did turn out to be an excellent choice for me. I like my work, and I think substance abuse treatment, rather than doing something like working as an operating room nurse, suits me. I guess I like working with conscious patients," I smiled.

"You said you had been married, back when we met for the very first time out at the beach."

I nodded. Okay, we're starting to get into it, now, I thought.

"Yes," I said. "It didn't work out. We were too young, I guess, and too different. Maybe it would have worked out if we were older, but I doubt it. I think I just looked past our differences when we were dating because I loved him."

Did I ever tell Jerry that he had died? That day we first met? I knew we'd never talked about it since. I waited to see if Jerry would give me a clue as to where he was headed with this.

"What ever happened with him? The guy you married. Are you still in contact?"

I shook my head. "No. He died. I guess I don't remember if I already told you that or not." I really didn't.

Jerry shook his head and waited. Cassie didn't seem like she was going to volunteer anything else. She would make an excellent poker player, he thought.

"Is it still painful for you?" he asked. "Or can you tell me about it?"

"It's not painful, not anymore. He died of an asthma attack, apparently," I said. "We were already divorced by then." I paused. "Are you sure we didn't talk about any of this that first time we met? At the restaurant at the beach? And then we came back here?"

Cassie lowered her eyes, flirtatiously Jerry thought, maybe trying to change the subject to sex, to get him off-track.

"Not much. Maybe you said he died. I don't remember, or I wouldn't have asked. We were sort of going from one thing to another that day."

"No, I guess we really didn't stick too long to any one topic that afternoon. I couldn't take my eyes off you. I couldn't believe I was really with you, both of us all grown up."

Jerry smiled but continued with his train of thought. "So, how did it happen?"

Cassie shook her head. "His death? I don't know, exactly. I heard that he was at home alone in his apartment when he had an asthma attack. I do know that he had asthma and that he had all these inhalers around that he used, ever since I first met him. He always had one in his shirt pocket or in his pants pocket.

"How did you meet him?"

"In school, not long after I started there. He was a year ahead of me."

"Why did you get divorced?"

I sighed, like I was remembering something bitter-sweet.

"We were not really compatible, but I didn't find that out until a while after we'd married. It was all fun and games while we were dating. We had really great times together, and I just thought that marriage would be more of that. It wasn't very long before I found myself really busy with classes and labs and hospital and clinic rotations. He knew how hard I was working, but he left all the housework and all the shopping for groceries for me to do.

"He wasn't very engaged in school, but he did love his parties. But he sure didn't like doing things like laundry or even making the bed. He would go out drinking with his friends in the evenings while I studied or worked at one of my part time jobs. He fell behind in school and started talking about dropping out. He'd take classes and then just drop them by the middle of the semester if he got behind in the work.

"Basically, I fell out of love with him after I got to know him better. I guess I lost respect for him. And I left."

"Sounds like it wasn't a very equitable arrangement," Jerry said.

I stared at him. "That's right. But I didn't know that concept at that age. It had never occurred to me to give any thought to how two people arrange their lives to fit together in a marriage. It was just frustrating to me, and then I kind of quit trying."

"How was it for you after you'd split up, when you found out that he'd died?"

"Shocked. I was shocked. I knew he had asthma, but I didn't understand how serious it could be. I didn't really know anyone before him who'd ever had asthma."

"What about in your nursing classes? Hadn't you studied that kind of thing?"

Okay, so this *was* an interrogation.

"Sure," I said lightly. "In theory, at least. My clinical rotation at the time was in surgery, and that's what I was focused on, not on respiratory conditions. That came later, in pediatrics. The asthma, I mean." I sighed a little, and I imagined I looked sad. "I kind of blame myself, in a way."

"What do you mean?"

"I don't think he was taking particularly good care of himself after we split up. He took our divorce harder than I did. He was surprised and angry when I told him that it was over. I told him soon after I'd graduated and had taken my national nursing exam."

"What was his name?"

I didn't even hesitate. "Jack Hartford," I said.

There is not one detail from that time in my past that Jerry or anyone else could dig up which would be substantially different from what I'd just told him. That I can think of.

CHAPTER 14

Isabella picked up her phone as soon as it rang, thinking it might be Jerry or Carlos or, even better, maybe a call from someone who wanted to buy some real estate. Instead, it was Sofia on the phone, Jerry's co-worker at the station. Isabella knew her casually and liked her. Her first thought, though, was that something terrible had happened to Jerry, and that Sofia had been nominated to be the bearer of the bad news.

"Nope," she said, "Jerry's fine, as far as I know. I'm calling to see if you would like to get together with me and maybe a couple of other women, or maybe it will be just us, for drinks and something to eat."

"Okay," said Isabella, "when were you thinking?"

"Can you make it tonight, about 5:30? That's what time I'm getting off."

When Isabella arrived at the casual restaurant, Sofia was already there with a couple of her friends from the station. The were all drinking draft beer, so Isabella ordered one, too. After about twenty minutes of pleasant chit-chat, the other two women said they had to get home to feed their kids, so Isabella and Sofia were left alone together.

A few tables over, a group of young men in baseball uniforms had noisily plopped themselves down in a booth.

"I thought those recreational teams went drinking after their games, not before," Isabella said.

"Before, during, after, who knows?" replied Sofia. "When I used to play in an evening co-ed league, that's sure how it was. Although, to be fair, it was mostly after the game. Although we did keep a cooler under the bench. So, during, too."

Isabella and Sofia hit on a number of topics, including some work gossip Sofia shared about people with whom Isabella was acquainted. They also complained about the crazy traffic around town these days, what with the all the forever road construction in South Florida, and how the real estate business seemed to be going pretty well for Isabella. Isabella was surprised when the next subject Sofia brought up to discuss was the problems she was having meeting men.

"You work around all kinds of guys, Sofia. It seems like you could pick and choose."

"You're right, I'm around men all the time, but I'm picky about who I choose. Do you know who I meet?"

Isabella shook her head. "Cops?"

"Married cops. Criminals. Crazy young single cops who really aren't good husband material, at least not until they grow up, and in the meantime, they would give me a bad reputation if I went out with more than one of them. You can have a steady relationship with a cop if that's what you want, but they'll talk all over the station if you date more than one. I hear what they say."

"What about lawyers? Judges? Don't you meet any of them?"

"I do meet a few, but it's mostly in the courtroom, and it's in-and-out with them. No time to really get to know them. There are some nice court officers who I do see somewhat regularly, but no one I'm really interested in."

"Do guy cops have the same problems meeting women?" Isabella asked.

"Not as much, I don't think. There is a certain segment of women who find the idea of dating or even settling down with a cop extremely attractive, at least maybe before they realize there's going to be more to it than just the steady county paycheck. There are the weird work shifts and the fallout at home from the stressful job. A lot of cops are kind of moody during their off-time and some of them cope with the job by drinking way too much. Of course, you know all that from personal experience."

"Jerry has been quite moody lately, but I ask, and he says it's not the job."

Sofia sighed. She weighed what, if anything, she should say. It had been her idea to meet with Isabella, but she hadn't really thought much farther than arranging the meet-up. She wasn't sure exactly what was okay to discuss and which topics to leave alone. She definitely had no intention of letting it slip that Jerry was seeing someone else…that was Jerry's problem to solve. He was the one who had gotten himself into the mess.

"Guys can be such jerks," said Sofia under her breath.

"Why, do you know something?" Isabella asked.

"I didn't realize I had said that out loud," Sofia said. "I meant in general."

"Do you think you're going to try to meet a special guy?" Isabella asked.

"Not right now. And I'm okay with that. I have a really good relationship with my dog. Did you ever meet Ollie? She flunked out of drug detection school, and I adopted her. Jerry met her once or twice when I had her out for a run."

"Yeah, he said something about you having a dog now. Is she a lot of work?"

"Depends on how you look at it. She seems to need to have a real relationship with me. And dogs ideally need other dogs or some other pet around, too. They're pack animals, at heart. I can't just leave her home alone all the time and expect her to be happy. It gets so their entire world revolves around you, so you have to acknowledge that and respect it and meet all their needs. But she gives me back love, and companionship, and loyalty. And, for me, there's another living creature in the house. So, I really never feel alone. If I find the right dog, though, I might get another one, so she has a friend when I'm not there."

Isabella sighed. "I think Jerry is drifting away from me. Even when he's there, it's like he isn't, not really. He's on his phone a lot. But even if we are watching a TV show together or talking, there's not as much connection between us as there used to be...not as much as I'd like. I don't know if we are going to last."

Sofia was quiet. Is it my place to say something, or not? She waited for Isabella to go on.

"You know how like on Valentine's Day?" Isabella continued. "I realize it's just a stupid fake day created to sell candy and flowers, and it probably makes a lot of people who are alone feel bad for no good reason..."

Sofia merely nodded. She had a feeling where Isabella was going to go with this.

"Well, Jerry came home late. He brought me a sweet but impersonal card and some okay flowers. We had a little dinner outside on the patio that I quickly put together from leftovers, and we had some wine, and it was...okay. But I was disappointed, probably because I wanted more. Like an engagement ring, or even just a more planned and special celebration."

"Such as what?"

"Something to show he cared enough to have put some thought into it. A really nice, personal card. Decent quality chocolates. Is that asking too much?"

"You're not alone. A lot of guys don't really read the room too well about Valentine's Day. The women plan, and the men just go along."

Not all of them, Isabella thought. Carlos would have made it very special.

"People make too much out of Valentine's Day, as far as I'm concerned," continued Sofia. "The greeting card companies, the flower vendors, the restaurants, and, of course, the jewelers... they all love it. But I learned in *catecismo* that February 14 was actually the day St. Valentine was brutally executed for disobeying some Roman marriage law. I don't think that chocolates and roses and going out to an expensive restaurant had any part in the original saint's day."

"If I tell you something, will you keep it private?" Isabella asked.

"Is it a crime you want to confess?" Sofia joked. "Because if it's that, don't tell me. But if it's not against the law, sure, I can keep a secret."

"It's not a crime. But I've started seeing someone else, and Jerry doesn't know," she blurted.

"Wow," said Sofia. "I had no idea." She sat back in her seat and looked at Isabella. Now I know what each of them doesn't know about the other one, she thought. But she felt better now for Isabella. What's sauce for the goose is sauce for the gander. Or vice-versa.

"Do you think I'm a terrible person?" Isabella asked. "For seeing someone behind Jerry's back?"

Sofia shook her head. "It's not really my place to judge what other people do in their relationships. I don't have all the facts. And it's not my life."

She felt relieved, even good, now that she had so much less reason to feel sorry for Isabella. She'd been viewing Isabella as a sad little victim of Jerry's obsession with the woman he was seeing behind her back.

"Can you tell me a little about the guy?"

"His name is Carlos; I met him at a condo I was showing. It started out casual."

"And now?"

"Not so casual."

"Did he get you anything for Valentine's Day?"

Isabella shook her head. "He knows I'm with Jerry. But every time I'm with Carlos it's like Valentine's Day."

"You sound enamored."

"I know it could just be that sweet rush you get when someone is new. Right now, I'm not sure I would leave Jerry for Carlos, but if our relationship doesn't get back on track soon, I couldn't say that I wouldn't. I hope you don't think I'm terrible," Isabella repeated.

"I don't think you're terrible, Isabella. I think you're living your life. Just be careful. Take that as you will."

"What do you mean?"

"You're on birth control, right? Using condoms for protection from diseases?"

"I'm on birth control, but we haven't been using condoms..."

Sofia gave her a look. "You need to be careful. Since you're not exclusive, and he's not exclusive either, probably..."

"He? Do you mean Jerry? You know something?"

"I don't know anything. I was thinking of the other guy, Carlos, when I said that," Sofia lied.

On her drive back home to take Ollie out for her evening walk, Sofia started thinking about praying mantis insects. She pulled out her phone and called Jerry's personal number.

"Hey, Sofia," he answered. "What's up?"

"Not much. I just had a drink with Isabella."

"She called me on her way home just now and said you had."

"Yeah, we were just catching up, talking a little girl talk. She'll probably tell you all about it. I wanted to let you know, if she says anything, that I didn't spill any of your dirty little secrets."

"I admit I have secrets," Jerry said, "but I bet we all have some, Sofia. And I don't like that word 'dirty.' I'm struggling with this. It doesn't feel dirty, it feels painful."

"Painful. Hmmp. Do you know anything about what a praying mantis is, Jerry?"

"No, not much, other than that it's an insect. Sort of like a thin, green grasshopper?"

"Kind of. You know what happens when they mate?"

"I don't know, the guy mantis gets on top?" Jerry asked irritably. "I'm a little busy right now. What's your point?"

"They have sex," Sofia said, "and then the female bites off the male's head and she eats it."

"You mean, the male praying mantis has sex once in his life, and then he dies doing it? That doesn't make sense."

"I read where about sixty percent get their heads eaten, whether you think it makes sense or not. But some of the guy praying mantis insects wise up before it's too late. Maybe they take advice from their buddies or learn something from what they've seen happen to their headless friends. They approach the female very, very cautiously. They maybe bring her something else to eat to keep her occupied while they mate. So, the smart ones might get away before their heads get eaten, Jerry."

"Your point is?"

"I wonder if those guys, the praying mantis guys, know that it's probably going to happen to them eventually, but they just go ahead and do it anyway. What do you think, Jerry?"

"Fuck off, Sofia," Jerry said, as Isabella walked in the door.

****

I think Ashley wants to be my friend, for real. She took a little break, doing what I have no idea, but recently, she's started back to texting me again every couple of days, asking how things are, and giving me some little update on her life. Which I really don't care about. And I don't know what to do about it except to ignore her. That would be easier to do if she didn't keep trying to be my friend.

The Miami Night Nurse

I've never had a best friend in my life besides Jerry. I mean, I wasn't ever lonely or without companionship. There were always people around, all my life. But I remember being very young, well before my parents died, and hating being in groups with other little kids, like play groups or in nursery school. Other kids bored me and confused me. Before I even had to go to The Home, I had become fairly skilled at avoiding any kids my age who tried to get too close to me. I just didn't know how to relate to them, other than by avoiding them, or by punching them if they were too persistent. I didn't like them.

I remember my mother tried to start me at a preschool when I was maybe three years old. That must have been not too long before the car crash that killed her. I didn't have these words for it at that age, but I was painfully bored at that place. Cutting and coloring and using messy white paste to put pieces of paper together seemed so pointless. I just wanted to be at home so I could be free to do whatever I wanted to do. I was glad when my mother said I didn't have to go back there anymore.

That happened after my mother was told by the nursery school teacher that I had taken the classroom turtle out of its terrarium and had deliberately stepped on it. I don't remember if I really did that or not, but I was very happy to be back at home.

Lest anyone think I have no social awareness, I do understand that Ashley is most likely lonely. Her boyfriend is away, meaning in prison, and she probably misses him, even though she said she helped to put him there. I can certainly understand having mixed feelings in her circumstances.

I guess I could try hanging out socially with Ashley sometimes. She could end up possibly being helpful to me at some point.

I don't know why I am the way I am. I just never had, and never wanted to have, a best friend besides Jerry. He's everything to me.

But I have something of more immediate concern to deal with right now, much more important than working to pry Jerry out of

Isabella's clutches or dealing with Ashley. A friend at work told me on the hush-hush that he's heard that Melissa hasn't given up on trying to destroy my career or at least get me terminated from my job. She seems to have decided that I am the one who set her up to get fired from the hospital. Not that she's wrong about that, but I need her to just let it go.

My work buddy, one of the orderlies, said that Melissa has supposedly asked a couple of her former friends who are still employed where I work to keep a close eye on me and to tell her everything that goes on. Since I have apparently taken up full-time residence in Melissa's head, my plan is to just be super-perfect in everything I say and do at work until this blows over. The perfection part should be no problem since I'm already very careful. I guess the one area that needs more vigilance would be watching even more carefully what I say to the co-workers I'm friendly with. I'm not a paranoid person; I'm simply aware that people aren't always who they seem to be.

Just the other night, though, something happened that has made me totally rethink my laissez faire approach to the Melissa-warnings I've been given.

I had driven straight home from work to the condo where I now live, parked my car in my assigned space, and headed across the parking area to the elevator. It was about 11:30 pm.

What happened next was that I saw Melissa's husband sort of hanging around near the building. He was wearing a hoodie in the ninety-degree evening air and smoking a cigarette. When I looked at him, he quickly turned his head away. I know it was him. I saw his face because he was standing under one of the security lights. Moron. I can't think of any business he could have at my building except to try to do something harmful to me or to my property.

I guess there is an outside chance that he was just hanging around waiting to do some drug deal, but my building is populated by mostly older retirees and is incredibly quiet. It's part of the reason I chose to live there. I'm not aware of any drug activity on the property at all, apart from some of the old former hippies smoking weed in the privacy of their own homes. I do sometimes catch a whiff of cannabis from my balcony.

So, what should I do? I'm completely sure that the losing team of douche-bag-husband and bitch-Melissa want to enact some kind of revenge on me. I would love to just eliminate them both entirely, but that would be *so* much work. They're already apparently tracking me and know more about me and my daily habits than I know, or care to know, about theirs. So, something needs to be done. I just don't have the energy or the motivation to take them out myself right now.

I wonder if my persistent little shadow Ashley could do something about them. Unfortunately, I don't really trust Ashley all that much. I don't understand her. I don't know what she really wants from me. It doesn't seem to be money, although I doubt that she would turn it down. It doesn't seem to be sex; I don't think she's gay or bi. Does she see me as a kindred spirit, maybe because of our boyfriend issues?

The simplest thing to do about Melissa and her goon of a husband might be to just move away to different, but nearby, location. I could sign up to get all my mail sent to a postal box from now on, and just not tell anyone at the place where I work that I've moved my actual, physical residence. I could change my address with Human Resources to the rented mail drop; then no one at the treatment center would know my street address.

I could easily find somewhere new to rent, but, at this point, I have enough money saved so that I could buy someplace nice, maybe even at the beach. Or maybe someplace on the Intracoastal Waterway that comes with a boat slip. And with building security. Maybe a gym, too.

I could even use Jerry's girlfriend Isabella as my buyer's agent. And, of course, I would use my real name, because it would be for a real purchase, pun intended.

It would no doubt give Jerry quite a jolt if Isabella ever talked about her new client, Cassandra Couri.

The next day, I called Isabella's real estate agency and asked to speak with her. I gave them my real name and cell number, and a few minutes later, Isabella called me back. I told her I'd met her at an open house several months ago, we had spoken briefly, and that I was now interested in buying a condo somewhere near my job. I neglected to mention at exactly which open house we had met, or that I had used a fake name then, or that I had cancelled an appointment at the last minute she'd set up for fake-me to see a high-rise condo with a great view. Or that I had sent an assassin to meet her there, instead.

Two assassins, if you count Ashley. Who I didn't really send. She was just sort of free-lancing.

Anyway, we arranged an appointment for the real me to look at some condos in my price range convenient to where I work. I wanted parking, security in some form, and some good light and space. I didn't care too much about the view, as long as it wasn't horrible, like staring at the wall of an ugly building.

"A city view, then," Isabella said diplomatically.

"But not in some building that has a lot of deferred maintenance and inadequate reserves," I said. "Please make sure you have access to the condominium documents and all that for any place you show me." I'm sure I sounded serious about buying, because I was.

Isabella did a good job of choosing listings for me to look at in person. I'm someone who makes up her mind easily, so I quickly found a place I liked well enough to buy and to live in for the time being. My ultimate plan, of course, was for me and Jerry to get a place together in the not-distant future. I didn't see us ever living together in either his little house that he now shared with Isabella or necessarily in this new condo I planned to purchase.

The deal went through quickly, and Isabella and her broker both came to the closing with me. I walked out of the room with the keys, the mortgage documents, and a promise from Isabella to stop by two weeks after I moved in, to see if I needed any help with anything at my new building. She was no doubt trying to make sure I had a good buying experience with her so that I might someday refer buyers or sellers to her, and she was doing a pretty good job with that.

I imagined she might go home after the closing with a bottle or two of champagne, waving her commission check. Perhaps she'd tell Jerry that the sale she'd made was to a registered nurse named Cassandra Couri. I expected Jerry to call me a short while later if she mentioned my name.

I could either tell him the truth—that I knew who Isabella was all along—or I could be surprised at the coincidence and tell him that I'd met Isabella at an open house months ago when I was out looking at properties and I did not even know she was his girlfriend.

If she didn't tell Jerry my name, that would be okay, too. I could just drop her name if I ever wanted him to know for some reason that Isabella had been my buyer's agent. And that she'd done a good job. And that she'd survived the experience unscathed. So far.

CHAPTER 15

Jerry sat outside with Julio, drinking a beer. The sunlight was fading. Spears of orange light were breaking through the mounds of purple rain clouds to the west. Mosquito activity began to pick up as the sun sank lower. Jerry slapped at a sudden buzzing near his left ear.

"Let's go in," he said. "I hate these little blood-suckers. I have something I need to run by you."

"Sure," said Julio. "Would it be okay to talk if Alejandro is out in the garage working? He's supposed to come by here pretty quick so I can get him started doing an oil change on his truck."

Jerry shrugged. "I wouldn't want him to overhear us..."

"That's ok. I'll get him set up and then just check on him a couple of times."

They settled down in Julio's front office. Julio lit a cigar and twisted open a beer.

"You want?" he asked, gesturing in Jerry's direction with the bottle. Jerry nodded, and Julio slid him the beer and opened another for himself.

"So, *que pasa*? You have something going on?"

"Cassie has been seeing Isabella."

"Seeing her?"

"Stalking her, I think."

"Your girlfriend on the side is stalking Isabella? What happened?"

"Isabella came home the other day, all excited because she sold a condo to someone. I looked at the paperwork she left out on the kitchen table, the sales contract. She was so happy about the amount of the commission. The buyer was Cassie."

"Are you sure?"

Jerry nodded. "Cassie hired Isabella as her buyer's agent. When I asked, Isabella said she'd originally met Cassie at an open house quite a while back, she wasn't sure how long ago. A few weeks or months or maybe even much longer than that."

"Did either one of them ever say anything to you about having met the other before this?"

Jerry shook his head.

"What do you think happened? Is it by chance, maybe?"

Jerry shook his head again. "I'm sure Cassie knows who Isabella is, but Isabella doesn't have any idea who she's dealing with."

"You think Cassie did this on purpose?"

Jerry nodded. "She's been talking about buying a place, so that's legit. And she knows Isabella is in real estate. But the contract said Isabella was the buyer's agent. That means Cassie, who is the buyer in this deal, deliberately hired Isabella out of all the hundreds or thousands of agents in Miami-Dade to help her find a property to purchase."

"Why would she do that?"

"I think she's fucking with my head."

"Again: Why would she do that?"

"I don't know. Maybe to try to speed along our break-up."

"Your break-up with Isabella or your break-up with Cassie?"

"I think Cassie is trying to push me in to breaking up with Isabella. Not that she's ever asked me to. But I know she wants us to be together."

"What do you want?"

"I'm not sure. I hate the thought of hurting Isabella. That's probably why I'm still with her. She's been nothing but good to me. She's a really kind, caring person. Cassie… I don't know what she is, but I do know she's the most amazing lover I've ever had. But she might be too much for me."

"You need to give this whole matter some very careful thought, little Jerry. And then you need to take some strong actions. Something is very wrong about your situation with Cassie. You need to find out what it is and deal with it. It seems like you have been just drifting along with the currents, like it's a sunny day at the beach. But, soon, you could be too far out in the ocean to make it back to the shore. And there you'll be, all alone. Except for the big sharks."

Jerry opened another beer. It was dark now, and the night bugs, as Julio referred to them, had started up their chorus. He could hear them through the window in Julio's office as clearly as if they were sitting outside. Cicadas, katydids, and crickets, sounding like the buzz of a live electrical wire, grew louder and louder. Then, abruptly, the cicadas dropped out of the ensemble, and the insect-serenade quieted to a rhythmic background hum.

"Let's go through this, step-by-step, ok?" said Julio.

Jerry didn't say anything, so Julio continued.

"You grew up around here, you go to work for me, you decide to join the police force, you buy yourself a house, you're a cop. You're a young guy, so you go out with some women, and then you meet Isabella, a nice girl with some ambition and some common sense. So you settle in with her. Things are going good to this point, am I right?"

Jerry nodded.

"Then, almost out of nowhere, a girl calls you, someone you knew when you were a child, someone you haven't heard from in what, twenty years? And you just go and jump right in to the deep end of the swimming pool."

"You don't understand what we went through when we were little kids, Julio. Our parents had died, mine very suddenly. We were orphans; all of us at that place were just clinging to whatever life rafts we could find. Cassie and I became best friends. I don't know how I would have coped with my grief and my confusion if it weren't for her. But I was one of the fortunate kids, because my aunt and uncle took me out of there and brought me down here to Miami. Cassie got kicked around from one unstable place to another for years."

"You wanted to save her, but you had to leave her. Then, when you meet her again, she's all grown up, and you fell in love with her."

Jerry was quiet. "I don't know if I'm in love with her."

"No? Then, why are you still with her? There's no reason to protect her any more, she's not a little girl. She's a grown woman with a good job, right? She has other friends besides you. She can manage her own life now, very well apparently. She doesn't need you to save her any more. Right?"

"So maybe I am in love with her, I don't know. Whatever it is, there is something so strong there that I just can't give it up. I'm trying, I really am. I don't call her that much, certainly not every day. I don't see her very much. But every single morning, Julio, I wake up thinking about her, and she is always the last thing I think about before I fall asleep."

Julio was silent.

"I'm going to have to tell Isabella. I just can't keep going on like this."

"So," Julio said. "You are choosing this girl Cassie over Isabella, jumping from a solid relationship with a good woman to something you don't know how it will even go."

"Isabella *is* a good woman. So she deserves more than what I've been giving her."

"Are you going to tell Isabella the real reason you are breaking it off with her? That there's someone else you want to be with?"

"I don't know how the conversation will go. I just know I'm dreading it."

"Well, be a man, if you can. Tell her only true things. Don't make her doubt her sanity with more lies and halfway true things."

"I don't want to hurt her."

"You don't want to be the bad guy. But you are, in this situation. So own it, *peque*."

****

Carlos woke from a restless sleep. Someone was knocking hard on the door of his apartment. He looked at his watch. 1:30 am. Maybe it was a drunk neighbor or a drunk friend of a neighbor, hammering on the wrong door. Then he heard the lock click and the deadbolt snap into the doorframe. He sat up and pulled his weapon from the nightstand drawer.

"Carlos?"

Isabella's voice. He slid the handgun back into the drawer and went out to greet her, tying his silk robe as he left the bedroom.

She was standing in the dark, holding something. He turned on the light and saw that it was a small overnight bag.

"I hope it's okay that I came here," she said. "I've left Jerry."

****

Three weeks later, Jerry and Julio were sitting inside Julio's auto repair shop on a Sunday, watching the Dolphins game on the small TV and drinking their way through a case of beer. Julio was trying to hold back his *I told you so* comments to the best of his ability.

"Is at least your other girlfriend, that Cassie, happy now that Isabella has left you?" Julio asked.

"I don't know. I haven't even said anything about it to her. I haven't talked with her. She hasn't tried to contact me."

"Are you doing okay at work?"

"I do better at work than I do at home, Julio, because I'm able to keep busy. I volunteer for extra hours whenever there's a need. I'm thinking about changing my schedule to a dogwatch shift so I don't have to feel so alone at night."

Jerry's phone pinged, and his heart rate spiked. A message from Isabella. He opened it.

I wanted to let you know that Carlos and I were married on Saturday at Saint Mary's. I invited Sofia to the wedding and to the little reception we had at a restaurant, so don't be mad at her when you see her. I wish you all the best in your future.

****

Well. Too bad nobody thought to tell *me* about any damn wedding.

As a result, I went to a great deal of completely unnecessary trouble making all the arrangements, setting up my alibi, and making sure I had witnesses who could attest to my whereabouts during the time period when Isabella was killed. I'm exaggerating; it was easy enough, since I worked a double shift that day and tons of people saw me at the treatment center over a period of sixteen hours. There is no way I would be a serious suspect in Isabella's death.

I tried to make sure Isabella would die quickly and painlessly, which was better than she deserved, at least in my opinion. But, I had to arrange the hit rather quickly; not sloppily, you understand… just fast.

It apparently happened just as she was getting out of her car on the way to a nail appointment at a storefront salon run by some tight-lipped Vietnamese women. I had no idea why someone would want to drive all the way up to Miramar just to get her nails done, but that's the way it went down.

I didn't ask Ashley for any of the particulars; nor did I care to know them. Why exactly Ashley had thought it was a good idea to stalk Isabella up in Broward County in broad daylight was beyond me. I have always found her motives to be somewhat opaque.

I guess, though, I will never be able to find out any more details about the hit Ashley did on Isabella even if I wanted to. Ashley was dead less than an hour after I met up with her that same evening.

We rendezvoused down near the beach when I got off work at midnight. I brought the rest of the agreed-upon cash in large bills and she stuffed the roll in her pocket, but, of course, she didn't get to keep it. I thanked her, I left, and then I immediately sped all the way out to her place.

Ashley pulled in to her parking space about forty-five minutes after I arrived at her shabby little apartment complex out near the edge of the Everglades. The dismal parking area was pitch black. She got out of her car carrying a bag from a Cuban take-out joint and a six-pack of premium beer. I left her body and her purchases next to her vehicle, but I took back what was left of my cash.

I'm surprised she ever thought I would let her keep it.

The story about Isabella, when it came out, was splashed all over the Miami and Ft. Lauderdale papers and was featured on the television news stations: *Newlywed bride murdered in daytime blood-bath in Miramar*. Poor Ashley, found face down in the parking lot of a run-down apartment complex, barely got two paragraphs.

I imagine all the people who were close and even not so close to Isabella, like Jerry, her grieving widower Carlos, her friends at the real estate company, Isabella's family, her former and current clients, *et cetera*, were all under some suspicion. I know I certainly was. I was interviewed by the cops both at home and at work, and so were some of my work colleagues. But I had prepared my alibi very carefully, because I knew that Jerry would bring my name up as a possibility, no matter how unlikely he thought it was that I had killed Isabella.

I sent Jerry a nice text and left a voice mail after the story became public, letting him know how very sorry I was to hear the news. I just said I wanted to be there for him whenever he was ready to talk with me, but that I wanted to give him his privacy at this difficult time. I worded it like I thought a respectful friend would, not like a gleeful woman who sees the finish line just ahead.

I didn't say anything at all to Jerry about me and my work colleagues' short interviews with the cops, even though I believed the reason they showed up at my door was due to Jerry giving them my name. Jerry may have played down any suspicions he had about me, though, because the cops' questions were rather *pro forma*. The fact that I was at work when Isabella died, with multiple witnesses to my whereabouts, put me way down the list of potential suspects.

Carlos had quickly gone from being a single man about town to besotted newly-wed to grieving widower to possible murder suspect. He told the police investigators about the suspicious thug, my old buddy Danny, who'd threatened Isabella at the real estate showing where Carlos had first met her. He also told them that Isabella felt she was being lightly threatened at some additional real estate open houses. He gave a pretty good second-hand description of my now-deceased friend Ashley, telling the investigator about one specific incident when someone who fit Ashley's description showed up at a real estate open house on a Sunday afternoon all the way out near the edge of the Everglades.

Carlos himself was never a serious suspect, though, mainly because of lack of motive and an air-tight alibi.

However, Carlos or somebody close to him did leak to the press that his dead bride had been made to feel uncomfortable at several real estate open houses over a period of a few months. The press jumped on that information like a duck on a June bug. As far as I know, it was only twice she was stalked, whoops, three times if you include my own open house visit with her very early on, but that one little leak put a serious chill on the number of real estate showings scheduled in South Florida for a couple of weekends. And, of course, the number of new sales contracts for homes was briefly impacted.

After nearly a month of extremely circumspect behavior, I finally texted Jerry again to offer him my sympathy and to let him know I would like to see him whenever he felt up to it. I was kind of surprised when he called me back right away.

"Sure, I'd like to get together with you sometime, Cassie." He didn't sound excited or happy, though. He sounded defeated.

"I'm so sorry for what you're going through," I said. "I want you to know that I'm available whenever you might want to talk. But I don't want you to think I'm putting any pressure on you. Just do what you need to do, and if I can help, you can certainly count on me."

I'd read up on death and stages of grief, and had taken a semester-long course in nursing school on death and dying. Patients and families of patients sometimes welcome someone to talk with about their loss, someone who isn't even a good friend or a family member of the person who died, since those people closest to the deceased are often immersed in their own grief.

I can't say I've ever felt anything like that, myself, when people close to me died, but I'll take the experts' word for it.

Jerry finally asked if he could come over to my new apartment.

He stood at the balcony slider looking out over the city. Then, he walked around the place, looking at the rooms.

"Why did you hire Isabella to help you find this condo?" he asked, with almost no small talk first.

"I knew she worked in real estate sales," I said, totally cool, "and I didn't know anyone else in real estate in the Miami area, so I called the agency and asked for her specifically."

"Why her?"

"I thought I might as well have you and her get the sales commission instead of someone I didn't even know."

"Did you spend much time with her?"

I shook my head. "I provided a list of specific things I wanted in an apartment, and what my price range was. This was actually one of the first places I looked at."

"Did you ever see her after that?"

I nodded. "Both Isabella and the broker came to the closing. That was the last time I ever saw her."

"When was that?"

I told him the date I had closed on my new place.

"You're sure you never saw her after that?"

I shook my head. "I don't think so."

"Is there anything at all you can think of that would shed some light on why she would break up with me? Or who killed her?"

I shook my head. "Maybe she broke up with you because she wanted to get married, and didn't think you were ever going to ask her?"

"Did she say that?"

"No, Jerry," I said. "We never discussed anything personal at all. I'm just guessing."

He looked so sad. I wanted to help him get through his grief, so I told him I would just really like to be his friend.

"I blame myself for everything," he said.

I walked over to him and wrapped my arms around him. At first his body was stiff and rejecting but then he relaxed into my embrace and began to sob.

I wondered how long he was going to cry over her. I mean, she had already dumped him and married another guy. I guess I hadn't really taken Jerry's feelings fully in to consideration when I had arranged to get Isabella out of the picture once and for all.

I led Jerry over to the couch, and served him a plate piled with green grapes, tangy slices of cheese, small, round slices of dark bread, and a glass of a nice French white wine. I sat quietly with him, my arm resting along the back of the couch behind his shoulders. Once he began to eat, it was like he couldn't stop. I poured him and myself another glass of wine.

I was about to get up to open another bottle of chilled wine when he pulled me in to his arms. I hugged him back, fiercely.

"Promise you'll never leave me, Cassie," he said, burying his face in my hair, and then our clothes were coming off and we were in bed, and he was inside me and we were coming and he was crying and then we lay on our backs looking up at the ceiling, holding hands.

"I'll never leave you, Jerry," I said. "I've never loved anyone but you."

He squeezed my hand. "Could you ever think about us getting married? Someday soon?" he asked.

I inhaled sharply. I had never imagined it would happen so quickly after Isabella was gone. I expected to have to go through a long, depressing period while he mourned and then a painfully slow courtship until he was ready for me. Like I said, I had even read up on how to help a person with their grief so I would know how to act.

"I would like that, Jerry," I said softly, my heart singing with a joy I had never known, the joy of my wildest hopes coming true.

I imagined a small beach wedding, early in the morning before the wind picked up from the east. The sun would be coming up through the clouds as the dawn brightened into full daylight. I would be wearing an ivory silk gown and I would carry a bouquet of yellow and white rosebuds. I hoped Jerry wouldn't want to invite too many people, since I have no family left, or really, any friends. I guess some people from my job would want to come.

CHAPTER 16

"You're shitting me!" Sofia shouted. "You are fucking shitting me!"

The guys in the station barely looked up. The sun rose this morning. Sofia was pissed off about something.

Jerry took her by the arm and led her outside. "Can you please calm down and just listen to me?"

"Fine," Sofia said, crossing her arms. "Speak."

"I made mistakes with Isabella. I knew she wanted to get married and start a family, but I didn't feel any rush to commit to a marriage. I did love her."

"So, now, just like a roller coaster or a freight train with no brakes, you're going to head in the exact opposite direction. Move crazy fast with that Cassie, not do any thinking at all. You can't fix what you did wrong with Isabella by going to the opposite extreme."

"I've known Cassie for…"

"I know, I know, since you were little kids. But you didn't really know her whatsoever as a grown woman until just a few months ago. So, you are moving very fast. But I understand. You feel like you can neutralize your grief and maybe somehow fix your regrets by taking the other path."

Jerry didn't say anything.

"But, you can't just stuff down those feelings of pain or they'll always be there. They'll keep influencing your life choices. You have to feel them, get through them, and learn what they have to teach you. *Then*, you'll be ready to move on."

Jerry sighed. "It's different with Cassie. We were children together. We are the only ones left in the world who can understand what we went though."

"Ok, fine," said Sofia. "All that will still be true if you just wait a few months. Say, maybe give it six months before you let her bite off your head."

"She wants me to move in to her new apartment, the one Isabella found for her."

"What do you want to do?"

"It's a beautiful place. A fresh start would be good, I think."

"What would you do with your house?"

"Rent it out or sell it. Maybe sell it, for a total fresh start."

"I suggest renting it out, if you do anything. You've had it for a very long time. It's part of your past, not just yours with Isabella. You'll know better what to do about it after a year or so."

"The memories I have would always be too painful. There are reminders of Isabella in every room..."

Sofia sighed. "So, change the paint color. Remodel the kitchen. Get new furniture, or something. You're doing too many drastic new things at once so you can try to bury your feelings about Isabella. Slow way the fuck down, *asere*."

Later that day, Jerry got a call from Carlos.

"I know who you are," Jerry said, when Carlos began to explain why he was calling and who he was. Jerry felt like saying *you're the guy who stole my girlfriend* but he knew that would make him sound childish and would also be untrue.

"The reason I am calling you is both because you are a police officer as well as my late wife's *ex-novio*."

Jerry froze for a second at hearing himself referred to as Isabella's ex-boyfriend and Isabella as Carlos' wife. "Go on," he said.

"Did Isabella ever talk to you, Jerry, if I may call you Jerry, about the incidents of stalking, maybe we could even call them very close calls, *por los pelos*, she had at some of her real estate showings?" Carlos asked.

"What do you know?" Jerry asked. "She might not have told me everything."

"She might have told *me* everything," Carlos said, "in order to keep *you* from worrying. That's how we first met, at a condominium showing she was having. I lived right across the hall at the time."

"Go on."

"She asked me to come in to the unit, to be company for her. I thought at first it was because she wanted me to pretend to be competition, to pose as another buyer. So I went, to help her out. She was alone, and a big guy had showed up she wasn't expecting. She felt threatened. I sent him on his way. From there, we became friends."

"How good of friends? She never said anything to me about you."

"I courted her. I admit it, I stole her."

"Get to your fucking point, if you have one. If not, just stay the fuck away from me."

"Another time, she called me to help her after some crazy woman was making her worry at an open house, at a place way out to the west."

"She never told me these things."

"She said she didn't want to cause you any concern, because then maybe you would give her a hard time, try to get her to stop with some of these open houses."

"Or, maybe I would have sent someone to be with her, if I couldn't do it myself on some particular occasion. *If* I had known there was trouble. What is your point here, Carlos, aside from telling me what an asshole I was to her and what a great guy you were?"

"My point is that we both lost the same woman. You are a police officer, no? Maybe you could use the resources you have at your disposal to get her some justice. As for me, I'm going to talk to some people I know who may be able to find some different answers. *Yo hago lo que haga falta.*"

Jerry stared at the wall. He felt the not-subtle rebuke, less in what Carlos had said than in the controlled anger of his tone, and in Carlos' confident determination that he would be able to avenge Isabella's death. Isabella had chosen this powerful, successful man, and had left Jerry behind.

That evening, Jerry came to a skidding stop on the dusty alleyway behind the tire shop and carried in a cold twelve-pack of Julio's favorite beer.

"I heard what happened," said Julio.

"What did you hear?" asked Jerry.

"That your ex, Isabella, was killed up in Miramar and that they don't know who did it."

Jerry sat down. "No, they don't know. The Broward cops are on it. They're asking around for witnesses, but no one has come forward. It wasn't Carlos. And I talked with him. He seems pretty determined to dig up some more information, to find out who killed her."

"Could it possibly be your…?"

"Cassie? No. She was at work. She was interviewed."

"How did they get her name?"

"I gave it to them."

"Does she know that? Cassie?"

"I would assume."

"What are you going to do about Cassie, *chiquito*?"

"I think someday soon, after things are settled, I'm going to ask her to marry me."

"Ok. Then, what? Live happily ever after, like in a fairy tale? Have babies, maybe make some little Jerrys?"

"I don't know, Julio. I'm just trying to keep myself from going crazy at this point."

"*Tal vez tengo algunas sugerencias.*"

"Like what?"

"Give me some more time. I will get back to you. Or maybe to Sofia."

****

Jerry sat at a table in back of a neighborhood bar none of the cops from the station ever went to. He watched a couple of men watching Sofia as she sashayed her way back to their table for four. She set down two fresh mugs of beer next to their plates of hamburgers, medium rare, with fries.

"I like my burger cooked a little more," Jerry said, as he lifted the bun to inspect.

"It'll be fine," Sofia said, pushing the bottle of ketchup across the table to him. She picked up some fries with her fingers and stuffed them in her mouth.

Jerry lifted his frosty mug and took a long swallow. "At least the beer is cold here."

"What's on your mind?" Sofia asked. "I don't think it's anything good or you wouldn't be buying me dinner."

"I plan to ask Cassie to marry me." Jerry was expecting Sofia to spit out her half-chewed fries and launch in to a rant.

Instead, she said, "Ah. I see you've decided to go headless, after all, Senor Praying Mantis."

"C'mon, Sofia. I think it could be the right thing for me to do. You and I have talked about it, so I know how you feel. I'd thought about marriage quite a bit on and off, but I never came close to proposing to anyone I dated. Then, when Isabella left me for that guy Carlos, it really shook me up. I don't want to lose Cassie, too."

"Has she put any pressure on you? Hinted that she wants to marry you?"

"No, not at all. She bought her own condo, a nice one, not very long ago. Isabella was her buyer's agent."

"Really? She knew Isabella that well?"

"No, I don't think so, not really. They'd met at an open house once quite a while back, I guess. Cassie had kept her card and called her, because she wanted the commission to go to us, to Isabella and me."

"How nice of her. And now you want to marry her because she threw a few bucks your way?"

"You've made it very clear that you think there could be something ...not right about Cassie. But she really does manage her life very well. You know: her career, her money, her investments. She takes good care of her health, she doesn't do drugs that I know of, and I don't think she drinks too much."

"All that might be a good enough resume for a friend, or a roommate, or a business partner. But why marry her?"

"I love her and I want to protect her."

"How would marrying her protect her?"

"I'd be able to keep a close eye on her, help her, make sure she's always doing well, that she's solving any of her problems in the best way..."

"But...you just listed all the ways she's doing so great. Sounds like what you're saying is that if you married her, it would let you protect other people *from her*. What exactly do you think it is that all the rest of us might need protection from?"

Jerry was silent for a moment. "I didn't mean it that way."

"Do you remember that I had a background check run on her back when she first showed up in your life? And that I originally met her while I was on the job up near where she was working, and she told me how you guys first knew each other way back in elementary school, and I told her you were with Isabella?"

"Yes, I remember that you met Cassie, and then you gave me kind of a hard time about her. I know how much you liked Isabella. I think everybody liked Isabella. I honestly can't believe that she's gone."

"I do get that you're still grieving. Some of the rest of us are, too. So, just wait for a while. Don't jump in to something with Cassie that you would have a difficult time extricating yourself from. Could you maybe just shack up with her, but don't make it legal?"

"Lately, I've been reading up on all the advantages there are to marriage…"

"Yeah," Sophie said. "There definitely are some. Like spousal privilege. You won't have to testify against her, if it comes down to that. I bet she'd consider that a big advantage."

CHAPTER 17

Things aren't as good as I thought they would be.

It seems like years and years since I first moved down to Florida, looked up Jerry almost on a whim, fell in love with him, and then set about to do absolutely everything I had to do in order to make him all mine. And now he *is* mine. We aren't married yet, but, strangely, I find myself less gung-ho about tying the knot than Jerry is.

Although I'm not ruling it out. Marriage does have its advantages. And Jerry bought me the nicest, biggest diamond engagement ring I could have ever imagined, after he very sweetly and subtly teased out my preferences. He said he got a great deal, which I believe, because he probably knows all the best pawn shops in Dade County from his job as a cop. I am not knocking how he went about buying it, if that's what he did. Diamonds are ridiculously overpriced and marked up, and I am all for saving money any way you can.

One fairly trivial issue between Jerry and me, though, which I don't really think I've ever mentioned, is that I am quite a meticulous housekeeper. I don't mean that I'm always doing housework, or that I even like doing it. I just mean that I like for things to be orderly and carefully arranged. I don't like dirty clothes to pile up...I have a nice stackable washer-dryer in my new condo and I do some laundry almost every day. I don't leave any dishes in the sink; they get rinsed and go right into the dishwasher. My drawers and closets are pretty well organized. And no clutter. I hate messy drawers.

But, nothing obsessive, I don't think, not really...although I do like the blinds arranged just so, to maximize my nice view and to also keep any creepy neighbors with a telescope or binoculars from seeing in at night. I know they could watch me if they wanted to, because I can see in their windows.

Jerry is just a typical guy. He takes off his clothes when he gets home from work and drops them wherever. He leaves dishes in the sink, even when the dishwasher is empty. He can never find his keys. But, again, it's nothing serious. He's nowhere near as bad as my first husband. It just grates on my nerves a little.

The bigger issue is that we don't spend as much of our waking time having sex as I thought we would once we were able to start sleeping together most nights. Meaning, once Isabella was out of the picture. I work mostly evening shifts now, although I do have some choice in the matter. But, if I get home close to midnight, and I want to drink and talk and have sex to unwind, Jerry is sometimes already asleep or just too tired to stay up with me.

I understand things between Jerry and me are fine and typical and that there aren't any real problems. However, I may have underestimated just how much of a role "the hunt" has had in helping me keep my life organized and interesting and focused. Now that Jerry is actually mine and I've achieved all the goals attached to getting him, I find myself becoming a little bored. And kind of moody.

Whenever I do get bored, it's a very uncomfortable feeling for me. It feels like a blankness is closing in, much the way a slow, stealthy New England fog floats in to the shoreline from the sea. As it gets "foggier," I start to feel like I might not really exist.

Once that fog begins, and I always know when it's starting because it feels a little bit like I'm gradually starting to disappear, I usually act to quickly correct the situation by injecting some new, enticing stimulation into my daily routine.

I hate to say it, but I've killed people mainly out of boredom. Not that it's happened very often, but I do recall some guy a long time ago somewhere up in Boston on, perhaps not coincidentally, a foggy night…

Lately, though, I've been fantasizing about how my level of excitement could be juiced up if Jerry and I would start to try some new things in bed. Something I'm sure I would love is having two guys at the same time, both of them taking turns with me while the other one watches, waiting impatiently for his shot. Maybe the one would push the other guy off before he was finished, and then the new guy would bury himself in me. The guy who got pushed off would maybe start kissing me and sucking on my nipples or trying to get his dick in my… well, you can use your imagination.

The main roadblock to that deliciously erotic—at least for me—scenario is Jerry. He wouldn't want to be one of the guys. I know he wouldn't go for it at all, ever, because I once dropped a little hint and his look of shock told me everything I needed to know.

Aside from Jerry's lack of interest, the other problem pertaining to sex with strange guys, is that sometimes, if a guy I've picked up says or does the wrong thing, I just feel like killing him, not screwing him. Maybe I picked him up hoping he *would* say or do the wrong thing. Or, maybe on that night, anything he could do would be wrong.

Still, I fantasize more than Jerry needs to know about getting with two guys at the same time. Finding candidates for my erotic scenario really wouldn't be too difficult around here, I bet. After all, this is Miami. There are bars known for that kind of thing. But I would never want Jerry to find out.

This is what I think could work for me: first, locate the right bars and check them out, both according to their reputation around town

The Miami Night Nurse

and by dropping in briefly some nights after I work an evening shift, some nights when the city seems hopping. Next, I would call and tell Jerry one evening that I needed to work a double shift, or half a double, and then go out to the bar I've found and do what I want to do. Definitely wear one of my cute wigs for a little disguise. Come home. Take a shower like always. And then wake Jerry up for some... dessert. That finish would be the part of the adventure I would be most turned on by.

You might think what I've just described is highly erotic; or simply sick; or not what the Bible says. Whatever. I'm not saying *you* should do it. But, if you think it's not anywhere in the Bible, you haven't been reading the right parts.

Anyway, things do seem like they are falling apart a little bit. I came in to work one day, thinking about how after my shift that night would be a great evening to go out prowling the city for some excitement. I even told Jerry I might work late. I was in a really good mood. Then, right off the bat, during report at shift change, we were told that Melissa is coming back to work on the unit. She got rehired after she threw a stink-fit with HR. She had an attorney and everything. The hospital decided, rather than risk an unlawful termination suit, they would give her back her job.

I feel like since I learned that my Melissa-plan failed and that she's come back to haunt me, it's like I'm unraveling a little bit on the inside.

For example, I apparently forgot to order some meds from the hospital pharmacy that this one bitchy doctor wanted *stat*. Instead of calmly explaining to him that it was his fuck-up, because I definitely would have put in the order as soon as he either wrote it or called it in to me, I realized that I just wasn't all that sure about the details. Because I'd been overly-focused on Melissa. Just that one little bit hesitation on my part seemed to give the doctor the impression that he could start unloading on me. Now, ever since, it seems like he's doubtful about my accuracy. He keeps double-checking all the orders he puts in, which pisses me off. I'm not used to being questioned professionally.

Melissa, as soon as she did come back to work, seemed to pull out all her stops, and is now openly hostile toward me. She still jokes and interacts like she used to with the rest of the staff. I'm ashamed to admit that I have even started to try to be nicer to her to maybe get her to let up on me. But me being nice hasn't slowed her down any. I know she feels empowered now and she's looking to really push my buttons. It's like she's started an actual campaign to try to ruffle my feathers. If she doesn't back the fuck off, she's going to regret it.

Another thing I've noticed is that Jerry is acting kind of weird around me. I say things, maybe just give a description of how my day went, and he looks at me with just a hint of skepticism.

For example, one day after I worked a day shift, I got held up in traffic and was an hour later than he expected me home. I told him about the construction backup and it was like he doubted it. I think he even looked it up on his phone, to see if there really was road work going on in the area where I said. He's a fucking cop. He knows what's going on around the county. He ought to realize that *I* know that, too, so I wouldn't lie about something he could easily check. And why would he want to doubt me about something so trivial in the first place? I hope it's just my imagination.

****

Carlos came back to the table from the bar with drinks for Jerry and Sofia. They were sitting in a quiet, slightly run-down joint on a side street located a few blocks from Sofia's house.

"I want to say I'm very sorry for your loss, Carlos," Sofia said, shooting Jerry a quick look.

Carlos lowered his chin. "The pain I feel from the loss of my wife has been great, but I'm sure Isabella's death has been no less a loss to

Jerry, as well as to her family and to her friends. She was a wonderful woman. I am mourning her deeply."

Sofia sighed. "Let me just cut to the chase," she said to Jerry. "Carlos has approached me more than once since Isabella's died…"

"If I may," Carlos interrupted gently, "I have also approached the investigator assigned from the precinct where she was killed."

"Okay," Jerry said. "And?"

"Not much from him. But what I wanted to say to you both is that I do have some information about a woman who had frightened Isabella at an open house she was hosting east of here. Isabella had called me to come assist her with a situation…"

"I never saw a police report about any incident out there," Jerry said. "I wasn't aware of it at the time. She never told me."

"There was no police report," Carlos said. "I was able to simply look at the sign-in sheet that Isabella kept for that day, the record she maintained for the broker who employed her as well as for the associate whose listing it actually was," Carlos continued. "The agency keeps those on file to develop their mailing lists."

Jerry nodded. "And?"

"It wasn't a busy day for her. Isabella filled in one of the lines herself, writing that a woman came to the house who said her name was 'Ashley' but the woman wouldn't provide her last name or sign Isabella's sheet. Isabella also made a note on that sheet in pencil, describing the vehicle; she was unable to get the license plate number. She noted that the woman was slender and dark-haired, and described the outfit she was wearing."

"Why did she write that information down?" Jerry asked. "Was there a problem?"

Carlos hesitated, and decided not to say anything about Isabella subsequently coming to his place, so as not to embarrass Jerry in front of Sofia.

"It was my impression that this Ashley may have been sent to do a hit on Isabella, but she decided not to for unknown reasons. I later read in the papers about a woman who was left dead in an apartment complex parking lot, along with her groceries, late one night. You might of heard about it?"

Jerry nodded.

"This was also the very same day that Isabella was killed up in Miramar. I almost missed seeing the news about the apartment killing, because it was so small. Isabella's murder was a much bigger story. However, what is big about this is that dead woman in the parking lot was the same Ashley, according to my sources."

"You're saying that a woman who once made Isabella feel uncomfortable at an open house was the same person who was murdered in that apartment complex on or about the same day that Isabella was killed? That Ashley?" Sofia asked.

Carlos nodded.

"To be clear," said Jerry, "you are speculating that the murders of Isabella and this Ashley are related, rather than just that they happened within a close time frame."

"Possibly so," said Carlos. "It would be strangely coincidental if they were not, no?"

After Carlos had left them, Sofia asked Jerry if he would like for her to help him, off the record for now, access information about the Ashley investigation.

"I could find out the estimated time of death and any other details in the report that was filed. I could also look up to see if this Ashley has, well *had*, a criminal record."

"Well, what I would most like to know is the estimated time of death," Jerry said.

I'd also really like to know if Cassie was at work when it happened, he thought, but he didn't say that part out loud.

"We can find that out," said Sofia. "I'll get on it. I know Lorenzo Perez up there."

Two hours later, Sofia called Jerry. "Approximately 0100."

Jerry sighed. "Thanks, Sofia."

"What's the problem?"

"No problem," Jerry lied.

"I heard you sigh."

"Just tired, I guess."

After he ended the call with Sofia, Jerry went out on road patrol. He wrote two tickets for improper lane change and issued a warning to new teen driver he pulled over for failure to signal a turn.

He also clocked the distance from Cassie's place of employment to Ashley's apartment and from Ashley's apartment to Cassie's condo. He estimated the amount of time those trips would take at night around the time Cassie normally got off work, after most traffic had cleared.

The problem was he didn't know what time Cassie had actually left work that night. Her shifts were a little variable and sometimes they ran over by as much as an hour or two. She might have been at work later, or she might have left right at normal shift change. There was no way he could find that out except by asking her or by somehow accessing the employee clock-in records at the hospital. The latter were impossible to obtain without an insider providing them. Or a court order. And, in any case, he didn't know what time Cassie had arrived home, because he'd still been spending nights mostly at his own house, reeling from the immediate news of Isabella's murder.

The only date-time information he had for that day was a *hi, honey, work's going* OK *hope you had a good day I miss you*-text Cassie had sent him that evening at 8:41pm. She probably wasn't aware yet that Isabella had been killed when she sent that, Jerry thought. He felt a weight dissolve within his stomach, and then he realized that he had just decided that Cassie had had no part in either of the murders.

****

"I don't know," Sofia said to the Broward County investigator, who she had convinced to take another look at Isabella's murder. "It's weird. There's something off about this whole scene. That immediate area where she was killed just isn't that high in violent crime lately. There hasn't been a daylight shooting up there in I don't know how long."

"Twenty months. Last one was twenty months ago. Domestic violence. Man killed his eighty-eight year old mother after she refused to give him her social security check to cash."

"Jeez, these fucking crack-heads," Sofia said.

Cassie *could* have just driven up there, Sofia thought, broken the streak of daylight murder statistics, and then, after killing Isabella, gone on to work at the hospital. When her shift was over, she could have driven out and done the other murder. Then she simply could have gone home to her nice apartment in the sky. Maybe she had poured herself a glass or two of champagne and sat looking out at the city lights below her.

"Why would you even think like that?" Jerry asked when Sofia ran the scenario by Jerry. "There's no possible motive. Even if her goal were to remove Isabella from my life, Isabella was *already* out of the picture. She was *already* with Carlos. They were *already* married. And I was already with Cassie. And, how would she have even known the woman who was killed outside at that apartment complex?"

"When did you find out that Isabella and Carlos had gotten married?'

"Isabella texted me shortly after the fact."

"When did Cassie know?"

Jerry shrugged. "I'm not sure when, exactly. I told her at some point, but not right when I first found out."

"What did she say about it?"

"I don't remember. Actually, Cassie might not have even known about it until after Isabella was killed. I do know Cassie was quite upset, very upset, when she heard about it."

"Upset about which part?"

"That Isabella was dead, I would assume."

Maybe, maybe not, thought Sofia.

Two days later, after Sofia had finished some additional research, she called Jerry and asked if she could come over to his house and would it be okay if she brought her dog, Ollie. They sat outside on the patio drinking beer while Ollie sniffed around the yard.

"I'll clean up his poop, don't worry," said Sofia, waving a little plastic bag.

"If you can find it," Jerry said. "I need to cut the lawn and really spruce up this yard. I've been thinking about selling the place."

"Don't tell me that," Sofia said, opening another beer. "Just rent your house out if you really want to move in with her. I mean, seriously."

"I spend quite a bit of time over there."

"Yeah, well, so what? *Don't sell your house*. I don't think you should."

"What, exactly, do you have against Cassie?"

Sofia took a deep breath. "I think she's very possibly a psychopath and that you are walking willingly but blindly into a trap, a nightmare, *una trampa*."

Jerry sat shaking his head. "Where do you even get this stuff from, Sofia?"

"I've been doing some research. Do you want to hear?"

Jerry sighed. "Go ahead. I know you won't shut up about it until you say what you came over to say."

"What do you think of when you hear the word *psychopath? Sociopath?*"

"I don't know. Someone who's crazy. Someone out of control, someone who doesn't have a conscience. Ted Bundy. Hannibal Lector."

"Kind of, but psychopaths aren't necessarily out of control. Some of them are very smart and very careful, at least until something inside them starts to unravel. Enough stress will tend to do that to them. So, what do you remember about the Ted Bundy case?"

"He was on death row here in Florida for over a decade before he was finally executed. I don't think I was even born when he was arrested. But, of course, I'd heard about it. I was told he killed women, college girls. After he was already in prison, on death row, I had moved down here and was starting to think about becoming a cop. We heard he used to get love letters from women, and my friends and I would joke about it. Some woman actually found a way to get married to him while he was on trial. I heard she supposedly had a kid by him, too, while he was in prison."

"Carole Boone was her name," Sofia said. "She apparently believed he was innocent for a long, long time, but at some point, she realized she had been played. Or wanted to get played. And that she had massively fucked up."

"I guess in your scenario I'm supposed to be her, Carole Boone?"

"Well, hopefully not, but, yes to Cassie being Ted Bundy."

"Ha-ha," said Jerry.

"Yeah, well, watch your back."

"She *loves* me, Sofia. Even if some of the crazy shit you think about her were true, I'm the last person she would want to hurt. She's loved me ever since we were little kids."

"Psychopaths don't love. They want and they need. And when they don't get what they want or need, they'll hurt you, or move on like you never existed, or, usually, both."

CHAPTER 18

She's ba-aack!

Melissa has been reinstated at her job at the treatment unit for only three weeks, but she's already regained her stride. Her little friends are hanging around with her again, laughing at her jokes, fawning over her, kissing her ass. That's how it seems to me, anyway.

And I feel diminished. My confidence at work is wavering. I do fine with the patients, but I keep second-guessing how I'm approaching the staff I'm working with. I don't contribute very much in treatment team meetings any more, not when Melissa is in them. It's hard to explain, but I feel like her presence makes me smaller and less visible, like I start to disappear in everyone's eyes. I would probably switch to all midnight shifts so I'd never have to be around her if Jerry wouldn't object.

How that schedule *could* work is that I'd get home just as, or just after, Jerry was leaving for work in the mornings. I would try to go right to sleep, maybe after doing a little housework and possibly some grocery shopping. Then, I'd wake up by the time Jerry got home, we'd have dinner (breakfast for me), hang out, socialize, maybe go see some friends together, and then I'd get ready to leave for work at the treatment unit and he'd get ready for bed. So, we'd still have plenty of awake time together, but we wouldn't be sleeping together on the five nights a week that I usually work. Or, I could ask to do four ten-hour shifts.

I could live with either schedule, but Jerry would hate it, and it does seem pretty chickenshit to me. The best solution for everyone would be for Melissa to no longer remain employed at the same place I am. Or, ideally, for her not work any place any more, because she would be dead.

I'd like to think I'm up to taking care of that particular task, but I don't have as much self-confidence in my ability to pull it off all by myself right now as I'd like. I keep doubting my capabilities, which makes me feel even more diminished.

I suspect that Melissa has been talking behind my back about me to people at work, because some of them seem to be distancing themselves. That could be my imagination, but, still, I know I would be a prime suspect if she dropped dead. However, I don't see any reason why I should have to go find a different nursing job somewhere, just to get away from her insidious presence. She's the one who needs to go.

I keep thinking I should have the strength *to remove her*, shall we say, by doing the deed myself. I feel a familiar tide of rage building and building and building inside me, and it would be such sweet relief to stick a knife in that bitch's throat. But I do believe it would be much smarter to make a call up to Boston.

Danny had been pretty clear when we last spoke that I would be paying full retail for a job like Melissa. I don't know exactly how much that would be, but I'd guess *at least* $10k plus his airfare and other expenses. How I figure it, though, is that his fee would be cheaper than what I would have to pay for a top attorney for myself, which I'd need in order to fight a first or second degree murder charge. Assuming it came to that. Plus, there would just be so much hassle and bad publicity for me. So, like I said, I'm feeling a deep reluctance about doing her myself, a feeling that's getting quite uncomfortable to live with. It makes me feel weak.

Apparently, I'm concerned about getting caught.

So, I placed a call to Danny's cell phone as soon as I got off work. Actually, I was still in the parking lot of the treatment center. The phone rang and rang and rang, and then some old lady with a sleepy Boston accent answered. I wondered if I had tapped the wrong contact (I don't have him listed as one of my "favorites"). The woman said Danny had died in April.

"Oh, *no*," I said. "I'm so sorry to hear that…" I must have sounded very upset, which I was, because then she started trying to console me.

"There, there, honey, everything is fine now. My little boy is in heaven with his father and his brother. I know I'll see them all again when it's my time to go."

I doubted that, unless the old dear had been an integral part of their family hit squad and was expecting to have a big reunion in hell. But I didn't want to burst her bubble. I just said I was very sorry for her loss and hung up.

Now what the fuck am I supposed to do? I wished Ashley were still alive. She would have been perfect, as long as she didn't get caught. Because if she ever had gotten arrested, even for shoplifting, I suspected she would have instantly incriminated me. Which is why I took the precaution of eliminating her so quickly after she went up to Broward to do the hit on Isabella. I don't *think* I was wrong about taking that route…but it would be nice, now, to have her help.

So that leaves me with no one competent to do the job on Melissa. And I really, really do not want to have to go find a different nursing job. I have some seniority here, and the pay and hours are really good for my needs. The other treatment centers within commuting distance from me are more tailored for low-income addicts and alcoholics, so they don't pay as well. They are more like spin-dry's than true treatment facilities.

Anyway, I'm sure anyone could understand why I'm feeling that my choices are limited here. Melissa has planted some very negative lies about me at work. And me finally living with Jerry, while it's delightful, makes carrying out any plans to eliminate that bitch myself all the more difficult. I know Jerry is aware that some of the people I have had contact with over the years are now dead, and he isn't stupid.

Thus, I imagine most people could sympathize with how seriously upset I became when I heard that Danny was no longer available. I would have gladly paid him double his asking fee for an untraceable, pro job.

Until I come up with a solution, I guess I'll just have to put up with Melissa being around. Maybe she'll eventually get bored with trying to annoy me if I totally ignore her. Maybe she'll move on to another job of her own accord. Or, maybe something bad will happen to her.

I got a sudden burst of insight with that thought.

Melissa would be traumatized if her little pimp of a free-loading, free-basing husband were to die. I imagine she might quit her job here and move back somewhere to be with family.

Her husband probably sleeps all day while she is at work. If she's ever scheduled for an early evening shift, which the counselors here occasionally need to do when coverage is required, he probably hits the streets as soon as the sun goes down. What if we were to cross paths some dark evening?

Maybe we already have.

It could easily have been him lurking around that time at the apartment I used to rent, the place I had before I moved into my new, more secure, condo. I had decided back then, you might recall, to get a postal box for all my mail for an extra layer of security, so no one in HR could give out my street address to anyone, either accidently or on purpose.

I don't think I am becoming clinically paranoid. I'm just being realistic about my situation.

So, what I decided to do was to follow pimp-boy around for a while to learn where he goes to buy his crack. His binges almost certainly take place when Melissa is at work. I started thinking about tailing him when she's at work and I'm not.

Fortunately, a wonderful, totally unexpected opportunity for me arose just the other night after I worked an evening shift. I was cruising by their place at about eleven-thirty, and decided to pull in to their apartment building parking lot merely to reconnoiter. After about twenty minutes, I saw the lights go off in what I was pretty sure was their unit. I was just getting ready to go home to Jerry when I saw them both come outside.

It sounded like Melissa was screaming at him. I rolled down my window to hear better. She was shouting that he was a fucking crack whore. Did that mean Melissa thought her pimp-boy was having sex with either a dealer or with someone else in exchange for crack, which is how the term *crack whore* is usually applied? Seems like it would fit what *I* thought of him.

Then, Melissa jumped into her car, and squealed the tires on the pavement. She turned west, in the direction of the Everglades. I followed at a bit of a distance, just keeping her in sight.

She really started to speed up once she got to the outskirts of the city, but then one of our sudden South Florida deluges began with a sharp crack of lightening. The skies just unloaded torrent after torrent of wind-driven rain. I had to slow way, way down, because the roads out to the west of the city can get covered with dust and dirt, and then when they first get wet, they can be very slick.

Her car began to round a curve at an insane rate of speed, and then, when I finally caught up, I saw that it had plunged off the side of the road into one of those Everglades canals that have ten or fifteen feet of water in them during the rainy season. The car's headlights were still on under the water, lighting up the clouds of silt that had been disturbed from the muddy bottom of the drainage canal.

I lowered my car window to get a better look. Large bubbles broke the surface of the greenish-brown water as the car settled deeper into the muck.

As I sat in my car, the frogs across the road resumed croaking their evening songs. The rain had stopped as suddenly as it had started.

What popped into my mind then was Ted Kennedy and Mary Jo a long time ago, up on Chappaquiddick Island, racing for the last ferry on her last summer night. I don't know what Melissa was racing to or from.

I suppose I could have called 911, but I decided to get out of my vehicle to take a closer look. The rear end of Melissa's car was still out of the water, so I stuck out my foot and gave it a hard shove. More bubbles came up and then it sank.

I certainly wasn't going to jump into the water and try to pull Melissa out. When Fate hands you a gift, it would be pretty unseemly to refuse it.

I remembered, of course, to run my car through an all-night car wash before I got back to my neighborhood. I also remember thinking, now that Melissa was gone, that my very last problem was taken care of.

Boy, was I wrong.

****

Jerry had spent most of the evening over at Julio's drinking beer. A college basketball game was on the television. Florida was ahead of Auburn. The volume was turned way down. Julio's white pit bull, Andre, lay at their feet, his pink tongue half-way out, a contented look on his chubby face.

"Sofia has been feeding your own doubts about Cassie, little Jerry. She didn't just pull them out of the air and give them to you. You already had them, am I right?"

"Maybe. I don't know. I look at her sometimes, at Cassie, and her face is as calm and perfect as an angel's and her eyes are such a clear, innocent blue. Then, I think, am I nuts or paranoid or just wrong?" Jerry sighed. "Isabella's death was traumatic for me. Maybe it made me crazy."

Julio nodded. "You had been together with Isabella for quite a while. She left you for another man. They get married. She is murdered."

"All within a few weeks. My head spins when I think about it. It's my fault that she left me. Maybe she wouldn't have died if we had stayed together."

Julio shrugged. "You didn't want to get married. She wanted to start a family, maybe. Some other man found her and wanted her and offered her what you wouldn't."

Jerry stared at Julio. "That makes me sound terrible."

"It isn't terrible to want something different. And it isn't terrible that Isabella knew what she wanted and found it with someone else."

Jerry nodded.

"What's only terrible is that she died," said Julio. "And now you have Cassie."

Jerry nodded again. "Cassie really loves me. I believe she would do anything for me. I don't think I ever really understood how intense someone's passion could be until we found each other again. It's not just the sex. It's that her commitment to me, to us, is so total and so unshakeable."

"What is stopping you from making Cassie your wife, little Jerry?"

"I need to figure out why my gut is telling me to slow down. Maybe I still need to put more closure on Isabella."

"Jerry, what if it is just some more hesitation, like you had with Isabella? What if the answer is in you, not in either Cassie or Isabella?"

Jerry looked up at Julio, who was changing the channel to a soccer game. "I think I'm going to talk to Carlos."

"Will he want to talk with you?"

Jerry nodded. "He's *un tipo chévere*, I think. He will."

****

Carlos readily agreed to meet Jerry at a café near the station after Jerry's shift was over.

"I must travel to Venezuela again soon, so today was best for me."

"Isn't it kind of dangerous down there these days?" Jerry asked once they were seated and had their drinks ordered.

Carlos shrugged. "Yes, to a degree."

Jerry waited, but Carlos didn't say anything more about his travel plans.

"What did you wish to discuss this afternoon, Jerry? Police Sergeant Jerry Cabot?"

"A woman named Cassandra Couri."

Carlos looked up from his plate of seafood empanadas, and regarded Jerry.

"You know her," Carlos stated.

Jerry nodded.

"You have been in a romance with her." Again, it was a statement, not a question.

Jerry nodded again.

"Why have you come to me?"

"How do you know her?" Jerry asked.

Carlos shrugged. "I don't, not really. I've never met her."

"I need your help," Jerry said. "I've been involved with her. I met her while Isabella was still with me."

"What are you looking for from me?" Carlos asked.

"Isabella led me to believe that you most likely have connections in Miami that I don't have access to, at least not without an arrest warrant. I need to find out some things about Cassie. She wants to get married."

"The most beautiful women in Miami all want to marry Officer Jerry Cabot," Carlos said with a slight smile. "And he thinks he needs assistance from me."

Jerry waited.

"How would you like me to help you, Officer Jerry Cabot? Jerry?"

"I want to know everything I would need to know if I were thinking about marrying her."

"You can run a background check on her yourself." Carlos smiled slightly. "With probable cause of a crime, no?"

"Her background check was clean." Jerry smiled back. "I was told."

"So?"

"Isabella met her. Isabella was her buyer's agent for the condo Cassie purchased a while back. When I noticed Cassie's name on a contract Isabella showed me, I questioned her about it. Isabella said she had originally met Cassie at a house showing quite a while ago. I didn't know anything about it until then. Cassie had never told me."

"What did Cassie say when you eventually asked her?"

"Her story checked out with what Isabella had told me."

"You don't think it could be a coincidence? Cassie is shopping for a home, she meets Isabella, they hit it off, Cassie hires Isabella?"

"Nothing is a coincidence with Cassie."

Carlos nodded and smiled tightly. "You think Cassie stalked Isabella, knowing all the time Isabella was with you, and she hired Isabella because…?"

"To give the sales commission to us, to Isabella, rather than to a stranger, is what she said."

Carlos shrugged. "That's nice, no?"

"I'm not sure now if it was nice, or if it was something else. It can be hard to tell the difference with Cassie."

"What would you do if you were to discover that Cassie is a very different person from whom she appears to be?" Carlos asked.

"It would depend on how different," Jerry said. "I've known her since she was a little girl. She was very high-spirited then. She still is. I've investigated her marital and legal background, off the record, and I've questioned her about what I found. So, I would probably be quite surprised if I learned something that I didn't already know, or at least had an idea about."

"Do you know how many people have died around Cassie?" Carlos asked.

"I know about her parents," Jerry said, "who died in a motor vehicle accident when we were children, shortly before I originally met her, and I know about her ex-husband, who died of an asthma attack after they were divorced."

Carlos placed his palms together and touched his fingertips to his lips. Jerry could imagine Isabella, or any woman, being attracted to his graceful manner and to his good looks.

"There are many more, Jerry. Quite a few associates and acquaintances of Cassandra Couri have all died. Probably an uncountable number of strangers, as well. You know better than the average person how many unsolved murders and unattended deaths there are."

Jerry gave a shocked snort. "Is this to imply that my childhood love, my girlfriend, is a serial killer?"

Carlos shrugged. "*A quien le pique, que se rasque...*"

"Where did you get your information?"

"I pay people to obtain it for me. In this case, only since Isabella died. I'm sure the list of Cassie's...actions...will grow longer as more information is retrieved."

"Do you think Cassie killed Isabella?"

"No, of course not."

"Do you know who did?"

"Not for certain. My sources point to a woman who was acquainted with Cassie and who was then herself murdered."

"Is any of your information actionable?"

"No, not legally. Your Cassie is very intelligent, very bold, and fairly careful."

"What am I supposed to do with all this?" Jerry asked quietly, almost to himself.

"It depends, I suppose, if you believe what I've told you and if you think Isabella deserves some measure of justice."

Jerry took a deep breath.

Carlos left cash on the table for the bill and stood.

"And," he said with a parting smile, "you should at least consider that you may someday find yourself on Cassie's list."

CHAPTER 19

When I heard Melissa didn't show up for work for her scheduled shift, I acted surprised. Her supervisor called the house and her cell phone. The call to her phone went straight to voicemail. People started to worry, because despite her rather chaotic life, she rarely called in sick and was always on time for work. A friend then called her husband's phone. He said they'd had a big fight, he'd left, and he hadn't seen her since. Nor was he at home, he reportedly said. I imagined he was still out on the streets on some massive drug and alcohol binge. He probably only answered his phone because he thought it might be some dealer.

Ellen, one of Melissa's little work friends, volunteered to stop by Melissa's apartment after her own shift to try to find out what was going on over there. I could tell that some people were starting to worry that she might have relapsed, what with all the stress with her husband and the job. I said that I didn't think that was the case at all, that Melissa had a very strong recovery program. People nodded.

It wasn't too long before someone, an airboat tour operator, found Melissa's car in the drainage canal. Everyone at work appeared shocked and saddened at the news. I mimicked their facial expressions, shook my head, and said I just couldn't believe it.

What I couldn't believe was that I hadn't needed to plan her death or do very much to cause her death. It was as if fate were on my side for this one. I imagined, though, that Melissa's husband was going to have some pretty intense interviews with Miami-Dade law enforcement personnel.

When I got home, Jerry called and asked if he could come over. I was delighted, of course, and I fixed us some snacks and drinks and made sure my nice, new condo was straightened up and that the bed linens were fresh and clean. But I didn't really think this was going to be a social visit, because Jerry's voice on the phone had sounded tense. Maybe it was about Melissa, since, of course, all the area cops would have heard about the incident.

I made sure it was the first thing I mentioned after he walked in the door.

"Did you know her very well?" Jerry asked.

Wow. Right to the interrogation part. "Yes, of course," I said. "She was a counselor. When I work days I see her, *saw* her I mean, and at shift change if I was on another schedule. We weren't what I would call good friends, but she had a lot of respect on the unit."

"What about her personal life?'

"That was maybe a problem," I said. "She was married to a guy who couldn't stay sober. He was in and out of detoxes, and had all kinds of shady dealings around town."

"How so?"

I shrugged. "Cocaine. What you would expect with cocaine. Money issues."

"Did you like her?"

I shook my head. "I wasn't close to her, but she was very good at her job. She had a lot of respect from the staff, I would say. I learned a lot from her in treatment team meetings. It's going to be a big loss to the patients and to the treatment team."

Then Jerry's work phone went off.

"Gotta go," he said, and was out the door.

I guessed I'd just had an official police interview.

****

On the way to his vehicle, Jerry stopped by Cassie's car, got down on his knees, and inspected the underbody. It was clean, just the normal road dust, and there were no new dents or dings. He looked through the tinted windows. Just Cassie's usual stuff: a coffee cup and some fast food wrappers on the passenger side floor. When he exhaled, he realized he'd been holding his breath. He looked up at Cassie's window, but he couldn't see if she was watching him because of the way the shades were.

When he got back to the office, Jerry looked up the accident report. The vehicle most likely went off the road between 11:30 pm and midnight, during the rainstorm. Cassie would have just finished her shift, unless she worked late. He decided to call her and ask.

"No, I didn't actually *work* late," she said. "But I sometimes drive around for a while when I get off. I went down to the beach that night and parked for a little while to chill. Then I came home."

"Did it rain?"

She shook her head. "No, but I thought it was going to. I could see some lightening off to the west."

****

"Why don't you believe what your girlfriend tells you, Little Jerry?"

Cassie was at work. Jerry was over at Julio's shop. The TV was on at background volume. No one else was there.

"I don't really know. She's pretty blunt and honest in what she says. She's not evasive. You know how some people won't look you in the eye, or how what they say one time doesn't match what they said before?"

Julio nodded. "She doesn't lie. But maybe she doesn't tell you everything?"

"Oh, she definitely doesn't tell me everything, and not it's not with just me. It's like everything she says is true, but she leaves things out. She's been doing it all her life. She was doing it when we were little kids. I'm not sure how good she was at it back then, because I was pretty gullible."

"All children are gullible, Jerry. We can easily lie to them…Santa Claus, the Easter Bunny…"

"I know, I know, but… I ran a background check on her…somebody I know did. I've never done that before with a friend or with anybody I had a personal relationship with. It's against policy, but it's not technically illegal, depending…"

Julio raised his palm as if to say, 'spare me the justification, I don't really care' and said, "And you didn't find anything, did you?"

"Nope."

"But you can't let it go. Once again, why is that, Little Jerry?"

"I guess because I think there *is* something."

"You can't arrest her on suspicion of…something, Officer Jerry. Right?"

"Only if there's probably cause. And I would never arrest her."

****

When forest animals first smell the smoke of a fire, they raise their heads and work their nostrils, assessing the danger. The large ones begin to move away. Smaller ones may deepen their burrows and head far underground.

Cassie listed her new condo with the agency that had sold the most units in her building.

"I would like to sell this very quickly, so please advise me how to price it," Cassie said. The realtor inspected her apartment, evaluated the view, and looked over the condominium documents.

"How fast do you want to sell it? I may have a buyer waiting for this view."

Cassie set her price, and told the realtor she was selling it furnished, as is, with no negotiations. She sold her car, and acquired a similar, newer one on a short term lease. She gave two weeks' notice at work, updated her resume', packed up some of her favorite clothes and her important documents, and ordered her cable and internet services to be stopped in two weeks.

Then she went over to see Jerry.

"Can I stay with you for a while?" she asked. "I'm having my apartment painted and I'm re-doing the kitchen counters. Things are going to be a real mess."

****

Carlos invited Jerry over to his condo. "I have some news and some difficult information for you."

Jerry paced around Carlos' luxury apartment. This is where Isabella had been living when she had left him for this man. She had kept her clothes in his spacious closets, rested on his fine leather furniture, and enjoyed his magnificent views of the city. She had made love with him in the king-sized bed with its silky sheets and quality mattress. Then, she had married him, and had put Jerry behind her.

Carlos handed him a thin crystal glass of the best red wine Jerry had ever tasted. Carlos watched Jerry's reaction as Jerry's taste and smell receptors were fired by the silky liquid.

"It's very good, no?"

Jerry nodded.

"You want to talk about Cassie?" Carlos asked.

Jerry sighed. Was he ready? There would probably be no going back once he crossed that bridge.

"Yes."

"Okay, then. Let's sit down." Carlos gestured to the brown leather sofa. "I will tell you everything I know. I will not tell you how I know what I know. It was very difficult in some instances to obtain reliable information. In other cases, not so hard at all. You may not record this conversation. You may take notes, names, dates, places, but I will most likely not be available to make an official statement on the record. If you think I must at some point in our discussion, I will probably no longer be able to continue to help you."

"Fine," said Jerry. He had decided before he arrived that he would treat Carlos and whatever information he provided as if Carlos were a CI, a confidential informant.

"Well, Sargeant Cabot. The Cassie you say you knew when you were but two small children living in Massachusetts is…an unusual woman. She has been responsible in some manner for an exceptionally prolific number of deaths. She first killed a man when she was a child, before you ever met her, in a foster care arrangement, in a very disturbing manner."

"I have to know something before you say anything more, Carlos. Is it absolutely certain that Cassie didn't kill Isabella?"

"It is certain. A woman named Ashley St. John killed Isabella."

Jerry nodded. "Where is she now?"

"Dead. She was killed in the apartment complex parking lot where she lived. My assumption is that Cassie killed her, this Ashley St. John."

Jerry nodded again. "How did *you* know about Ashley St. John?"

"From a private source. And, of course, it was in the news."

"What are you going to do with all this information you are about to tell me?"

"Provide it to law enforcement if that time comes."

Jerry took notes as Carlos unspooled his threads of information, and he drank Carlos' wine, and by the time Carlos was finished speaking, most of the wine was gone and Jerry's notebook was filled. He looked down at his writing. It was clear and organized, even though he felt like his guts had been slowly pulled out and smeared across the pages of his notebook and on to Carlos' fine floors.

He had taken statements from witnesses of horrific child abuse, from nursing home employees detailing cruel mistreatment of helpless elderly residents, and from drug kingpins speaking of crimes of spectacular violence in exchange for reduced sentencing. None of these accounts had left him with the desolate feeling, the utter emptiness, that had settled over him as Carlos continued talking about Cassie's trail of death.

He didn't know how much admissible evidence there really was, or how many witnesses would be available to corroborate Carlos's information. It sounded like Cassie didn't leave many witnesses alive.

Jerry envisioned Cassie sitting in a Dade County courtroom dressed in a conservative business suit or in a feminine, flattering dress and groomed as carefully as conditions in the Miami-Dade Pre-Trial Detention Center allowed. She would make a good witness on her own behalf; calm, attractive defendants frequently swayed jurors. He would be called to testify, most likely as to her schedule and other such details, since he had no direct knowledge of any crimes she may have committed.

The next morning, Jerry woke up with a hangover. Cassie was supposed to come over to his house in a day or so, after he got home from work. She had said she wanted to begin moving some of her things in temporarily while her condo was being refurbished.

She would want to sleep with him. Jerry didn't know if he was going to be able to share his bed with her, after his meeting with Carlos. Would he make desperate love to her anyway, one last time, even though he knew what she was, even though he knew that he would have to end up breaking his own heart by having her taken in to custody?

****

Ecuador. Ecuador currently has no formal extradition treaty with the United States. I double-checked that.

Getting work in the medical field down there shouldn't be a problem. The money from the sale of my condo will be enough for me to make an excellent start in a good section of Guayaquil or Quito. I'm not sure if my Spanish is quite up to the challenge yet, but I've been studying hard and practicing with the Spanish-speaking patient care attendants every single shift I work. Plus, I've already picked up plenty of Spanish colloquialisms and swear words, just from living in Miami.

I have booked a round trip ticket to Quito to avoid any of the red flags that would come with a one-way ticket. I tucked some brochures from a travel agency into my carry-on. I look forward to getting out to the Galapagos Islands at some point, as well as to visiting archaeological sites in Peru and other locations in South America.

I have communicated with a local Quito real estate agent to help me find an apartment to rent near the hospital district, and I've located an immigration attorney down there to assist me in securing my work permit, visa, and all that. I withdrew slightly less than ten thousand dollars cash from my bank account, and checked to make sure my credit and debit cards, attached to my Miami bank account, would be accepted in Ecuador. Thank god for online banking services, although I think I will immediately transfer everything to a local bank down there after my last pay check is direct-deposited.

Then I thought about what I would say to Jerry. I want to tell him how much I love him, but I also need to keep him from immediately taking me in to custody. I don't know for sure if that's his plan, but

I think it could be. I have a lot of tingling, spidery feelings going on, which I never ignore. I'm sure he loves me, but he is also a duty-bound cop.

I had hoped we would be together forever. Once we reconnected here in Miami, I knew for certain that he was my one true soul mate. We will always be joined together, in some way, but possibly only in my heart from now on.

Maybe someday he'll come down to visit me in Ecuador. Maybe one day, after he's come to better terms with things, he'll even leave Miami and move down across the equator to share his life with me.

I dreamed last night that he was standing with me in the late afternoon sun in an old plaza in some South American colonial city. We were looking up at a statue of a Spaniard on a horse. Maybe Pizarro? Pizzaro was a pretty terrible conquistador, at least from the perspective of the native people, but in some respects, he was a hero. After someone is gone, what other people believe determines their reputation. I don't know what Jerry is going to decide to believe about me.

****

Cassie was supposed to come over very soon with some of her things. Jerry paced his house, nervous, alert, and still torn. He wasn't going to be around when she was taken into custody if it was tonight, no.

He was staring out into his side yard at a bird feeder when she knocked on the front door and let herself in. He turned and looked at her. The sun behind her was lighting up her beautiful reddish-blond hair like a shimmering halo. Were all the angels who were left up in heaven after God cast out Lucifer and his minions really good, or did some of the bad ones get to stay, the ones God couldn't bear to be parted from?

Jerry took Cassie into his arms, and she melted against him. He brought his mouth down on her lips and then they were on his bed, their clothes stripped away, joined in their need and lust and pain. He had never loved her more than he did at this moment.

At 6:20, the chime of a text message woke them from their nap. Jerry picked up his phone and looked at it.

"Cassie, you need to get dressed."

"Why?" she asked, trying to pull him back down to her.

"I have to go out to pick up a pizza I ordered for us."

"Why didn't you just have it delivered?" she asked sleepily.

"I don't know, I really don't know."

He pulled Cassie to her feet, and wrapped her tightly in his arms. "I'll always love you, Cassie."

Then he was out the door, practically running, yelling, "You need to get dressed!"

Cassie instinctively sniffed the air, and instantly began pulling on her clothes. She grabbed her pocketbook, locked the front and side doors, and was over the fence to the street behind Jerry's house where she'd parked her rental car in less than two minutes. As she turned on to a main road, she saw the cop cars at a distance in her rearview mirror, their lights flashing, their sirens off, silently approaching Jerry's house in a line. Had he sent the whole squadron to arrest her?

****

I was able to return my rental car successfully and make it safely with my one piece of luggage to Concourse D of Miami International Airport. American Airlines was able to rebook me for tonight on their evening flight, no problem, which was leaving in forty-five minutes. There were two seats available in economy and one in first class. I knew I was going to need to have a drink or two or three, so I chose the first class seat.

I called Jerry a few months later while I was off on a trip to Peru, exploring Machu Pichu. I didn't tell him where I was. Right away, we got in to an argument. I just wanted to tell him goodbye properly and that I'd always love him. He wanted to rehash the past.

"Jerry, a lot of bad things happened to me when I was a little girl. My parent died. I got taken advantage by Herman at The Home. Did you even know that? You were safely down in Miami with your aunt and uncle. You were my only friend, and you left me behind in that snake pit. Bad things happened to me," I repeated.

"You were like that before you even came to The Home," Jerry said. "You got sent there for what you did when you were in foster care."

Ah. Someone had been doing some research. I sighed.

"I hope you'll get help," he said.

"I'm going to be fine, Jerry. And, please know that you have been the best thing I've ever had in my life. I will always, always love you. Maybe someday I'll call you again." Then I hung up.

****

A few weeks later, Jerry and Sofia were sitting outside at Jerry's house. He'd repainted the exterior and the entire interior, and had replaced all his old, worn furniture, except for his bed, which he couldn't bear to let go. He'd saved the sheets he'd slept on with Cassie during their last night together, unlaundered, stored on the back of a shelf in the linen closet. Her scent lingered

Sofia knew Jerry was still suffering, first from losing Isabella so horribly, and next from Cassie leaving him just as he was finding out what she really was, abandoning him with all his unanswered questions. Sofia would bring Ollie over once or twice a week to romp in the backyard while she sat with Jerry on his patio, drinking beer.

Sometimes, he had wine or vodka. It seemed like he was going through a lot of alcohol.

She looked over at him, and patted his hand. Jerry smiled back wanly.

"No need to be so sad, my friend. She'll no doubt turn up again somewhere, like a bad case of herpes. And," Sophia grinned, "at least you still have your head."

"Some days it doesn't feel like it."

"You sure you don't know where she is? We could get the FBI or Interpol on it."

Peru. Ecuador, maybe. "No," Jerry said. "I don't."

The End

ACKNOWLEDGMENTS

First thanks goes to my husband, Robert Mullennix, for his patience and support during the months I spent writing this novel.

I am especially grateful to Christine Linder and Don Weimer for their valuable editorial assistance and suggestions.

Thanks also to the excellent marketing support team at *Best Page Forward*.

Cover design and formatting by *100 Covers*.

Also By This Author

Stop Him For Me (Psychological Thriller)
The Soldier's Wife (Psychological Thriller)
An Everglades Romance (Contemporary Romance)
I Could Never Forget About You (Psychological Thriller)
In The House Of The Seventh Messenger (YA Historical Fiction)

Writing as "Jane Wesley"
Nicole's Halloween Cat (Children's Picture Book)
Nicole's Christmas Kitten (Children's Picture Book)

Author Website www.lesliejanelinder.com

Printed in Dunstable, United Kingdom